Busking Blues

Recollections of a Chicago Street Musician & Squatter

Westley Heine

Roadside Press

Busking Blues: Recollections of a Chicago Street Musician & Squatter
Copyright ©Westley Heine 2022
ISBN: 979-8-9861093-1-2

Editor: Michele McDannold
Cover Art: Waylon Bacon

Roadside Press
200 W. Main St. Unit 209
Trinidad, Colorado 81082

dedica-tion

Dedicated to all the people who inspired the characters in this book and to Chicago itself.

TELL ME YOUR PROBLEM!
AND I'LL WRITE YOU
A
BLUES SONG

*"I love to write songs all the time about what's up on these streets.
I write songs about people getting killed; I write songs about people
getting beaten up; I write songs about people getting taken to jail
by the police; and I also write songs about love and happiness."*
–Wesley Willis

I have questions. Questions no man can answer and God won't bother. In the still morning I'm walking down the alley behind 18th Street in Pilsen the Mexican neighborhood on the near South Side. In Chicago dawn is the only time there are patches of silence. Third shift hasn't gotten home yet and first shift is just waking up. The only sounds are my own footsteps and the freight yard clanking in the distance. Now even the rats are asleep. The occasional breeze stirs a newspaper and wafts the stench off the tired old trashcans. The sky has that cool blue tint streaming up from Lake Michigan out east somewhere.

For a moment the silence feels out of place. My lips purse together and a happy whistle cuts the air. Some half forgotten song is in my head, "Rambling. I got rambling on my mind." The blues lyrics make light out of an otherwise somber morning.

At the corner of Wood and 18th everything is still like the after effects of a neutron bomb. The brown brick buildings hang motionless to the horizon. But it's all in my head. It's early. Soon the music of the street will be humming with activity. The sun will thaw people from their sleep. There will be brushes on teeth, spoons ringing in bowls, arms in coats, the white noise of traffic will rise like the tide. Laughing school children, delivery trucks, commuters, crossing guards will click into position.

Only later do the hustlers come out. The perpetual street corner spirits, miscellaneous sentries, sometimes menacing figures wandering the pavement at a slower pace looking like they have nowhere to go because they are already at their destination somewhere between a borrowed bed and the curb. Today I am joining them. I have just walked out on my girl. I tell myself this is the last time. This time I'm leaving for good. We've been together for three years, but that's another story. Right now I'm homeless. I need a plan.

As I walk guitar case in one hand and a steel folding chair in the other, I ask myself how did I get here? The brain offers flashes of reason. Memories reel in my mind like scattered clips. The housing bubble burst two years ago right after I got out of school. I studied art. For a few months I was freelancing doing video production. It seemed possible. There were some jobs doing lighting and audio-visual gigs. I was making money. Not much but enough to make rent. Then there was nothing. I got a job as a deliveryman until my car gave out. Now my old green station wagon is crushed into a cube somewhere on the West Side. Unemployed I finally landed a gig at a grocery store which would throw me a few hours per week. It's 2010. No one knows how long the recession will last. As usual it's all up to us. We're on our own.

Still I have questions. Despite the news, scapegoats to point at, and all of the excuses, I question myself. Maybe there are some good jobs out there. Maybe I'm not looking hard enough. Maybe I'm not competitive enough. The truth is I'm beat. I'm tired. I'm tired of looking. I'm tired of pretending to care. I'm tired of interviewing against people who have been doing it longer. I'm tired of acting excited for a job I truly need, but really don't want. Now I'm on the street.

Is this my own failure or is it the failure of the world? I count the clichés that put me here. They parade through my skull: the break-up, the economy, the country, my own cynicism… I could blame Wall

Street, 9-11, or George W. Bush, but all my questions are met with the silence of the cool blue morning. There's no sense looking for blame. It wouldn't do me any good. There's little point in asking the big questions when I need to ask only one: Where am I going to sleep tonight? There are answers to my questions, but no solutions to my problems… All the reasons for my troubles are there, bleak as the dawn, but the real question is always: What to do right now?

As I walk down 18th Street common sense clicks in my head like a reflex. I should scramble looking for a better gig. I should stop spending all my time playing guitar and writing songs. I should go back to Wisconsin with my tail between my legs. Things are cheaper up North where I grew up. I should beg my folks to stay with them until I figure out my next move. I should go to the library, log onto rommmates.com or Craigslist, and find some people to split rent. I should be concerned about getting my life together. I should be worried about getting a ceiling over my head. I should be worried about getting my clothes clean. I should be scared.

But the truth is I don't give a damn. I'm not afraid at all. My feet are light. My pace picks up. I skip between the cracks in the sidewalk. The melody I'm humming is stronger than all these thoughts. "Rambling. I got rambling on my mind." The day is getting brighter. I catch my reflection in a store window. I'm still young. A weight has been lifted. The air feels cool in my lungs. Today anything could happen.

As long as I have this guitar I'm not homeless. I'm a street musician.

Waiting for the bus at the corner of 18th and Damen the romantic notion of a guitar player, axe in hand, running out on his old lady at dawn quickly fades as I check my pockets. I have twenty bucks left. This kinda thing happens every day: Broke. Heartbreak. Kicked out. Moved out. Ran away. It happens to people all the time, and most don't play guitar. Most don't sing about it. Most people have families to worry about. Most have car payments and mortgages. It's hard times for everyone. I am lucky. The less I have the less I worry. Until I get hungry.

The Damen bus slides up. The rusty brakes moan like a sick dog. The driver is a pasty guy with a q-ball head. He looks half asleep. The only other passenger is a tall black lady with two milk-crates taped together. Inside the crates a spotted kitten is mewing. The lady is skeleton thin, smiling pleasantly at her makeshift cage.

Morning dew still on the window I see the looming towers of the Loop in the distance. They shine like crystals in the sun good times or bad. When I was a delivery boy I'd been in just about every building downtown. I've seen all the views. Still those heights seem unattainable. Do I even want to be on one of those lofty perches? No. I'd rather be just another ghost down in the grid.

Deep in my heart I know I want to be right where I am. No longer restrained by my ex-girlfriend, by school, or even a regular job I am free to seek adventure. I am free to explore. I can finally prove myself as a musician. I can prove that I can survive in the city on my own. I feel like a hobo looking for the next freight train to hop on. I feel like Robert Johnson, the greatest of the Delta blues musicians, standing at the crossroads. I want to play the blues like him. The pavement under the wheels of this bus has absorbed more sweat and sorrow than a slaughterhouse. It can take a little more.

The pleasant lady with the kitten in the crate asks me for the time with a dreamy look on her face. I tell her I'm not sure. I have no watch. I have no cell. I stopped paying the bill months ago. She just nods and drifts away. The kitten meows.

Time is the strangest thing of all. It feels like time has slowed. The past doesn't add up and there's no future. There only is today: the next dollar, the next meal, and where you're gonna lay your head down. I'm about to turn twenty-seven. Sometimes I feel older, sometimes younger, but never twenty-seven. Robert Johnson had found fame and died before reaching this age. Meanwhile here I am. I've been wasting my life. I've bounced around worrying about rent for too long. It is time to completely dedicate myself to music. Like so many kids music was my first love. Music was the first dream. I am going to live for my dreams even if it kills me. If I am going to die in the gutter I might as well do it playing music.

Loraine's Diner is a greasy spoon at the corner of Damen and Chicago Avenue in Ukrainian Village. It's a modest street-level hole in the wall with loft apartments above. The sign above the door is hand painted. Nothing fancy. If you blink you might miss it. Never crowded, the food ain't bad, but it ain't too good either. It's perfect.

Loraine herself is behind the counter. The only soul inside, she's a big polish gal with short red hair fading grey. She wishes me a happy Cinco de Mayo. Oblivious to the fact it is a holiday I mumble a likewise answer.

Placing myself in the booth by the window I scroll the menu. Keeping it under five bucks I could have a light breakfast of soup and toast. That should keep me going for a while. I have a bus pass that's good to the end of the week. After I eat I could easily hop on the Chicago Ave bus and head straight downtown. Maybe I could play the blues for some drunken tourists. If it's Cinco de Mayo I figure that some out-of-towners would dig some Chicago color. Hopefully I could relieve them of some of their money. I'm ready to sing for my supper.

The modest meal arrives. Steam rises from the golden broth filling my nose with love and life. As I eat I think: What came first? The blues? Or the blues music? Was it the hard facts of life in America that made me love this music, or was it the love of this music that made me romanticize the streets? Perhaps subconsciously I always wanted to drop out of the machine and cheat the game.

Whatever got me here I have no choice now. I have to hustle. I have no time to think. Despite the reasons it feels like fate.

They call Michigan Avenue "The Magnificent Mile." Commuters rush by. Cabs honk. Buses cut the air. Fur clad ladies window shop. Behind glass the bland inoffensive wares hang on headless mannequins. The smells of the city are blown breathless by the lake winds. I have my folding chair out. I'm tuning up my guitar. My pageboy cap is on the pavement. Inside I place a few bills weighted down by some change so people know where the money goes.

I've never done this before. This is my first day on the job. I tell myself I'm a street musician. Sure, I've performed with garage bands, but this is different. Growing up I sang with metal and punk groups hiding my heart behind the guttural groans that would pass for singing.

More recently I had a band here in the city. We played roots music, blues, folk-rock. That is, until the bass player went to jail, the lead guitar player became an elementary school music teacher, and the drummer's visa ran out and he had to go back to Australia. It seems my band fell apart along with the job market, the girlfriend, and everything else. No worries. Whatever doesn't kill me… Nietzsche and all that shit.

Over the roar and rush of traffic I *think* my guitar is in tune. I begin to sing low. I'm plucking *Love in Vain* by Robert Johnson. "Well I walked her to the station… suitcase in my hand…"

I feel like I don't have any clothes on. Commuters pass as if I'm not here. Occasionally someone gives me a look like they smelled something bad.

Next, I break into *Hard Times on the Killing Floor* by Skip James. "Hard times are here, and everywhere you go. These hard times will get you down long, hard, and slow…"

This is different than playing a club or a coffee house. There's no stage saying it's ok to be there. There's no spotlight just for you. Your name isn't on the flier or on the chalkboard above the bar. No one is paying for this. No one is expecting this. No one is requesting this. What I'm dishing out is at best easy to ignore or at worst unwelcomed.

I pull myself together and start *One Bourbon, One Scotch, One Beer* by John Lee Hooker. "Well I ain't seen my baby since the night before last. I'm gonna get drunk, man I'm gonna get gassed…"

Maybe no one can hear me. I miss having a microphone. I bring up the volume in my voice. Most people are wearing earbuds for iPods. It's no use. Where are the drunk tourists for Cinco de Mayo? By the fourth song I'm pouring my heart out like Howling Wolf. By the fifth song my voice is raw. My throat is starting to hurt and not one penny has dropped in my cap.

Pulling out my glass slide I begin *Death Letter Blues* by Son House. "Got a letter this morning, how do you reckon it read? Hurry, hurry, the gal you love is dead…"

I love these songs. For the past couple years I have worked hard to learn them. I just hope I do them justice.

My guitar ain't much either. It's a classical Spanish style acoustic guitar with nylon strings. It has a soft pretty tone for a hundred dollar guitar but it has no volume to compete with the traffic. My parents bought it for me for my birthday when I was a kid. Besides the sentimental value my axe ain't worth much.

Perhaps no one can hear me, but I begin to think it's me. Maybe I really need the band. In the group I wrote a lot of the songs and tried to sing but the lead guitarist, Guitar Mike, did all the heavy lifting. He was the real musician. He backed me up. He believed in me. Mike and the other guys had all the talent. They made me look good. They did all the work and I got all the credit. No wonder they're gone.

Meanwhile the sun is climbing the big blue dome above. It's getting hot. The excitement I felt a few hours ago is fading. I wish I could get a cold beer but I have to save my money for food. Slowly I pack up my guitar, my folding chair, and my pathetic cap. Bearing my burden I make my way towards the Loop.

The way is paved with real street performers. Most I've seen over the years. The man painted silver standing like a statue until enough bills are laid down then he begins to dance like Michael Jackson. The lady drawing caricature sketches for tourists and couples. The mustached man whose sax echoes down by the Chicago River like a forgotten dream. The elderly Asian man playing a cello that breaks your heart. Now I realize I am far from being one of them.

These performers have become part of the landscape. Their spots on the sidewalk have been staked out over years of defending their territory. Now I have a renewed respect for them. It's hard work. They sit out in the elements. They have to indulge the clueless tourists. They have to put up with the Chicago natives who are numb to peddlers or look down on them as scam artists.

Below the El-tracks at Clark and Lake I see a familiar face. There's a guitar player who I used to stop and listen to back in college. He's still there. He's dressed in black head to toe. He sports a bowler hat and a scarf. He has a soulful voice, which he turns on and off as pedestrians drift in and out of earshot. He does this seamlessly as if to save his voice. He has the right idea. Strapping my pathetic axe on my back I squeeze through the turn-style at the Clark and Lake CTA station.

Up on the platform I settle on a bench to rest my dogs. A few minutes later I see my mysterious singer friend coming my way. Sitting next to me he asks me what kind of guitar I have. I tell him. He nods. I realize that even though I know his face I have never been this close before. For all my eavesdropping on his music I never got close enough to drop him a dollar, even when I was a spoiled art student. That seems like a lifetime ago. He's a skinny black dude with a neatly kept goat and sharp brown eyes. A silver cross dangles from his ear.

"What's your name man?" I ask him.

"Billy. Yours?"

I tell him.

"How you do, Mr. Wes."

Billy pulls out a roll of bills thick as a Campbell's soup can. He licks a finger on a hand studded with silver rings and begins counting the bills.

"Damn," I say. "You've had a good day."

"I did alright. You?"

"I didn't make shit."

Billy tucks his roll in his breast pocket. He seems to ponder my complaint. "How long have you been busking?"

"Busking?"

"Yeah busking. Maaaan, you don't even know the lingo. Busking is playing music on the street for *cash*."

"Just today."

"You have a street performer license?"

"No."

"You gotta get one, son."

"You mean you have to have a license just to play on the street?"

"You bet your ass! The City of Chicago don't let no one do shit for free."

Billy reaches into his chest hair and produces a lanyard with a card on the end of it. His picture is on it. It reads: Chicago Street Performer.

"How much is that?"

"Hundred."

"A hundred? I don't have a hundred…"

"Well you better get it. Get one of these or be light on your feet. The Chicago police come up on you while you're playing they liable to fine you. Don't give'em no lip neither. The boys in blue have been known to throw a busker in jail, and leave his guitar and gear on the street for the vultures."

"Damn… No way."

"Soon as you have the cheddar get yourself down to City Hall for that license." Without skipping a beat Billy asks, "What kind of music you play?"

"Blues."

"Blues is cool." His eyes narrow in thought. "The thing about the blues is that everybody in Chicago says they like the blues because it's an issue of pride because Chicago is the city of the blues. But the truth is most of these people don't really listen to the blues. No sir."

"Damn. What about all the blues clubs?"

"What about them? You ever been in those joints?"

"Can't afford the cover charge."

"Right. If you do go in there you won't hear much blues neither. You'll hear blues-rock. Or some funky blues inspired dance music. It ain't some cat with an acoustic guitar singing about love and life. No Sir, it's some hot shot playing electric guitar solos that last twenty minutes."

"Yeah?"

"Yeah. Those clubs are for tourists. They're museums. The people that go there are paying to see an old black guy howl. Let's face it, no matter what you sound like you're just a young white boy. Nobody wanna see a young white dude sing the blues."

"Maybe you're right."

"I know I'm right. Listen, I've been doing this a long time. No day job. No one telling me what to do. But I know what people like to hear while they walk to work. They like to hear songs they already know… They don't want to hear no blues."

"What do you play?"

"My favorite is Counting Crows, but I play everything. Listen, you better learn some oldies or The Beatles on that thing otherwise you're gonna starve."

The Green Line pulls up to the platform. Without looking back Billy hops on the train and is gone. I wait for the Pink Line back to Pilsen.

Pilsen is lost in time. It's as if a Mexican village dropped from the sky into this massive metropolis. The old brick buildings are decked in beautiful murals. Fire-escapes zig-zag like black ink across soft orange windows. In crumbling corner bars a guy can enjoy a quiet beer because there's no TV and all the clientele speak Spanish. Cobblestones rise out of the cement on dead end streets. A teenage boy croons under an open window. Schoolgirls always traveling in twos giggle at him. A hairy little man in a wife-beater sweats on the corner his eyes going two ways. The concrete sections under the Metra tracks have illustrated scenes of all styles creating a montage of visions shrinking to the horizon.

On Ashland I know a place that has tacos for a dollar fifty. Sticking with water, I order two carne-asada tacos so I can use their bathroom. Coming back to the table my lunch is ready. After eating I go to the park off Blue Island Avenue where I lay in the grass under the bronze statues rusted green. Under the likeness of heroes from Mexican history, presidents, Aztec kings, and revolutionaries I cloud watch and think about my next move.

Most of my books, clothes, papers, and junk are stashed at Guitar Mike's place in the South Loop. He swooped up these boxes, milk crates, and bags in his van the other day while my ex, Linda, was at work. That was one thing, but Mike's girlfriend didn't want me crashing around. Plus, Mike was cleaning up his image. He cut his hair and shaved his beard. Being a music teacher at an elementary school now the PTA couldn't find out that he was in a dirty blues band playing raunchy ruckus with lyrics full of innuendo.

As the sun descends I know I don't have much choice. Standing on 18th Street across from my old apartment, now my ex-girlfriend's apartment, I can see lights on in the window. I'm not going back there. Not for anything. The lease is in my name, but I really don't give a damn whether she pays the rent or not. Assuming she won't, I figure she'll squat until evicted and my credit gets ruined. Big deal.

The old street lamps wink on like dominos westward chasing the sun.

Linda and I must have lived in four or five rooms like this across Chicago. Bad jobs. Bad weather. Bad food. Cheap wine. Staring at each other. Deserving each other. Not deserving this. Two lost souls perfectly fitted to jab into each other, rub you wrong, and then suddenly just right. Like aroused demons we clawed at each other in an ocean of pain, tears, screams, lust, and childhood trauma.

She was the only person that understood. I was the only person who understood. Maybe we understood too much. We were so much alike we couldn't stand each other. We cared for each other, but we couldn't stop fighting. It was all passion. But there are two sides to the fire.

We had our own kitty-cat language. We had pet names and insults. Linda would scream, claw, hit me, once flicked a cigarette in my eye. Linda would bait me till I'd smash a bottle over my head cutting myself to keep from hitting her back. Usually, if I started crying she would stop. Then she knew I felt something. But I was tired of feeling. I was tired of feeling this. It was all too much.

We tried everything. Nothing worked. She was on meds.

Then she stopped taking her meds. Then she took all her pills at once. Hospitals. Psych wards. She got worse. She got better. No matter what I did I couldn't make her feel loved. I couldn't make her love herself. She'd push me away before I would even think about leaving. Finally, knowing it was useless to try any longer, I actually did leave. I waited until she was having a manic upswing, when she could take care of herself without going over the edge. That's when I went out the door.

I walk away from these bad memories. There's a bodega under the 18th Street El Platform. Garlic cloves and pictures of saints hang behind the counter. In the back there's a butcher shop. Cardboard boxes on the floor soak up the blood from the hanging carcasses. A metallic taste catches in the back of the throat. Across from the display case complete with pig's feet and a goat's head are some coolers full of cheap drinks. After grabbing a forty-ounce bottle of MGD from the bodega I walk up Wood Street and hang a left down the alley. Behind my old building by the trash cans I look down the slender walkway between the sleepy homes.

This neighborhood has buildings that survived the Great Chicago Fire. After the epic tragedy 18th Street was one of the roads that was raised above the existing houses when the new sewer system was put in. This means that the 1st level of my building is below the sidewalk. The 2nd level, where I used to live, hovers at the street level across a cement bridge leading to the front door. There's a second door leading to additional stairs up to the 3rd level. Each level has a front and a back unit, which are separated by another stairwell in the middle of the building. This stairwell is only accessible from the side door in the alley. It's rarely used.

Not much choice. I slink down the alley hoping that my ex doesn't decide to look out the side window in the kitchen at just the right moment. As usual the side door is unlocked so I tiptoe up the stairwell creaking quietly past the backdoor of my old unit and up to the 4th level: the attic.

As I pass the back door of what used to be my place I hear voices. Linda's friends were due to visit from St. Louis. Maybe that's them talking. At least she will be safe. I hope. Right now I'm sure she's telling them how much she hates me, which is probably the best way to feel right now if only to leave the past behind.

The attic is merely a storage space under the triangular roof. There is just enough space to stand in the middle before it narrows. The insulation is exposed. There's no lights just one window facing 18th Street and one in the back facing the alley. Only the maintenance man comes up here and he seldom visits. Lucky for me the door to the attic is unlocked as well. I used to practice guitar up here when my strumming was too annoying for Linda. Most of the attic is used for storage. In fact, I have hid a good amount of my stuff up here. In a crawl space by the back window I have concealed canvass bags filled with clothes and other odds and ends. When I saw the writing on the wall I set these things aside.

Setting my guitar and folding chair down I rummage through the piles of junk. I thought I had seen an old mattress up here. I try to step easy so the people in the unit below won't hear that someone is in the attic. Sure enough I slide out a mattress between a table-saw and a stack of boxes. Laying it on the ground below the yellow street lamp streaming in the front window I take off my shirt and dust off the mattress. After finishing my big baby bottle of beer I lay down using my shirt as a pillow.

Thinking I'm pretty slick I shut my eyes. Soon I drift to another place.

It's hot. I wake up with cottonmouth. Staggering to the window I slide open the glass for the occasional breeze. The sun has been beating down on the attic roof all morning. My makeshift dwelling is like an oven.

Unwrapping last night's forty-ounce from the plastic grocery bag I take the bag back to the opposite corner and squat over it. Then I take the bag back to the trashcans in the alley as if I had just picked up after a dog.

In the light of day I can see what else is stored in the attic. Among all the junk I notice some cans of paint and used brushes. Also there's a stack of particleboard for some shelves yet to be assembled. One of the pieces of wood is a foot and a half square. It's the perfect size to make a little sign. In my sleep I've hatched a new plan.

Carefully cracking open the cans of paint I begin neatly writing on the particle-board using the corners of the bulky house brushes. After about an hour I have a bright sign that reads:

Tell Me Your Problem &
I'll Write you a Blues Song

As I put the paint away I muse that my art school degree has finally paid off. Maybe I'm not the best guitar player in the world, but I bet I could write some songs for people. As far as the street performer license goes I'll just have to be careful and watch out for the Chicago Police.

The paint is still wet so I leave it there to dry in the heat of the attic. Meanwhile, I have to make a few bucks. Sneaking down the stairs I slip down the ally to the 18th Street El-Stop. I take the Pink Line to the Loop and transfer to the Brown Line. At the Sedgwick stop I exit and walk down to the Dominick's on Division Street nestled between the Cabrini Green Projects and the condos in Old Town.

Dipping into the deli department my co-worker Bandi sees me. She knows what I'm thinking before I even open my mouth.

"Go on check the schedule Wes, but there ain't no hours for you!" she barks but when we make eye contact she bursts into a smile. We both know her teasing is just a way of making light of a fucked up situation. Bandi is about four feet high but a bundle of energy. She's always speaking her mind with humor, anger, wisdom. Despite her stature she has become like a big sister. Like any older sibling she never shows that she cares until she has to. She narrates the goings on in the deli out loud. She always tells it like it is even if no one asked. Mohamed or "Moe" might be our manager, but everyone knows that Bandi really runs the deli department. Moe usually knows better to stay out of her way and just make sure she has the supplies we need. He spends most of his time in the stockroom or in the cooler loading pallets.

The grocery store is at an interesting nexus in Chicago. Directly to the east is Old Town at the end of the Magnificent Mile where trendy condos have popped up along with trendier clubs. Just to the west is the notorious Cabrini Green Projects. The store serves as a friendly stage of class warfare where both crowds mix.

When I first started Bandi told me about Cabrini Green. "You know the buildings they used in *Good Times*, like during the credits."

"Vaguely."

"Well that's them. How about *Candyman*?"

"Yeah, I've seen that flick."

"That was filmed there. After seeing that shit everyone started nailing boards in the back of the bathroom mirrors so no one could push through from one unit to the next and attack you."

"Damn, like the Candyman."

"Right."

"It's a shame they be using the playground between the buildings to sell them drugs. Policeman just gets paid off. They don't care bout us anyway."

Most of my co-workers grew up in the projects. The party line at City Hall is that as the blocks become more gentrified Chicago becomes less segregated. But the reality is that gentrification is not a melting pot situation. Instead, the cost of living goes up and the people who were there first get pushed further south, out west, or even to the suburbs. This area between Division and North Avenue is one of the last strong-holds for the black community anywhere near downtown. Bandi, Gloria, Charlotte, and my other co-workers were reasonably defensive of their neighborhood. This included my pale face applying for a job at the store. But soon everyone grew to accept me as an ally and a friend. When there's work I work hard. I snap back jokes and insults with Bandi. A few times Charlotte even lent me a few bucks while waiting for payday.

Every day our customer service skills and patience are tested between the snooty rich people from Old Town and angry poor people from the affordable housing. We cut lunch meat using industrial slicers *thinner, thinner, too thin* for the rich folks. We make five-dollar pizzas on Fridays and the line goes out the door. We make fresh fried chicken for cheap with all the sides: mashed potatoes, greens, and rice. With the exception of working on a farm when I was a kid, the grocery store is the hardest job I have ever had. At least I work with the best people.

In this world it seems like the harder the work is the less it pays. We're all living paycheck to paycheck. After taxes and a bus pass I net about $100 a week. I can't make rent on that. Though, right now, having a job at all is something to be happy about.

The schedule is in the back by the dishwasher station. I just want to see it with my own eyes. My name isn't on the schedule for two more days. I go back out front and get in line at the deli counter with the customers. I ask Bandi for a sample. At the deli we are allowed to give samples of everything we sell. The idea is to entice people to try the food and then they will buy it. What happens is we give away mini snacks to the local kids and hungry co-workers. The security guards manning the surveillance system can see all this. But their hearts aren't made of stone. We found a loophole and until the rules change we can use it all we want.

Once a ghost thin homeless man wandered in just before closing time. I was the only one there just mopping up before shutting down the deli. It was hard to understand him because he was missing most of his teeth. One side of his face was a net of scars like the melted marks of a burn victim. That night he got about ten samples of mashed potatoes and gravy the only thing he could gum.

"So what you want to try?" Bandi asks me with a smirk.

"Let me get one of those hot wings. Oh and a thick slice of pastrami."

She hooks it up. At least I won't go hungry.

Stashing my guitar in a locker in the break room I see Chet from the produce department. He notices I'm not in my work shirt or apron. Chet is an energetic teenager with a pubic mustache and ice in both ears.

"Hey Wes. You don't work today?"

"Nope. No hours."

"I hear that. Hey, I tell you what. I work part time at a dry cleaner in the South Loop."

"Yeah? I need a second job too."

"There's work at the dry cleaners. My boss said to find him a white guy to work the front register."

"A white guy? He said that?"

"Yeah he wants a white guy. You know, for the customers. It's dry cleaning. All these rich white people have to clean their suits every week."

"Ok. I'm down. Thanks man."

Chet gives me the address and tells me to show up and interview with his boss the day after tomorrow.

Heading back towards the train I run into Rodrigo. His face has that bruised look like he has been drinking for days. He used to work at Dominick's. Now he's vague about what he does all day. Rodrigo is in his late forties, but has the energy of a man half his age. After some mumbles and gibberish he finally spits out, "Come on, let's hit up the plasma clinic."

At the end of the Brown Line is the one and only blood bank in Chicago. Rodrigo and I get off the train, pass the all night diner the Huddle House, and hang a right on Lawrence Ave. Two blocks later is the blood bank in an unassuming little storefront with blue trim. Above the door are some ornate Art Deco engravings of swirling seahorses. It makes me wonder what the building was originally built for.

Through the windows we can already see the lobby is full. We shuffle in and squeeze our way to the nurse's window. We put our names on the clipboard. There's standing room only. Some of the guys slip out to smoke a butt as quickly as possible, but most hang tight because if the nurse calls your name and you don't answer you'll lose your place.

It's always a long wait. Sometimes it takes two hours before you get called in the back to donate plasma, which takes at least forty minutes in itself. At the end of this long wait a full-grown man can get thirty bucks for his trouble. If you don't weigh much the payoff is even less. Rodrigo and I are both six foot and worth our weight in platelets.

After a half hour some chairs open up and we take a seat. Rodrigo bunches his brown leather jacket against the glass window and tries to take a nap. I look around. The faces are black, brown, white, most are unshaven, tired, there's no eye contact. Some are in overalls or old work uniforms. Some are in white t-shirts and baggy jeans. Some are older workingmen without a job. Some are young kids who may have never even had a job yet. Only once did I see a lady here.

These are the heroes that donate their precious life force so someone in a hospital can get an IV full. Obviously, no one here is patting themselves on the back. We wouldn't be here for free. Hard times make capitalists of us all.

The kid next to me gets up. That must have been his name that was just called. But as he heads to the back I see he has a clipboard full of forms. That means this is his first time. The nurse is calling him back to complete the screening process. After that he'll be sent back to the lobby to wait in the general line. The first time donating plasma is the longest wait.

During your first visit they test your syrup to make sure you don't have AIDs. They check your arms for track marks to make sure you don't use needles before they stick you with one of theirs. I remember my first time. A tiny nurse ran me through a page of screening questions.

"Have you ever shot heroin?"

"No."

"Have you ever visited Africa?"

"No."

"Have you ever had sex with a man, even once?"

"No."

One can't help but wonder what would happen if you said yes to any of the questions. Are you dismissed or is it just a guide to double check the sample? I assume people lie all the time so they don't get disqualified.

After all the questions with the nurse I waited until a middle-aged doctor came in to talk to me. He was a slender Asian gentleman. His hair looked unwashed. He yawned as he skimmed my blood test. I told him I had type O negative hoping I would get more money for being a universal donor. He explained donating plasma was different than donating blood. I pointed out it wasn't exactly a donation was it? At this he finally made eye contact with me and chuckled politely. As he phoned in the rest of the screening questions he kept trailing off. He wanted to talk about mircro-robotics and remote control surgery. It seemed he wished his career had taken him somewhere other than milking a waiting room full of desperate men.

Meanwhile in the lobby things have livened up. Some kids in white t-shirts are arguing about which rappers are the best. Rodrigo stirs awake and looks around with his eyes half closed.

"I make my own beats in my room," says the most animated kid.

"Yeah, how? What you use?"

"Garageband. It comes with most any computer."

"Garageband..."

"It's on my daddy's laptop. I'll show you after we get dis money."

"And you can record your rhymes on there?"

"Yeah. You just layer another track over those beats and go at it."

Rodrigo interjects, "Hey young-blood. Let me hear you rap."

The kid licks his lips as if to get ready. As he begins he's looking around like he is pulling the words out of the air around him.

My baby needs milk and I can spit.
Gonna make money by talking that shit.
So hook me up doc with that plastic vein.

Soon's gonna be my big break.
Any man that can get his pen in his hand
can record that shit on Garageband.

Then the words get too fast for me to follow. Anybody who wasn't listening to the kids can't help but hear them now. It's pretty sharp that he can just rhyme about whatever is going on at the moment even if it's only waiting in line at the plasma clinic.

My name gets called.

In the back is a large room with four rows of beds. Next to each bed is a machine about the size of a bathroom sink. Tubes hang out of each machine. The nurse directs me to my bed. Rolling up my sleeves I lie down. The bed smells like bleach.

There are old TVs hanging from the ceiling by chains. Every time I come here they have a different vampire film playing. This keeps the atmosphere light. Today they are screening *From Dusk Till Dawn*. At least the plasma clinic has a sense of humor about itself as they harvest our life-blood.

The nurse wheels up a tray with gauze and instruments. She puts her gloves on with a snap. Cleaning my mainline with alcohol she explains the process again. The needle she holds in her hand is thick as the ink tube in a Bic pen. The point is slanted at the end. I can actually see the hole in the needle. Once it is connected to the tube in the machine she asks if I'm ready. In my experience it hurts much less if I watch it go in. This takes away the element of surprise. Wide eyed I give her the okay. She jabs my blue vein and a shot of red liquid flares up a tube.

Just then a vampire bites a pale neck on the screen above. I'm given a squeeze ball to help pump the juice into the machine. I pump away vigorously. Let's get this over with.

Rodrigo is getting seated across the room. His nurse eyes him suspiciously wondering if he's been drinking too much to donate. No one says anything. Soon both our plasma machines are purring away like coffee makers. I wonder if his recipient will get a buzz from his boozy blood. Probably not, because during the first cycle the blood is sucked into the machine where it separates the red stuff from the white platelets. Next to me there's a large cylinder filling with the milky medicine.

A bell goes off and the nurse comes around for the second cycle. This is the worst part. She switches out the tube and hits a button on the machine. Now the blood is returned back to my veins minus the plasma. It comes back cold. I get a chilling sensation in my arm and chest.

Rodrigo is trying to flirt with the nurse. Broke and wired up like a lab-rat doesn't discourage him. He tries the same line every time. As he pumps the squeeze ball he tells her that he's pouring his heart out just for her. She rolls her eyes.

It's over. Rodrigo and I are standing on the sidewalk blinking in the sunbeams. Our blood is thin, our heads are light, our eyes are spotted. Pixels and stars are dancing in a cloud of subatomic activity. Angel ladders follow us like spotlights. We have cotton swabs over our mainlines held down by pink Band-Aides. We look beat, but we're both thirty dollars richer. Rodrigo elbows me. "Let's make the most of this. It won't take much to get a buzz on now."

We mosey to a liquor store off Lawrence and Kedzie. The shopkeep has a Syrian flag behind the counter. He sports a comb-over, a silk shirt, and a gold chain. He greets us. "Hey buddy." He seems to know Rodrigo.

We peruse the coolers. "Here, this won't break the bank." Rodrigo scoops up a bottle of Wild Irish Rose from the bottle shelf. "Wine is the best thing to rejuvenate the blood." I don't think even Rodrigo really believes his own words. After donating plasma the veins are thin. A full-grown man can get drunk off one drink. Using the blood bank is not only a way of making money but saving money.

Cutting down the alley we come to a vacant lot and pop-a-squat behind a pile of gravel. Rodrigo breaks the seal of the Wild Irish Rose. I take a hit and start humming *Where the Wild Roses Grow* by Nick Cave. "They call me the wild rose. But my name was Elisa Day..."

This wine is as sweet as Kool-Aide. I can already tell there will be a headache right after the high. Soon the afternoon sun seems to swim around us slowly.

It doesn't take long to finish the bottle between passing it back and forth and Rodrigo occasionally pouring a swig on the ground for his dead-homies.

Time has slowed down. I'm ruminating on the ambitious young guys back at the clinic practicing their rap skills in the waiting room. I guess I am not much different than these would-be hip-hop stars bleeding away. There are so many kids who are sure that they are gonna be the next urban poet. There are just as many open-mics for MCs around Chicago as there are for us wannabe singer-songwriters.

At least hip-hop still has a pulse in the media consciousness. Yet underground, there is an emerging scene of alt-country, alt-blues, and folkies in Chicago. Maybe it was the hard times, or maybe roots music began to appeal to those of us living in the city as we began to miss the farm country we once ran away from. I miss the smell of plants, rivers, and the feeling of life all around. Growing up all the prepackaged pop-music and especially pop-country music was the enemy. Pop music was a lie. The music was more concerned with sex appeal than substance. Back in the nineties I wanted to play the angst ridden chords of punk and metal. The thundering guitars and industrial drums called me to the cities. It took years of living in the city to appreciate real country, real folk, and most of all the blues. There's an eternal haunting quality to roots music. That twang of the guitar rings through the mind in a tunnel of nostalgia for the agrarian life.

It's easy to think that musicians these days find wealth and luxury as a valid subject to sing about. "Bling" and glamor has become a staple in pop music. Yet there are whole subcultures that reflect and even romanticize the poor state that most Americans are in. You might not see it on TV but punk, blues, and bluegrass are still favorites in working class circles. Also, rappers who write about being rich are not writing for other rich people. It's a fantasy that lets those without money feel better about being broke. It's an escape. Just as often hip-hop contains stories from the streets about real life drawing from personal experience which is exactly what folk singers do. By default, artists often have more realism than they bargain for. Economic pressures can kick the pretense out of a songwriter. Even if you have surrealistic tendencies in this climate pretty soon we're all keeping it real.

In industrial parts of Chicago there are hidden communities of artists who illegally live in warehouses, build rooms, create indoor tents with sheets, and spray-paint the city by night. My buddy William Leland's loft in the West Loop is like this. Makeshift rooms divided by tarps and sheets. There are those that still hop freight trains and criss-cross the country despite the surveillance systems of our time. Some of these futuristic hobos are hybrid hippie-punks, sporting dreadlocked manes, face tattoos, bandanas. They call themselves Crusties, Travelers, or nothing at all.

There are still more artists like myself who after college have not been able to translate art school to employment. Us damn geniuses wake up facing an ocean of debt and a sparse job market. The cry of depression often turns to America's roots music, and Chicago is still the world capital of the blues.

On the outskirts of this scene was my old band. Using the name

Cousin Bones we played all the clubs: The Green Mill, The Double Door, Reggies. A summer of steady playing and recording demos we seemed to get a foothold in the business. But now the guys have left. Now I am on my own.

Getting up I tell Rodrigo, "I better get something in the breadbasket otherwise I'm gonna pass out."

Clutching my arm I help him up. "Suppose I should eat. It's been a couple days."

Staggering in the afternoon delight we make our way to the Huddle House on Kimball Avenue.

We slide into a booth and watch the bustle out the window: the man with a hotdog cart, the meter maid, kids skipping school. The waitress comes. She's in her fifties and has a black eye. For starters we just get water.

Rodrigo lends a pro-tip, "If you just get the burger without the fries you can eat for under five bucks."

"Two burgers please."

The waitress smiles and heads back behind the counter.

Leaning in to Rodrigo I shoot a thumb back at her. "We should give a fair tip. Did you see her face? Some jerk gave her a black eye."

"That's an old trick. You shouldn't fall for it."

"What do you mean trick?"

"That's makeup. Waitresses have been doing that for years. You put on a bunch of mascara on one eye and it looks like a shiner. Then everyone feels sorry and over tips."

"Looks real to me."

"Oh don't be a sucker."

A gaggle of ladies approach the window outside. They're in sweatshirts and baggy jeans. As they pass Rodrigo ducks down and turns his face away from the window.

"Damn, they're out early. I owe that bitch forty bucks."

"Why?"

"Those working girls hang out at this diner at night to stay warm. That one with the face tattoo serviced me a few weeks ago. Afterwards I reached in my pocket for the money and it's gone. She said I could owe her, which only had convinced me she picked my pocket while she was going south in the first place. She was trying to double dip: rob me *and* get paid. Otherwise she wouldn't let me slide. No sir, she would have called her pimp on my ass."

I'm skeptical. "Those girls? In the baggy clothes? They weren't even showing any skin."

"You can't show too much or the cops will bust ya. You know that they're working girls from the tattoos. That face tat with the claws by the right eye has been a brand pimps put on their stable in this part of town for years."

I should just nod and let it go. Maybe Rodrigo has had too much wine, but I press it. "So why would she steal your roll of bills, and then demand more knowing very well that she already has all your money?"

"So she can make me owe her! And you know what? I *did* have some more bills. I always tuck an emergency stash in my sock. I wasn't about to give her that after she had already helped herself."

Our food arrives and we eat in silence.

Streetwalkers in sweatpants? Branded ladies with face tattoos? Waitresses drawing fake black eyes with eyeliner? It's all too much. In this town when you hear a crazy story it's hard to tell if what you're hearing is some real crazy goings on, or if the person that's telling you the story is crazy. There may be a kernel of truth to every hip tip, but each time a story gets repeated it gets distorted like the schoolyard game of telephone. Multiply that by three million people in Chicago you have quite a yarn. It's hard to tell what is urban legend and what is that hidden knowledge, that straight dope, which everyone who thinks they are streetwise wants to know. Behind every door, behind every pulled shade, down every alley something is going on. You can feel it. Behind the vale of the everyday comings and goings on the avenues there must be some hidden pattern. There must be some criminal conspiracy just below the surface. Most of the time it's just the same old shit: people eating, sleeping, watching TV. For an old timer like Rodrigo the vast criminal conspiracy moving in every shadow has become just the same old shit too.

Making some excuse I leave him there picking his teeth. Not before placing another five dollars on the counter for the waitress. Even if the black eye is a hustle it's a good hustle. I could use a good hustle.

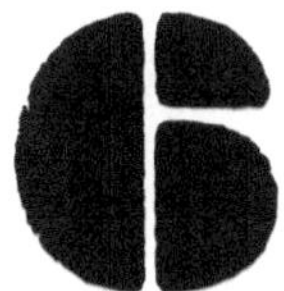

Since I'm on the North Side I take the Brown Line to the Belmont stop and walk towards the lake. A friend of mine from school has just moved into a studio apartment off Belmont and Broadway in Boy's Town.

Feathers from a discarded pink boa flutter in the gutter. A boy with blonde locks roller blades down the street singing a love song out loud to the world. A buxom lady with an Adam's apple gives me a wink and then adjusts her platinum wig.

Without a phone I am relying on luck that my friend Matt will be home.

At the front door I buzz his room number on the dial. There's only silence. Then the intercom sparks up, "Hello?"

"Matt! It's Wes. How's it going man?"

"Oh hey. I'll buzz you in."

Since the advent of texting the art of impromptu knocking on doors has been obliterated. Saying that you were just in the neighborhood is considered rude, if not laced with ulterior motives. But Matt and I are old friends. These types of mild shenanigans have come to be expected from me. Also, Matt is just about the most easy-going person I know. He has that rare calm energy that attracts stray cats and stray people. He's unpretentious and a good listener. I've seen complete strangers at parties puke their souls out to the guy for no obvious reason except that Matt seems openhearted.

The rickety elevator jerks up to the fifth floor. It's the kind with the accordion doors. Down the dim yellow hallway I come to his door, which he has left open a crack. As I step in his cat runs under the bed. It's a one room joint with the radiator under a window. There's a kitchenette and a bathroom. Otherwise the studio has enough room for his bed, a desk, and an easy chair. Matt is a slight but handsome Italian kid with a full black beard. He offers me the chair and he sits on his bed.

Rolling himself a cigarette he asks me how things are going? I update him on my comings and goings. He nods thoughtfully. Before I ask he offers, "You can crash here tonight if you want. I don't have to work at the thrift store until noon."

Thanking him we head down to the end of the hall where the door to the fire escape is open like the end of a tunnel of light. We peer down through the grates of the poor man's balcony as he sparks up his roll.

"What's your next move?" he asks.

"I have to figure out someplace besides lurking above my ex-girl-friends' apartment. That attic is dirty and it's only a matter of time until I'm found out."

"Right."

"I gotta get some money together and find my own place. I've got an interview at a dry cleaner in the South Loop. Also, I'm gonna try this angle writing songs for people on the street. In the meantime I've been thinking about getting a practice space. I could keep all my shit there for cheap, and I bet I could keep myself there too."

"A practice space? Like for bands?"

"Right. To rent one is usually pretty reasonable. There was a building of storage units on Western and 15th by the rail yard which was recently converted to practice spaces. I went there to take a look. It had showers and everything. You know for washing off the sweat after rocking out. Those places are usually unventilated warehouses. This one had air-conditioning. But the owner had security cameras everywhere. He was eyeing me suspiciously in my dirty clothes. It was a bust."

Matt takes a second look at me. "You can take a shower here."

"Thanks man."

"There's a washer and dryer in the basement too."

"You're a lifesaver."

Throwing down for beer Matt heads out to the corner. He lets me use his laptop to look up some practice spaces. The cheapest one I can find is way out west in Garfield Park. My band used it once last year to audition bass players. It's a red brick building from the 1800's originally an old YMCA. When Matt gets back I use his phone to call the owner and make an appointment to see what units he has.

While I jump in the shower Matt takes his homemade paintings off the wall and turns on his projector. With the white wall clear he plays a DVD of *Run Lola Run* from his laptop. Hooked up to the projector the wall serves as a screen. Images fill the room. Taking the cushions off the recliner I lay them on the floor and create a makeshift bed. The movie flickers away into dreamland.

7

Feeling clean and rejuvenated I leave Matt's place early in the morning. First I pick up my guitar from the locker in the break room at Dominick's. For breakfast I get another sample from the Deli counter. Then I dip back to Pilsen. After silently heel-toeing down the alley and up the stairwell I find my sign. The paint is dry from the heat in the attic. I slip it into my guitar case and retrieve my folding chair.

Determined to make this work I head back downtown. Knowing now that a street performer license is required I am even more nervous than the first time. I'll have to look out for the Chicago Police. My guitar is out. My sign is propped up against my guitar case reading: Tell me your problem and I'll write you a blues song. Some change is sprinkled in my cap hoping to take seed.

Minutes pass. People on Michigan Avenue rush in all directions their motivations unapparent. My fingers keep busy by noodling on the fret-board. A few people pause to read my sign. Most chuckle to themselves and keep walking. I ask myself: Do these people have any problems to write blues songs about? Taking the time to practice my songs I run through my entire repertoire.

A middle-aged man strolling with a tall lady stops about twenty feet away from me. He points at my sign. He has wispy brown hair and sad eyes. She is lanky and has dirty blonde hair. Thinking I have a bite I smile the best I can and wave them in. With a little coaxing he steps up.

"Howdy young man," he greets with a southern accent. "I've got more problems than I can shake a stick at."

"Sorry to hear that. Music always helps. You want a customized song?"

"Fun, fun. How much do blues songs cost?"

Nervous, I don't want him to sense this is my first time. At a glance I size him up: white tennis shoes, pastel colored shirt, kaki pants. He's probably from out of town.

"Just ten dollars," I tell him as I whip out a piece of paper from my pocket and click my pen. "Go ahead, tell me your troubles."

He produces the ten spot.

"Well, I have lung cancer."

My heart sinks. This is more than I bargained for.

"The doctors say I might have a year. This young lady here…" He pauses to take the hand of his companion. "Well she's my ex-wife. We were married for eight years. We've been through a lot together. But nothing like this."

"Oh wow," is all I can muster.

"She's come to visit me. We're gonna have a night in the big town. Dinner, dancing, Champagne, and song…"

I'm taking notes.

"The truth, if she don't know by now, is that I want her back."

Her eyes well up. This is heavy. I pegged him as a well to do middle class white guy from the suburbs. Book and cover right? Everyone has problems. From Michigan Avenue to 95th Street and beyond. That's the blues.

Asking for a minute I look at my notes. Keep it simple. Quickly crossing out some words and replacing them with rhymes and drawing arrows to rearrange the order of the phrases I have something.

Slowly I start a pulse on my old guitar. He takes her in his arms. As I strum a basic Willie Dixon riff I moan out:

Baby, I know you
And you know me
Greatest days of my life
Was when you were on my knee

Doctor say, a spot on my lung
Doctor say, maybe a year left of fun
Baby, I'm no longer foolish and young
Won't you hold my hand as I slip into that great beyond?

Darling, I won't treat you bad
Please, I won't make you sad
Baby, you make me so happy
Please, my wife, please come back to me

When I look up she has her hands cupped around her mouth like she's trying not to cry. He's down on one knee. He kisses her hand. She nods her head up and down silently as she helps him up. They embrace. Damn now I'm starting to tear up. A small crowd has stopped to watch. Everyone starts clapping as the couple kisses.

My first customer turns to me. This time he fishes out a twenty-dollar bill and puts it in my hand. "Thank you young man." They start to walk away arm in arm. Not before he turns and says, "Oh, and if you smoke. Try your damnedest to give it up."

He winks. She waves. That's it.

The crowd evaporates with the current of the street. I'm stunned. This could work. I'm actually a street musician. I'm holding my own with the toughest audience in the world. Robert Johnson would be proud.

Feeling lucky as the devil I'm grinning and waving at each passer-by. Pointing at my sign people smile, shrug, or look away. When anyone makes eye contact I wave them in. Step right up. Step right up. I'm the carnival barker of the blues. I'm the pitchman under the biggest big top: the clear blue sky.

Most ease up with a chuckle. Almost all my customers use the camera on their phones to film whatever I come up with.

Love problems? No problem.

Hate your boss? Gimme some details. Let's make fun of him.

As the day goes on I gather some more green in my pocket, but I realize it might never be as magical as that first customer. It's hard work. Honestly people approaching the sign are few and far between. But for an original song I'll average a five-dollar tip, which is better than singles and change for pouring heart and soul out hour after hour. I have found a good hustle. Soon I begin keeping a novel in my guitar case and reading until someone steps up. Even if I have to wait hours to find a customer I can at least make enough for a sandwich and a forty, and live to fight another day.

With a good hustle I might survive but getting a decent roof over my head is another story. After ringing the buzzer of my old friend William Leland's in the West Loop with no answer I am wandering down Sangamon Street. At the dead end where the road runs into Highway 290 I throw my chair and guitar over the chain-link fence and climb after. Making myself comfortable in a bed of tall grass on the slope overlooking the rush and roar of the glowing cars I fold my arms and tip my hat over my eyes.

After a restless sleep and a shower of morning dew I'm ready for my job interview at the dry cleaners. Itchy and yawning I take the Halsted bus through Greek Town, UIC Campus, pass Maxwell Street, and skim the eastern edge of Pilsen. Blue shadows dance in the delicate dawn. At Cermak I transfer heading east under a cathedral of highway overpasses, over a lattice of canals, and through the fading neons of Chinatown.

On the other side of the Red Line tracks is where the South Loop begins to feel like the South Side. Past the Hillard Apartments is Sharks Fish and Chicken, Reggies, and the Velvet Lounge. Round the way is the Blues Heaven Foundation, a nice little museum where the famous Chess Records once resided. Every Thursday in the summer I used to go to free blues concerts in the vacant lot next door.

At the corner of Michigan and Cermak I'm at my destination. There are racks of suits in the window covered in cellophane. Every now and then the racks start moving on an automated track. Inside there's customers lined up with their drops offs in hand or a pink ticket to claim clean threads. Chet is here. When he sees me walk in he waves me around the back. Just behind the cash registers it hits me. The steam from the pressing machines is overwhelming. Even with industrial fans blowing it's a jungle behind the counter.

Chet knocks on an office door with a glass window. I set my guitar and chair next to a filing cabinet. Inside is the boss. He's a skinny guy with a sneer on his face and his feet on the desk. It's air-conditioned in the office.

"Herman this is the guy I was telling you about," says Chet.

The boss vaguely looks in my direction. Never looking me in the eye he keeps grinning. His gums are bloody. He licks his teeth, leans over, and spits into a trashcan. Later I'll chalk up his constant sneer as some sort of birth defect. Herman mumbles to Chet, "Fine. You can start training him Thursday morning." Following Chet we go into another room where he starts rummaging through a box.

"I guess I got the job."

"Guess so."

"Easy interview."

"Like I said he was looking for a white guy."

Chet pulls out some blue shirts with the company logo on the breast pocket.

"What's your size?"

"Was extra large, but I've been slimming down these days."

I stuff the shirt into my guitar case. After wading through the gauntlet of heat and steam I'm back on the street. A cool morning breeze comes off the lake. It hits me like a kiss from God.

To kill time I go to the Blues Heaven Foundation. After ringing the buzzer a man in his mid-thirties greets me. He has kind eyes and says his name is Kevin. It's early. I'm the only tourist here. On a wall there are sculptures of the faces of all the greats: Muddy Waters, R.L Burnside, Charlie Patton, Bessie Smith, Koko Taylor, Blind Willie Johnson, Little Walter… I see the room where some of the most iconic Chicago blues and some of the earliest rock and roll were recorded. It's just a white room about ten feet by twenty. Chuck Berry recorded here. Etta James recorded here. In this room Muddy Waters recorded *Hoochie Coochie Man.* This room is where Howling Wolf recorded *Smoke Stack Lightning.* Kevin shows me the pipe that leads down into the basement. By placing another microphone down below Chess Records would create that great 1950's reverb sound long before it was reproduced digitally.

My tour guide tells me they still have recording sessions here sometimes. I ask Kevin how much they charge to record here. He says it depends who it is. "If a local group wants that Chess sound that's one thing, but if it's the Rolling Stones that's another. This is a foundation. All the money goes to trying to make young people aware of the blues. It's their musical heritage."

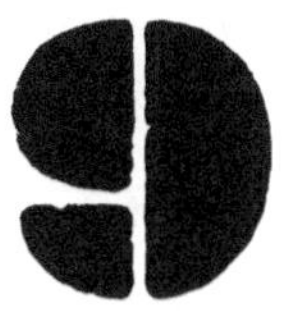

I need a place to call my own. I need sanctuary, safety, some peace and quiet. After the Ashland stop the Green Line doesn't make a stop until California Avenue. The train roars over the horizon to the West Side. At Kedzie you can see the old timers drinking their juice huddled around burn barrels. The light from the trash fire flickers under a mural of Dr. Martin Luther King. As the crow flies Garfield Park isn't that far from downtown but it's a world away from the likes of the Apple Store and Marshal Fields.

In the city you can't play music in the garage or the basement like you can back in the country. You certainly can't play in apartments without getting noise complaints from your neighbors. Instead smart businessmen take old warehouses and convert them into practice spaces. There a band can rent a room the size of a studio apartment and get as loud as they want. Afterwards they can store their equipment. The only issue is that these warehouses are often in the more rundown corners of the city. It doesn't take much common sense to watch your back if you are loading expensive amps and drums into one of the buildings. Otherwise your gear will end up in the pawnshop window.

My stop is Lake and Pulaski. At the end of the platform I take the stairs down to the street and turn north on Karlov passing a salvage yard. The next corner is clustered with three hard looking guys in the uniform: black jackets in summer, loose pants, durags. Like bees around a hive kids ten or twelve run up performing secret handshakes with the older dudes and then dart off again. Powder is in the air.

At the end of the block semi-trucks beep where Karlov is cut-off by the rail yard. A Metra train roars past running parallel with Kinzie Street. First there is a lot heaped with scrap metal mostly stacks of mattress springs. Across from all this is my destination.

It's the oldest building on the block. It looks out of place. The red brick climbs two stories high. There is a small spire like a castle. This is the YMCA from the 19th century converted into practice spaces. A large steel door leads to a stairwell with a large square window with black trim.

Waiting on the curb a beat-up white van pulls up. Out comes a bearded middle-aged dude. Under his baseball cap his blonde locks have shocks of grey. His suit-coat and tight pants are hipper than his age. I recognize the owner from the one time my band used the place for auditions. We shake hands. He doesn't recognize me. He looks like he just woke up.

"I'm Bret the owner."

At the door Bret seems to come alive as he punches in the security code on the steel door. He has the guided tour locked and loaded into his verbal ammunition. "If you get a space you'll get the security code numbers. It changes every few months. The new numbers will be on the envelope I'll place under your door used for collecting the rent. If you lose it just call me."

Inside the place is dimly lit and painted red which makes it glow like some medieval dungeon. It smells of dust and mouse droppings. In the narrow lobby is a vending machine and a torn leather couch. To the left there's a door labeled: Office.

"See the slot in the office door? Here's where you drop your rent envelope every month. Men's room is on this level down the hall to the right." A few forty-watt bulbs flicker down a dark corridor.

As we ascend the broad carpeted staircase he points out, "As you can see we have a very liberal graffiti policy." Rounding the large window overlooking the street I can see what he means. Across the landing and the wide-open space on the second floor the walls are covered with colorfully painted tags, band logos, stickers, some smut crudely drawn with marker. There are some old couches in the common area. The sound of water is dripping from the women's bathroom.

He shows me a few rooms large enough for a brass band. These rooms are pretty expensive. Then on the second floor directly across from the stairs on the opposite side of the common area he opens one of the white pinewood doors. This room has red carpet and is about ten foot by ten foot. In the back there is an opening to a closet of large shelves made of two-by-fours. Past the shelves is another room. This cubby is about eight feet by four feet. The ceilings are high. There are no windows. The air is stale.

The owner says, "I know this one would be hard to have a drum set in. How many people are in your band?"

"It varies." I begin to spin a lie. "You know how bands are. Members rotate. Usually four."

He nods. "Since it's such a squeeze this is the cheapest one I have. It's a hundred and seventy-five a month. Split that four ways and it's a great deal."

After my next check from the grocery store, the first one from the dry cleaners, and a few days busking on the pavement I should be able to make that.

"This could work for what we do," I tell him.

"What kind of music do you guys play?"

"Blues. Roots-rock. We do a lot of acoustic stuff. So this works."

For a second he eyes me wondering if I play acoustically why do I need a practice space? Just play in a living room. But he just shrugs and continues the tour.

As he locks the door behind him Bret says, "So with security deposit that will be three fifty."

I gulp. It will take a while for me to make that.

"That might take a few weeks. It's just three of us right now. We're looking for another drummer."

"Alright, I would be quick though. This deal won't last long. Someone will snatch this unit up."

On the way downstairs he lays out the rules. "Now I'm usually at the main location at Kinzie and Ashland. If you have any issues just call me."

In the common area he points to some security cameras installed in the corners of the ceiling. "Just because I'm not here doesn't mean that I don't know what's going on. You have some hangers on that are just hanging out? Fine. Your girlfriends want to watch you practice? Fine. I only care if punks break my shit." Looking around there isn't much to break. He goes on. "I'm old but I'm a black belt. If you break my shit all your equipment will go out to the curb for the hood to have."

None of this is actually directed at me. It's clear he says this every time.

In the lobby he shows me the vending machine. "This thing is stocked with beer. Here I think I have some change." He ruffles through his pockets. Coins tumble down the slot. Out clunks a can of Stroh's then another.

He hands me one. "I haven't seen this brand forever," I tell him.

We crack them open.

"It's cheap but good," which seems to be Bret's motto. He strikes me as a burnt out hair-metal guy from the eighties. I get the feeling that he really cares about music. This was his dream: just a place where people can party and play loud. His heart is in the right place. He just doesn't want any hassles. Since these old buildings are no longer zoned as residences there's minimal upkeep required. The rent checks just drop through the door every month.

Eyeing the vending machine full of beer I think: Well that's deadly. Even after bar time and the liquor stores close I could get a cold one in this stuffy old building. That is if I could spare the scratch.

Out of his back pocket Bret whips out a copy of the lease agreement. He proceeds to read it to me. He gets to the clause that states it is unlawful to live in the practice space. As he reads this I let out my most folksy laugh.

"Man, you must have seen everything!"

"Yeah, you know if you've had too many beers just crash on one of the couches. But if I start seeing your laundry hanging up we've got a problem."

Of course, my intention is to live here. I would have to see to it that I have one too many beers every night. As for my laundry and food I'll have to hide it in my guitar case when I come in and out.

Bret gives me a copy of the lease. I tell him I'll call when I have the money. We shake hands again and he leaves.

Walking along Kinzie and the train tracks I pass a sausage processing plant. Somehow it smells appetizing and horrible all at once. At Pulaski I decide to head north. At the bus stop there is no bench. The lot behind me looks newly demolished. I pull up a loose cinder block.

As I sit on the block picking my head a Crown Vic sedan rolls by. Out the passenger side a black dude around my age dangles out the window tapping ash off a blunt. His crown of dreads bursts in the breeze. When he sees me he yells, "Bitch!"

As I start to hangout on the West Side I am still maintaining the following assumptions: A.) If I am nice to people they'll be nice to me. B.) Only people who choose to be gangsters get hurt by gangs. C.) If I look poor no one will try to rob me.

Turns out, this is ignorance. None of these assumptions are true.

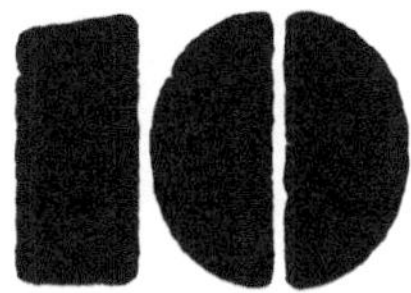

Back at Dominick's on Division Bandi sees me come in.

"Get your apron on Wes. You're on the schedule for five-dollar pizza day."

I don't even have to look at the schedule. "Of course I am. Moe only schedules me for the busiest day."

Bandi laughs and then snaps back, "That ain't nothing new. If you're good at your job you get punished for it. Meanwhile old junkie Joy over here gets the easy days because she half asleep from them drugs!"

She says this last part loud enough for everyone to hear. Leaning on the counter with both elbows Joy's face doesn't change. She brushes off Bandi's words with a wave of her hand like she's batting off a fly. Bandi grins at me. "Look at her with her nose dripping. That means she's coming off that stuff."

Joy sniffs, "I can't help it!"

Bandi continues her monologue. Sometimes she whips herself into such a frenzy her venting turns into a rant. "Moe! Where is he? I don't wanna work with Joy no more. She a bimbo! What do you gotta do to get fired up in here? It's the union. That's what it is. They take a bite out of our checks but they sure as hell make it impossible for anyone to get fired. I would know. Shit, I've pulled some shit up in here myself." Her fury doesn't taper off. She keeps going as she wanders into the aisles looking for Moe.

I always shave at work in the employee bathroom using disposable razors. Instead of shaving cream I use the pink hand soap from the dispenser. Before landing the gig at the grocery store I preferred to grow a beard and wear my hair long. Working with food that is no longer permitted. So now I look clean cut and despite all my troubles my co-workers assume I'm square. The guitar on my back usually just gets a laugh.

Today as I scrape my face the store manager Mr. Paterson walks in. He slaps me on the back and says, "Looking good for the customers? That's great!"

Meanwhile as I enter the deli my department manager Mohamed or "Moe" pulls me aside. "Westley you have to work on your personal hygiene. I was trying to tell another worker to clean their apron and they pointed you out. Your hair looks dirty, and your shirts are never clean. Please at least meet the bare minimum here. You're not the same Westley that started here."

"No problem," I tell him. Moe makes a check mark in his book noting that he talked to me. Bandi is right. If the union can protect the workers who don't pull their own weight they can protect me.

The only person I ever saw get fired was Chuck. Under the eyes of the security cameras he helped himself to a slice of pizza. He simply went in the back by the dishes and ate it. Sure for what they are paying us we will sometimes eat off the food that is right under our noses. Yet it is easy to get away with it if you bother to take some precaution. I'll bag up an expensive item like prosciutto, but when I punch in the code on the scale I'll punch in a cheaper product like turkey. If I place the bag on the scale but hold the bag the full weight of the item will not register on the scale and a lower price tag will print off. These items can be set to the side for a worker to purchase during break, lunch, or at closing time. I'll cut a slice of pizza twice the normal size for myself, go on break, and come around to the other side of the counter and purchase it for the normal price. I will use free coupons over and over. All this appears as normal activity under the cameras. Of course I wouldn't do this just for fun. If I could make ends meet I wouldn't put myself through the trouble. It's a matter of survival.

Working part time at minimum wage is a thin tightrope. Per week my check averages about one hundred and forty dollars. After taxes, union dues, and buying a CTA bus-pass at the service desk maybe one hundred goes in my pocket. It's barely enough to live on.

At closing I always volunteer to take out the trash. This way it is my responsibility to clear the unsold rotisserie chickens and take them to the garbage shoot behind the storeroom where there are no cameras. With some practice I have trained myself to devour a whole chicken in less than a minute. After being under the heat lamps all day the meat slides right off the bone and down my gullet.

Even on my days off I'll do the rounds at other grocery stores getting free-samples from other delis.

Most of my coworkers use food stamps through the Link Card. Though I am more than qualified I never have been able to breach welfare. Homeless people can qualify for stamps even if it's just hippie homeless like me. Instead of getting the Link Card mailed to a residence they can have it sent to a city office for pick up. I tried to go through the system a couple times. The lines are epic. Dealing with the bureaucracy is a job in itself. After being told to go to another location in a different part of town for the third time my efforts slowed.

One day I asked Bandi about her name. Sometimes people called her Bandit like she's a bank robber. She showed me her driver's license. "Look, my full name is Abbandit. See my daddy took off before I was born. So my mamma said, 'Well this baby is abandoned. I'm gonna name her Abandit.'" Somehow Bandi laughed. But what choice does she have? It's no wonder Bandi has such a strong sense of humor.

There's also Mr. Sunshine. He got his nickname because he's light skinned and smiles all day. As I'm prepping the pizzas for the oven he asks me, "Wes. Where you stay at?"

It would take too long to tell the whole story. I've found people just think I'm joking anyway. So I just tell him, "Well today I looked at a place off Lake and Pulaski."

"Damn. I don't even visit out west. You're blacker than me!" He laughs so hard he leans to one side and spins his whole body in a circle like a figure skater.

Joy is back in her street clothes. She's leaving for the day after the morning shift where she mills around trying to do as little work as possible. She's nice enough. But she puts on more miles walking around trying to look busy than standing in one place actually getting something done. At some point trying to avoid work becomes harder than just doing it. Joy rushes out the door as if she has something on her mind.

There's Roxy who is originally from Palmyra, Wisconsin. She does more than her share of work because she's on meth. She buzzes around mumbling to herself in run-on sentences, juggling hams, taking orders, cleaning up just as soon as she makes a mess. She's a model worker. Moe and the other managers love her. The managers at the store are so full of slogans and sales numbers that they are completely unaware of what is really going on between Roxy on uppers and Joy on downers. Maybe that's one reason alcohol is still legal. If someone shows up to work drunk you can see it and you can smell it. But all these powders are harder to detect unless you know the signs.

Clyde is the only other white guy at the deli beside myself. The black ladies don't take him seriously either. After a shave I look pretty wholesome. Clyde even more so. He has a baby-face and Ron Howard ears. Turns out he's the most twisted cat here. He's fresh out of jail for dealing meth. In fact he's Roxy's new supplier. He told me at his peak he was living in the Trump Tower and took weekly plane trips to Arizona and driving back with serious sums of crystal. He was always weary about getting busted. So he would hide pounds of meth outside his room in the Trump. After getting strung out and not sleeping for days he would forget where he hid the stuff and wander the hallways checking under ceiling tiles paranoid that the security cameras were watching him. Clyde only works here as a parole requirement.

Like I said Chicago has become checkered with housing projects on one block then condos on the next. The Old Town neighborhood is particularly surreal in how it shifts from block to block. I remember getting something from the service desk at the store and this older lady with a British accent was acting like she had never shopped for herself before in her life. She was asking the service desk clerk about everything on her list. She didn't have the cockney accent but that blue-blood aristocratic tone. "Oh dear, and where would I find the eggs? And steak? What about the juice? Oh dear, this is going to take a long time." She was waiting for someone to volunteer to shop for her. Hard times were hitting everybody. Meanwhile Lamonica the clerk behind the desk attended to the people who bothered to stand in line to get cigarettes and bus passes. Occasionally she'd answer this older lady, "That's in aisle five… steak is by the butcher counter… aisle eight… three… produce…"

It took a minute but my co-workers grew to like me. Bandi and the other gals could smell bullshit a mile away. Yet I never acted like I was from Chicago. I never acted like I belonged back in Wisconsin. I kept it real. Because the truth is I don't belong anywhere. I'm a natural outsider. So naturally I sympathize with all outsiders.

But not everybody liked to see my face behind the counter. One day I was working the hot food counter at the deli. A tall dark man in aviators bought a two-piece chicken meal with mac & cheese as the side.

"Lemme get some hot sauce."

There were no packets but we kept a bottle of Louisiana Sauce under the register for everyone to use. I put in on the counter so he could dowse his food. It's true you gotta add the heat.

"Can I get this on Link Card?"

"Sorry Link doesn't work for the cooked food. Basically it's any cold thing."

"Come on. Just put it through."

"Sorry I can't. For real the computer won't let it go through. The barcode knows what it is."

A line was starting to form behind him. He grumbled something and peeled off some bills. I gave him his change.

"Lemme get a bag," he barked.

I pulled off a plastic bag and wrapped up his food.

"Double bag it."

I double bagged it.

"Lemme get another bag."

I gave him another bag.

"Look I need extra bags."

The line was now six deep but the customer was always right. So I gave him another bag.

"Look I need more. I have a special project."

I finally snapped, "How much is enough?! Here!" I peeled off one, two, three, four, five, six more bags. "Just say when!" They were in a pile on the counter.

Without picking up the bags the man in the aviators turned and walked towards the door. Over his shoulder said, "Just wanted you to know what it's like to be ordered around. Come see how the other half lives!"

"I don't know what you mean sir."

Of course I knew what he meant. I just didn't want to give him the satisfaction. He thought he knew me. Did he think he was a mind reader? All that shit is the cost of what privilege I have. So I just counted my blessings and chalked up his anger to the guy having a bad day. Someone had hurt him. He was mad at someone. But whoever it was it wasn't me.

It's a shame. Most of us meet in passing. There's little time to get to know each other. To save time people run on generalizations. There's no time to see the individual. We're left ignorant of each other. The best we can do is be open and unassuming.

In a way he was right. I *am* seeing how the other half lives. Let's not kid ourselves. Once the recession lifts it will probably be easy for someone like me to move on. Shit, when I applied to this job I purposely left my Bachelor's Degree off the application. I didn't want to appear overqualified. After months with no callbacks for any interviews I quickly learned that my education was a hindrance rather than an asset. Employers could see I probably wouldn't stick around. I started leaving it off the resume and bingo I landed the deli clerk gig.

Some of my friends at the store have been working minimum wage all their lives, and many will be doing so long after the economy bounces back. It's hard times for me. For some it's nothing new.

At the corner of Grand and Milwaukee I'm set up where people can see me as they come out of the subway. On the wall behind me are the remnants of a shrine to my friend SOLVE. We were friends in art school. He became a prominent street artist with tags all over the city as well as official art shows in galleries at least once a month.

Last year he was murdered. He was stabbed to death by a member of the 77 Gang. This is a group of punk rockers who take themselves way too seriously. After his death fellow street artists erected a shrine to SOLVE on the vacant building here on Grand. Now the pictures that were plastered up, stickers, tags are all fading and peeling. Now it is a collage of ink, rain, wind, and tears. SOLVE's ghost seems to hang in the air. I wonder what he would think of what I'm doing? He'd probably have some advice. Like any creative critique he'd probably see something I don't see.

Coming up from the stairs of the Blue Line shuffles a young guy in baggy jeans and a black hoodie. He's unshaven. He has a long pointy face, buckteeth, and circles under his eyes. When we make eye contact I give him a wave. He stops and reads my sign.

"You write songs do you?"

"Sure do."

"That's cool."

"Tell me about yourself."

"Like what?"

"Anything. What do you do?"

"I work at a lab."

"What kind of lab?"

"I take care of the rats. I raise baby rats. Then when they are grown the scientists come downstairs and take them away for testing."

"What kind of testing?"

"Don't know. But they do experiments on them."

"Why do they use rats?"

"Well, there really isn't much essential difference between people and rodents. The organs are the same. They are very smart. They even have their own personalities. Each one of them."

"Rats?"

"Sure. I raise them. I get to know them."

"Do you ever see them again?"

"Sometimes. Sometimes they come back the same. Sometimes they come back different or scared. Sometimes they don't come back at all."

"I'm sorry."

"I just wish I knew what the studies were for. You know? That way I'd know if the scientists were learning something useful. I just wish I knew if it was all worth it."

He pulls the drawstrings on his hoodie tight around his face.

"Aren't you hot in that thing?" I ask.

"Yeah a little. I just don't want the surveillance cameras to see me."

I look around. Like most intersections there are cameras up on the traffic lights. There are more electric eyes monitoring the exit to the subway.

"They're everywhere. At any moment the state can know where you are. Not that I'm doing anything wrong. Just don't like being watched. You know?"

I'm taking notes. I think I have something.

"I might have a song for you. You can record it on your phone if you want?"

"Don't have one. They can track you on them too."

Testing, testing, 1, 2, 3
Hey big brother, can you hear me?
Testing, testing, 1, 2, 3
I'm running in your rat-race maze, so now where's my cheese?

You see me on your camera?
Yeah, I don't like that.
Watch my every move. Don't like that.
You tell on me, though I'm up to nothing, so you're the rat.

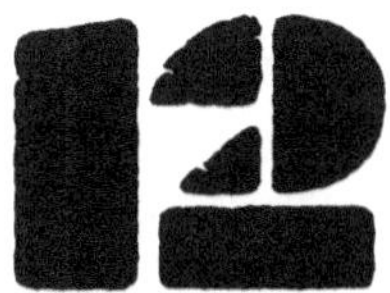

While saving money for the practice space I'm settling into a sort of mad merry-go-round routine. When I can get the hours I work at the dry cleaners in the morning and work at the deli in the evening. Any time off I hit the street and busk for the pedestrians all the while still saving for the license to do so.

When I need a place to sleep I split my nights between Matt's and the attic above my ex's apartment. From the landline at the deli I call Matt. Cheerfully as possible I ask if he wants to hang out. I only burden him when he's off work the next morning. We tie one on and have some laughs like it's old times. This way I keep things light. I arrive with antidotes, updates, and tell him about the characters I meet. I make it seem like adventure rather than charity. Matt is a kind soul, but no one wants the weight of being a life raft.

The rest of the time it's back to the attic in Pilsen. I live in the shadows like a ghoul. As I feel my way up the dark steps I hope tonight isn't the night someone finally locks the door at the top of the stairs. Dusting off the old mattress I bed down cold at night only to wake up sweating when the morning sun hits the roof. Then I dress in my dirty work clothes and sneak down the stairs.

Once in the alley I wet the ground behind a telephone pole, and then hoof it to the restaurant on Ashland for breakfast. As I wait for my food I pop into the bathroom to clean up. I have my toothbrush in my pocket. Just using water I brush'em up. My thoughts are filled with soldiers who had less. History is full of inspiring tales, and before written history there were eons of forgotten human misery. Smiling in the mirror because all my teeth are still there I'm whistling like a bird ready for the day. Plenty of people never had toothbrushes or Mexican restaurants. What a beautiful world we have. I fill up on the complimentary chips and order a steak taco.

The Chicago Reader is free on most every corner. Pawing through the pages on the Pink Line I realize it's already June. Blues Fest has begun down in Grant Park. Every year Chicago puts on the largest blues festival in the world. Plus it's absolutely free. The Reader has a foldout displaying all the performers. What a thing it would be to play there some day.

Checking out the lineup I decide to take a much-deserved day off and go hear some music. Crossing the Loop and passing the Art Institute Columbus Drive is blocked by police barriers for the festival. As I wander between the tents and the stages I hear the honking of harmonicas, the shiver of a brass slide against steel strings, and the growl of throaty crooners. This year is the celebration of Howlin Wolf's 100th Birthday, one of my favorite bluesmen. I don't like most modern blues. Often it's too jazzy. Too upbeat. Too clean. Too safe. Too damn happy to be called the blues. This is what I like to call BBQ blues, the kind of music you hear during a pick-up truck commercial or in the background at a rib restaurant. But this year the bands are playing mean, swampy blues in honor of Howlin Wolf.

In one of the tents there are blues scholars and old bandmates of Wolf holding a discussion panel. His adopted daughters Barbara and Betty are there. Now they must be in their sixties. Wolf passed away in 1976.

Betty has the microphone. "Oh he was a good man. He loved us as if we were his own."

"People think he was some kind of a wild man the way he sang," Barbara chimes in, "but to us he was just a big old teddy bear."

"We'd get red hots down on Maxwell Street and drive home while we ate'em. He'd drive so slow! People would be honking and he'd just wave them to go around."

"Yes, he was good man. Between sets with his band he taught himself how to read and write. Everybody thought he was drinking whisky and carousing, but those were just the stories he sang about in those songs. He loved us and stayed true to our momma."

"But he could be intimidating when a boy would come calling."

"Oh yes we were always brought home on time after a date."

"People forget how powerful his voice was. This is back in the fifties. It was shocking back then. Now all these heavy metal guys wanna sing like Howlin Wolf."

Jodie Williams is here. He's one of the original guitar players in Wolf's band. He is quieter than the other panelists like Eddie Shaw the sax player and Dick Shurman a blues scholar. Mr. Williams seems almost shy. As the panel breaks up I get in line to get an autograph. The other music nerds are more prepared. They are waving rolled up posters and have Sharpies in hand. All I have is a free festival schedule. One of the other fans lends me a marker.

Jodie signed my leaflet with a warm smile almost embarrassed to be getting so much attention. I'm stoked. I'm hanging out with one of the guys who wrote some of those old guitar riffs that we are all so familiar with that most of us don't know where they came from. Howlin Wolf's records document the point where blues turned into rock and roll. These riffs have been imitated and downright ripped off to the point that they are taken for granted. Jodie Williams doesn't seem used to the recognition he deserves.

Before the tent clears for a band to set-up Barbara and Betty announce they have a cake to commemorate what would have been Howlin Wolf's 100th birthday. I am by far the youngest person in attendance so I'm employed to help them pick up a massive sheet cake and place it on the table. Scanning the icing as I heave the cake it says: Chester Burnett aka Howlin Wolf born 1910 or there abouts. What luck I think. Everyone is so nice to me. Plus I have a free slice of cake under my belt.

Thinking nothing could top that I drift through the other tents looking for shade more than anything else. But as I venture I slip further back into music history. I see David "Honey-boy" Edwards the last of the original Mississippi Delta bluesmen. He's in his late nineties. He played with Robert Johnson back in the nineteen thirties. His voice is raw but strong. A white goatee dangles as he smooches the silver microphone. Hunched over his axe he goes into *Key to the Highway*.

> *I gotta keep to the highway, baby I'm bound to go.*
> *If you didn't want me baby why didn't you tell me so?*

At night in the attic I think of my ex Linda two stories below. As I tiptoe past her door and up the stairs I can smell the food she's cooking. I can hear her voice muffled behind the wall. Up there in the dark my life plays back like a midnight movie.

When I first met Linda I liked her right away. She had lived a lot for her age. I couldn't relate to most girls in school because they were like spoiled children. They were too innocent. But growing up outside St. Louis Linda talked about how she moved out of the house when she was just fifteen and got her own apartment. She spent a year on acid claiming she would dose whenever the effects began to wear off. She stopped when she learned this could enhance her PTSD from being abused by her mother. Then she became addicted to heroin for a while. She would reminisce about H by making yummy sounds closing her eyes and humming. She described being absorbed into the carpet and becoming one with the distorted fuzz tone of Sonic Youth. Yet, when she decided to get clean she stayed off H even when she was tempted with a loaded needle some pusher set in front of her.

On our first date I pulled up to her apartment in my green station wagon. She skipped out wearing a metal dog collar. Her un-styled blonde hair fell around her lanky frame. Her leg bounced up and down nervously as we drove listening to The Stooges. Her leg was bobbing so much that she was vibrating the car. I put my hand on her knee to calm her. She said this was my first act of affection.

We were going to a rooftop party. It was an art show for my friend SOLVE. He was becoming well known in the gallery scene, but also by the Chicago PD for his daring pictorial graffiti around town. Linda and I sat in the corner and spoke only to each other. Like a bemused poet, she told me that ants and prairie dogs are socialists. That man will have to evolve physically before we could reach the utopia in the back of our minds. That there is a "They" controlling the world and that "They" must be stopped.

Mississippi River so long deep and wide.
I can see my good gal standing on the other side.

After we moved in together I began to see that all her problems were not in the past. Memories of her mother and every man she ever knew haunted her. One night she swallowed what was left of a bottle of her psychiatric pills. These are the pills that were supposed to make her well. Now the pills were killing her. Together we took turns putting fingers down her throat until she threw up the pills. She was screaming and sobbing.

After she threw up her tone changed. Amongst the half dissolved pills on the floor she sat up and just said, "Oops-a-daisy…"

I said, "Do you think we got them all up?"

"I think so." She gave me a seductive look. "I can't fall asleep in case they didn't all come up. You have to keep me awake."

"Ok. I'll try."

Helping her purge the poison proved that I cared. She was painfully insecure. I didn't understand why I had to prove that I loved her all the time. The intense drama was constant and exhausting. She would push me away if I was too cool and casual. I wished she could just take me for granted. All the crying, screaming, and passion made her feel loved. That's what love was to her. But all that passionate insanity made me want to leave her. It was a tightrope.

Once she chucked a book at my head because I wasn't paying enough attention to her. She chased me into the kitchen and hit me over the head with a plate. Then she started punching me in the face. I was fed up. I didn't even block her blows. I stuck out my jaw and leaned into her fists.

"Yes. Yes. That's what I want! Keep hitting me! Show me you love me."

She kept slugging. The ring I gave her was cutting my face.

Then I reached over and pulled the bookcase over. It landed on my laptop and shattered the screen. She told me to leave. I grabbed a sleeping bag and went out the back door. I zigzagged through the back streets towards the vacant lots by the train tracks where Wood Street became pockmarked as the moon. Between an abandoned factory, and the freights there was a doorway where I'd regularly see a homeless man camped out. He wasn't there that night. Better than the doorway was the scaffolding by the factory, and probably how the graffiti writers were able to cover the massive exterior of the building.

I climbed the scaffolding. I laid down the sleeping bag and fell on top of it. Exhausted and in pain I passed out.

I was awoken by cold rain on my face. I pulled the bag over my head. I moaned.

In the morning Linda said she was sorry.

Another time I tried to leave for good. Linda cut her wrists and ended up on suicide watch at Weiss Hospital. When I heard about it I felt sorry for her and went back to her.

If there ain't one thing that give a man them walkin blues.
He ain't got no bottom on his last pair of shoes.

After I got laid off from dispatching for the food delivery service I went home to tell Linda. She took it calmly at first. "Not again," she said almost to herself. She said she could get the internet turned back on so I could job hunt from home. But as the evening wore on she wouldn't drop the subject. "We're gonna get evicted. I can't carry the both of us working at Potbelly's. The last time this happened to me I lived with this boy who wouldn't get a job and he wouldn't move out. I moved all my shit into the closet. I slept in the closet and I was the one paying the rent!"

"I'm not him. I'll get started applying first thing in the morning."

"You better."

I don't remember what did it, but she finally found an excuse to snap. Not that there had to be an excuse. We started yelling at each other. She threw a plate at me. It hit me in the shin. The cat hid under the desk. She ran out the back door into the stairwell. I slowly followed behind allowing her plenty of space. I just wanted to know where she was. I heard her sobbing and talking with Jonah the young property manager who lived in the back unit with his twin brother.

I went back downstairs and watched Matisyahu on Saturday Night Live waiting for her to come back. When she didn't come back I went upstairs and knocked on the door.

"There he is!" Linda yelled.

Jonah opened the door. Linda pushed past me and ran downstairs. "I want to talk to you," Jonah lisped. Or was it his twin? Who cares? I obliged.

I sat at his square kitchen table looking at a pot of plastic flowers and listened to his dewy drops of wisdom. It was all so simple. If only I was nice to her. If only I said nice things. If only I tried. Above all no matter what happens never get angry with a lady.

"Even if she hits you?"

"It doesn't fucking matter. You never hit a woman."

"I *didn't* hit her."

"Well, you scared her."

"I scared her? … Is this one of your property manager duties?"

"No Wes, it's not… So? So are you sorry?"

"Sorry?"

"Yeah are you sorry?"

"Sorry for yelling at my girlfriend? Sure. I'm sorry. I'm sorry for everything. Listen I understand why everyone always blames the male in a relationship. That's fine. I get it. But it's not like that. It's not that simple. I'm telling you I don't start this shit. And I never hit her back."

As I got up and went downstairs he said, "Next time I'm just gonna call the cops."

"Fine," I said. "Sure they'd be more helpful than you."

When next time came two officers stood in our living room. They made that squishy sound as all the leather in their utility belts shifted. Linda sat crying silently. I was confused why they were there. "I didn't lay a hand on her," I said. "I *love* her." Hearing this Linda sobbed more violently.

The officers didn't feel like doing paperwork. One of them turned to Linda. "Ma'am, would you like to make a report?"

Linda closed her eyes and shook her head. The officer turned to me, "Sir, will you try harder?"

"Yes. Of course."

He turned to Linda, "Miss, I know you two care about each other. If he says he will try harder, will you try harder?"

She nodded up and down.

Harder and harder we tried and tried. It's strange what you will go through when you've decided to commit yourself to someone. We always hoped things would get better. Maybe I'd get a better job. Maybe she'd get on the right meds. We'd stop drinking for a month or so but always find some excuse to fall off the wagon. I stuck with her, but I was never good enough. After being screamed at for no good reason for so long you begin to think that you deserve it just for being a man. In the end I can't blame myself. I did my best. I couldn't blame her either. There's a mental health element here. She wasn't always responsible for her actions.

She wanted nothing more than to be independent, but deep down she knew she wasn't. She needed help from someone, but I just wasn't strong enough. I came to realize that I couldn't save her. I could not make her feel loved. It basically came down to this: You must first love yourself before you can love someone else, and we hated ourselves.

We spent nights burning the four walls with words. We drank cheap wine on the beach. We watched too much TV. We never bought toilet paper, always stole it from jobs and restaurants. We shopped for food. I worked long hours. After work I did all the housework. Then I drank away my aching muscles. She overdosed, cried, screamed, loved me, hated me. We ate mushrooms trying to sew the holes in our souls. We were holy children giggling. We were hicks with mouths full of garbage. We had our own kitty-cat language. We had pet names and insults. We tried hole-in-the-wall restaurants that were all the same. We met each other's parents. We psychoanalyzed each other. We kicked each other's baggage. We made love like cannibals. We double dated with our demons.

I lost my car, my job, my lady, my home, then my mind. I'm sorry, but I can't care anymore. I'm sorry, but I can't feel sorry anymore. I walked away. I had nowhere to go, but I walked away. I was more numb than miserable. There's a point where things get so bad you're in survival mode. Fight or flight. There's only one thing you can do. So you see it, and you do it. Everything focuses to a point of clarity. There is no balancing of consequences because there is no choice. As easy as fate it was over.

I'm going to the bottom baby where I'm better known.
You ain't done nothing but run your good man away from home.

Now at Blues Fest David "Honey-boy" Edwards strikes the last chord of *Key to the Highway*. It's just another blues song with an ocean of pain and wisdom hidden between the lines. It fades from our ears. Time ticks on like a foot tapping to the music.

Linda lives in my bones and attacks me in my sleep. As I keep walking away from her I hope that she finally finds happiness. I hope more than anything that she makes it. I hope her mind will cease to storm. I hope she won't hurt herself again. I hope she won't treat other boys like she treated me. I hope somebody will succeed at making her feel loved where I failed.

In dreams I wish she were still lying beside me. When I wake up I hope I never see her again.

After another night crashing at Matt's he goes off to work at the thrift store and I'm roaming around Boy's Town. I'm set up on the corner of Halsted and Belmont where rainbow flags fly high with pride. After running through my covers and noodling on my originals I begin reading a book.

I'm about to pack it in when two strapping young lads stroll by arm in arm. Bandanas hang out their jean pockets. Though I don't know the color code one gent is beefier than the other. He is in the otter realm if not a bear. The other dude is firmly on the twink end of the spectrum. He has a blonde bop shaved on one side and his painfully boney spine sticks out a lavender belly shirt.

The blonde sees my sign and cries, "Hey boo! No one wants to hear the blues round here. We like dance music."

I play along. "You can dance to my music. See, I'll tap my foot so you know when to move." I begin stomping my foot like the bass in a techno song.

The taller guy slowly reads my sign out loud. "Tell me your problem and I'll write you a blues song…"

"Oh honey, where to begin?" his companion exclaims. "You have too many problems. You'll end up giving this boy all your money!"

"Bitch. You're the one who's a hot mess."

"Why thank you!"

"Tell me about it," I offer.

My slender new friend puts his arms on his hips, "My new apartment is full of fucking cockroaches!"

"Ewe," says his boyfriend. "Don't tell him that shit!"

"Bitch. At least it ain't crotch-crickets!"

"You're nasty."

"You love it. But seriously everybody here by the lake has a few bugs. It's because of the water in the soil."

"Oh, that's just an old wives tale."

"How would you know?"

"Listen," I interject. "I have a song for you, *and* it's a dance song." Over the last few weeks I've begun to find that people have a lot of the same problems despite all the surface differences. I've begun to reuse the themes and polish the verses accordingly.

"This is called the *Cockroach Crunch*. It's a song, but it's also a way to get rid of vermin. You know in the sixties when a new dance step would come out, toy companies would sell these plastic footprints to put on the floor with directions on how to do the dance. This is kinda like that. But the footprints are roach traps."

"What the fuck?" one of my new friends says as he places a hand over his mouth to shield a laugh.

"Come on kids! It goes like this…"

I begin picking an upbeat little riff and singing in falsetto.

I'm going downtown on a midnight train.
Going to that same old place.
I know the band they're a hell of a bunch
when they play that song–
　　　the Cockroach Crunch

Crunch! Crunch! Crunch!

I stomp my feet with every *crunch* as if I'm smashing bugs.
"This is cray-cray," says the slender one.
But I go on.

Well I'm gonna dance till it hurts.
Gonna drink until I lose my shirt.
I know the band they're a hell of a bunch
when they play that song–
    the Cockroach Crunch
    Crunch! Crunch! Crunch!

By the third verse my buddies are singing along and chanting, "Crunch! Crunch! Crunch!" They start swinging their hips and doing the twist to the twisted tune.

So have some snake juice and hear the word.
This is the truth now, sorry that it's slurred.
I know the band they're a hell of a bunch
when they play that song–
    the Cockroach Crunch
    Crunch! Crunch! Crunch!

I wrap up the song with a big crunching chord. My friends start clapping.
"Yeah, crunch that shit!"
"Give him some cash boo."
"I don't have any!"
"You lie. Here, I'll do it. Oh all I have is a twenty!"

"Hold on," I say. "I have change." I pull out my fold and peel off three fives.

"Let him hold ten you bitch."

"Fine!"

I take the twenty and give him back two fives.

They enfold their arms around each other and sway away up Halsted.

"Bye boo!"

"Bye." I wave.

High above my head the buildings cut the sky into baby blue paper dolls. Below I sing. I'm sitting in the financial district at Wacker and Madison. My guitar squeaks and hums under a glass slide as I contemplate the tall greasy crystals full of windows and eyes. As soon as the market closes stock brokers from the Board of Trade will pass me on the way to Union Station. I figured I would go where the money is. Slick soldiers in slender suits slide forward. Off they go hopping Metra trains to safe suburbs, yards like golf courses, a land of manmade lakes.

Five-o-clock and the gates open. Business people flood the cement river. The crosswalk signal feeds them past me in waves. Green light strums the blues, red light the sigh of my empty hat on the sidewalk. Passing by are iPod zombies. No one can hear me. Militant bike messengers pause in intersections like spinning trapeze artists. Cabbies jerk, jump, bob and weave like boxers. Traffic cops conduct the crowd in a silent symphony. Then engines, horns, the screech of metal on metal. Now an ambulance screams like a burning angel bending the air.

After an hour with no one stopping for a song my guitar seems to be strung with barbed wire. Between the notes are rusty gates, scarecrows laughing, beams of moonlight on soft hay fields. This music grounds me in the moment yet takes me somewhere far away.

Today I heard a security guard company was hiring. I lined up with a few dozen other men in the carpeted lobby of a hotel near Navy Pier. After filling out the application and snagging some free coffee I was called to the back room. An old man with a flat top proceeded to explain the merit of the polygraph machine despite that it is deemed inadmissible in a court of law. Next thing I know I have agreed to get wired into the box for the last portion of the interview. The rationale being that the security guards will have to be a hundred percent trustworthy. They will be guarding expensive property and valuable products.

So I got plugged in. I got grilled. My heartbeat drew pretty waves across a monitor. It was easy until he started asking about drug history.

"Ever tried marijuana?"

"No."

"Ever tried LSD?"

"No."

"Ever tried cocaine?"

"No."

"Ecstasy… Amphetamine… Opium…?"

"No… No… No…"

These were all lies. The truth is yes. Really I was thinking: Man, I went to art school. I experimented with psychedelics until there was nothing left to learn from them. I explored harder street drugs too not to soften reality, I had alcohol for that, but because I wanted to write about that world. The only one I could honestly say I hadn't tried was heroin. That's the one you don't flirt with.

I thought I could beat the box. I tried to be cool and clear my mind. It was hard after the cup of coffee in the lobby. Caffeine is an excellent drug.

Afterwards Flattop stepped away and reviewed the data in the other room. When he came back he said I should leave and not to expect a call back.

It felt like a punch in the gut. They were promising a high hourly rate, benefits, long hours, overtime. My father had been in security when I was a kid. He guarded a cat food factory at night while he put himself through college. My uncle is a security guard to this day.

What I should have done was just answer honestly and hope that there would be follow up questions. Like when was the last time? How much? When? Truth is I hadn't smoked pot regularly since high school. The street drugs were to have new experiences. Once I had those experiences I moved on. My goal was to find life not escape from life. So I never developed a habit. As for psychedelics, I thought they would help me be more creative. That was true for a time, but once they revealed their wisdom there was little reason to keep returning to the altar of altered consciousness. Even the voice of god gets repetitive. With a little onion peeling it would have been apparent I am just a garden variety booze hound. God bless America. Flattop didn't even bother to ask about alcohol.

My real addiction has always been the muse. Staying creative takes a lot of dedication. It takes a lot of sacrifice. I could say that art has enhanced my life, but just as much it has acted like a drug addiction. There are highs and lows. There's seeking inspiration desperately like a fix. When it comes there's the mania when possessed by the muse. Then there is the come down as the effects wear off and you start looking for the next project. Like a drug I dose my mind with art, music, poetry and escape from the world. But just like a drug the visions reveal staggering truths about the world and myself.

Like junkies some artists end up giving up all the middle class comforts for their work: cars, houses, lawns, TVs, pets, even family. We make these sacrifices willingly. We bring these things to the great pawn-shop in the sky. In exchange we are given a little more time and a little more freedom to dream.

I look at my reflection in a window. My hair is sweaty from sitting under my cap. My cap is on the sidewalk waiting for a tip. My clothes smell like grease from making fried chicken at the deli. The souls of my shoes are getting thin. If my priorities were to look clean and rack in as many material possessions as possible then I could have. Just down the street is Union Station. I could hop on a Greyhound Bus back to Wisconsin at any time. I could start over. Why do I stay? I stay in Chicago for the muse. I stay for my music. I stay here because there is a better chance someone will hear me. I keep playing here because there is a better chance that someone will care.

But at the moment it feels like no one in Chicago cares either. I was a fool to think that the folks in the business district would be loose with their money. They are playing the game where you don't give away anything for free. None of these suits ever said: Hey, it's only money. It's not: Here, get a beer bum. It's: Get a job bum. I've had better luck in the tourist traps. I've had better luck in Wicker Park where the hipsters care about culture. Where art is enjoyed and not just something to chase, possess, own, and flip for a profit. I've had better luck in every neighborhood in Chicago but here.

As I stare out into space thinking these thoughts some bills fall into my hat. I snap into focus and follow the shape that just passed me. It's a security guard walkie-talkie in hand who just dropped me three bucks. He must work at the building I am sitting in front of. How do you like that? A working guy, still on the job no less. Ironically this happens just a few hours after being rejected by a security guard company. He didn't tell me to move along. He didn't alert the cops that I'm singing without a street performer license displayed. Yet the colorfully dressed stock traders coming down the sidewalk don't tip. What's wrong? Too bummed about the housing bubble bursting? Too guilty about gambling with peoples hopes and dreams?

Maybe it's just me. No one wants to hear the blues. No one wants to hear the truth. It's rush hour. There's a five-o-clock shadow on my face. The shadows behind the skyscrapers act like sundials. There's a shadow in the heart of every commuter. It's time to go home. It's that simple. Everyone has somewhere to go but me. It's time to cut my losses and leave. So I snatch up the three bucks before the bills blow away. I pack up my guitar and head towards the park. I need to find people who are trying to enjoy themselves.

After another hour in Millennium Park with no takers I begin to feel that I should call it a day. Sometimes the cards are stacked. It's a slow night. The wind is picking up. People are rushing home. The air is heavy like it's about to burst. In my bones I can feel a summer storm about to roll in off the lake.

Guitar on my back I'm hoofing it towards the subway. I'm on a path in the park weaving through a newly planted garden. There is a fountain in the middle. As I pass a glimmer catches my eye. People have been using the fountain as a wishing well. The last remaining sunlight sparkles against the silver speckled water. Quarters, nickels, dimes, a million shiny eyes are winking at me. There's more money in the water than I made all day. Looking over my shoulder I take off my shoes and roll up my slacks. Soon I'm wading in the fountain fishing out the silver. Soon I have handfuls. I'm scooping the coins into my guitar case. I'm plucking and popping into my pockets. My slacks unroll and fall into the water. They need a rinse anyway. Lightning sparks in the distance. The whole atmosphere flashes. I've struck gold. I've found a silver mine.

Is this what people had in mind when they flipped a coin in the water for a wish? Did the fountain grant any wishes? Do wishing wells feel hunger? Do fountains need shelter from the storm? I don't know but my wish has been granted. Today no one wanted to hear the blues. No one wanted to hear the truth. The only thing anyone wants is wishes, prayers, silent words… The lightning gets closer.

Behind me I hear, "Hey, you! Get out of there!" A couple hundred feet away I see a security guard walkie-talkie in hand. "Hey! That ain't for you!"

I leap out, drop the coins I have in my hands into my guitar case, and scoop up my shoes quick. As I skip away I ask out the corner of my jaw, "Oh yeah? Who does all this money belong to?"

"It goes to the city. You better run punk! I'm calling the cops."

"Oh it goes to the city eh? Like taxes? I thought these coins were wishes."

While the security guard is still crackling on his walkie-talkie I have turned north. Good thing the cops in Chicago have better things to do than hassle the likes of me. That's another reason to stay in the city. Growing up in Wisconsin I would get stopped just for looking weird by bored country cops. Here a report of a kid skimming change from a fountain is not a priority. Before hearing so much as a siren I have long since descended into Lower Wacker Drive. The tunnels that run under the Loop lend shelter and security. What a day for security guards.

The thunder rolls like timpani above. Let it rain.

It's dark down here. Pipes drip overhead. Lights covered in cobwebs flicker from the ceiling. The occasional car roars up or down the ramps. The headlights blind me as I hope the driver sees me. I know these tunnels. Below the Hyatt Hotel and other buildings east of Michigan Avenue there are four levels of cement caves. During my days as a delivery driver I'd use the tunnels to park as I waited for the next order or when delivering to one of the fancy hotels above.

The first level there are unmarked doors, emergency exits, and service entrances to the Harris Theatre, the Radisson, or the Pedway that runs the length of downtown. The next two levels are auxiliary parking. At the bottom there is a homeless encampment where rows of mattresses and makeshift tents are lined up taking shelter under the four stories of concrete. Spelunking to the bottom there is a fifth layer few know about. There's a tunnel that runs under Millennium Park where the ceiling lights stop all together and the cement road turns to dirt.

On the same level of the homeless village is the downtown impound lot. When I was a delivery driver I had to visit the impound regularly. While bringing food to the well-to-do in River North my car would get towed despite the placard in my window for GrubHub and that I was using the loading zones. A car with its flashers on in a loading zone acts like a beacon to the city tow trucks. Attempting to fight the tickets and impound fees at traffic court proved useless. The city didn't care. It was a second tax the vampires.

Delivering convenient meals to people downtown I would be lucky to cover gas and feed myself let alone pay for the parking tickets and get my car out of hock. When I'd come out of a posh condo to find my car missing I knew where to go. These were dark days. I'd radio dispatch and let them know I would not be able to take orders for a few hours. Then I would start walking across town and descend into Lower Wacker. At the impound I'd wait in line to hand over more money than I had made all day just to get the car back. Eventually my car wasn't worth bailing out. After the miles I put on it delivering food and the damage done to it by the tow trucks themselves I eventually just told the city to keep it. I was losing more money than I was making. It made more sense not to work at all.

You could say things are worse now but I feel a hundred percent better. Rather than play the game only to lose it's better to drop out of the game all together. I know these tunnels. Anyone who might be looking for me will never find me here. At the bottom along Lower Wacker Drive columns line the south shore of the river like grinning teeth. Sheltered by Upper Wacker Drive I stop and sit on the cement barrier on the edge of the river until the rain stops. I let my legs dangle over the water and stare up at the buildings as the windows flicker awake like fireflies up to mingle with the stars. This is my own private Riviera. I wave at the boats and the people on the other side of the shore. Bewildered by my cheerfulness few wave back. I wonder how long it will be until the city paves the south shore and fills it with cafes and public parks like it has on the north side. For now it's all mine.

The night is official. I take the lower level of the Michigan Avenue Bridge and come to the original Billy Goat Tavern underneath the Magnificent Mile. Down the stairs I slip into the soft red glow of the Goat. The place is wallpapered with news clippings. Despite its fame being spoofed on SNL in the 70's a guy can still get a fresh burger for five bucks at this counter. The guys in the paper hats don't even blink when I pay using a fist full of wet coins. Soon I am sitting pretty getting a gut full as I eavesdrop on the newspapermen drinking at the bar. I overhear the real news. I hear what's between the lines.

The air outside is calm and cool after the summer rain passes. The streets are slick as mirrors. Oily potholes reflect rainbows back at the clearing sky. A soft breeze rolls off the lake. Just like the weather I feel my luck has changed. I come to the surface from Lower Wabash and step up the stairs onto Illinois Avenue. Here is the Jazz Mart the only roots music record store in the city or practically anywhere. I used to get my blues records here when I could still afford them. Next door is my favorite bookstore Afterwords which prominently displays a counterculture section by the front window. I set up my chair and pull out my guitar under the red glow of The Star of Siam's neon sign, which rests under the offices of the Chicago Reader. It's a quiet little street as far as foot traffic, but perhaps I could snag some music lovers coming out of the Jazz Mart after they pick up some dusties.

Not twenty minutes go by and a man steps down the stairs from Upper Wabash. He's in his forties, his fading hair slicked back, and shirt unbuttoned to feel the breeze. He sees my sign and gives a smirk.

"That's an honest proposition. Sure-nough," he seems to say this to himself more than to me.

"Would you like me to write you a song?" I ask matching his nonchalant tone.

"Ah hell, why not? Beats fortune tellers."

"So what's eating you man?"

He pulls a long comb out of his ass-pocket and proceeds to plaster his hair back nervously. "Just this town changes every time I turn a corner. Nothing lasts you know? I mean I just passed the Trump Tower. It don't fit the look of Chicago at all. Meanwhile, my old waterhole gets torn down so they can put up more yuppie condos."

I forget that just up Wabash is the Trump Tower. It was completed in 2008 just as the recession hit. It's a big blue phallus with the guys name printed across the side so it's in everyone's face: TRUMP.

My friend goes on. "That cocksucker comes into our town and puts his cheesy New York shit up, and we just have to take it?"

"Yeah I hate that guy."

"It's just everything that's wrong with the world. People with money can do whatever they want. He even has all the poor people thinking he's so cool with his little game show."

"Gameshow?"

"Yeah he's got this show where he shows people how to be greedy and fires the contestants one by one."

"Oh yeah. I've seen ads for that."

"The more he acts like an asshole the more everyone kisses up to him."

"It's sad. Well, that's human nature."

"You think so? That's caveman shit. You'd think there's been some progress. People seem more sensitive these days. Just listen to the music or watch a good movie. People are a little more enlightened than all that follow the pack bullshit. Right? I mean it's not the eighties no more. Greed ain't good baby. Maybe that's just me."

"Most people don't think about enlightening themselves. They just want to fit in."

"They just don't care about nothing. You know? Instead of preserving a historic place they'll just bulldoze it for the next new thing. There ain't nothing but trendy clubs in this part of town now. Pretty soon there won't be no reason to go downtown except to renew my drivers license. No one cares about history or what was there before. They just care about what's new and shiny."

"Man, I hear you."

"So yeah sing me a song. Maybe I'll feel better."

I've made a few notes about Trump and mixed it with some other stuff I've been working on called *Human Nature Show*. I strum a slow rhythm as my rasp begins to rise:

Let me tell you about cannibal Ed.
He ate until he turned red.
I asked how he got so full of hate?
He said, "It must have been something I ate."

I asked Lucy Jo
what about all the men she's known?
She said, "A man could help what he is,
they preach and preach yet never act like Jesus."

I'm just asking:
What is human?
No answer,
evolving faster.
I'm just asking:
What is human?
So what's human?
It's still a question.

I saw that golden CEO.
You know the one that owns every glory hole?
I asked 'em how he made his name?
He said, "Treat life like it was just a game."

I had an interview with the Terrorist.
I ask'em what's the twist?
He said, "I just want peace, just want to live simple,
but first I am gonna watch the blocks topple."

In the end we're just parasites
that inhale the sun and cough out the night.
A virus that multiplies,
drinks the air till everything fries.
So human, humor me.
Is this brain a curse, or to set us free?
Opposed to the thumb, pulled a plum,
now the tree's bare to the stump.

My friend's face doesn't change. He remains sour. Finally he says, "That's some fucked up shit man. But I appreciate the effort. Here take a fiver."

He gives me a five-dollar bill. "Fair enough."

"Man that ain't the blues. That's pitch black. Well, I guess I asked for it. You did your job, but I still feel bad."

He flashes me the peace sign over his shoulder as he strolls towards State Street. As he disappears I think that it was damn decent of him to still make good on the tip despite that I wasn't his cup of tea. That's integrity. Wish there was more of that.

He's right about one thing. Not much lasts. In a few years the Jazz Mart will be gone. Afterwords will have to sell half its floor space. The south shore of the river looks like a mall. The city is changing all the time. Everyone has their own definition of progress. Most of the time things get cleaned up and homogenized at the cost of culture.

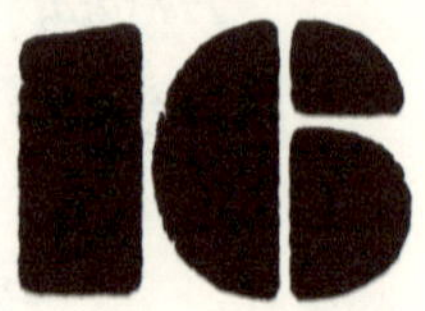

The dry cleaners is literally a sweatshop. My hair is sweaty. My brow is sweaty. It drips down my back. It swells in my pits. It stains my work shirt as people hand me their shirts to clean. The press machines ooze steam while I work as fast as I can but it still isn't good enough for the boss.

The boss Herman never speaks to me directly, but sends Chet over to tell me to work faster and be more chipper with the customers. Chet acts as an intermediary, like a ventriloquist. Herman just sits in his office in the air-conditioning with his arms folded, feet on his desk with his resting sneer.

The line is out the door. The customers don't want me to be chipper. They don't want to make small talk with me. They just want to drop off their wares and leave. I gather the suits, rack 'em up, stuff the shirts in laundry bags, and ring the people up. When presented with a pink claim ticket I run to the rack that spans the length of the joint and spin the motor. Ghostly garments without heads dangle forward their arms waving under plastic sheets. They dance forward like corporate automatons. When I find the number that matches the ticket I run the suit back to the customer. Despite Herman's feedback, which Chet regurgitates, I can't work faster and make small talk at the same time.

Though he won't speak to me directly I overheard Herman call

all the workers "lazy niggers." Then he spit blood into the trashcan. My coworkers are Black, Latino, some are Asian coming from Chinatown down Cermak Avenue. I admit I was shocked to hear him say that, let alone because he's of a minority himself. Being a Hispanic man I thought he would have been above racial slurs. He must have felt that since he was the boss he could suddenly look down on everybody.

Turns out I am not the white guy Herman had hoped for. He thought I would be extra chummy with the customers. He thought I would be preppy. He thought that I would somehow work harder than everyone else. The truth is no one working there is lazy. Everyone busts their asses. The only lazy person at the dry cleaners is Herman. Maybe it's dawning on Herman that there is no such thing as white magic. Or if he still believes in it I just don't have it.

Like the touch of mercy a lull in business hits just before lunch when I see a familiar face come in through the door. Ken has sandy blond hair and a wispy mustache. He's there to drop off his expensive suit. He's a college recruiter. He was my college recruiter. I would not have ended up in Chicago if it weren't for Ken. With all the pressure to make small talk here's a customer who I actually have something to say to.

As he steps up to my register he cocks his head to one side. My face rings a bell. After headhunting thousands of hungry hopefuls all dreaming of being the next Salvador Dali he actually remembers my face. There's a reason for that. In his eyes I can see the wheels turning as it sinks in. When the memory clicks his head returns to the upright position.

Back in 2002 I was eighteen and looking at colleges. I had legal troubles and I wanted to get out of town. I wanted to see what was beyond Wisconsin. I wanted to study art. After putting out applications a man named Ken kept calling from a school in Chicago. At the time I didn't feel that the recruiting process from this art school was aggressive. Ken said the school worked with employers in the industry and guaranteed employment in a creative field upon graduation. Honestly the calls made me feel appreciated. Perhaps they liked the slides I sent of my paintings? The calls made me feel it was worth traveling to Chicago to take a look at the school. At the time I was on probation and not allowed to leave the state. But no one said anything as my dad and I drove to Illinois.

When we got to the recruiting office Ken greeted us. He wore a sharp tan suit, had a pleasant effeminate voice, and smiled under his wispy mustache. We toured the classrooms that were spread out between the Sun Times Building and the Merchandise Mart. As we strolled the corridors Ken explained the programs in a general sort of way. I had been to the Art Institute Museum before to see the surrealist paintings of Magritte and Dali. I asked Ken how this school measures up to the programs at the School of the Art Institute associated with the museum. My dad suddenly became confused thinking that the school we were looking at was the same school. I explained to him that there is the Art Institute and this is the Institute of Art. To breeze over the confusion my dad made a joke. "Well you have to institutionalize artists somewhere."

Ken laughed pleasantly and said, "It's a common misconception. In fact, potential employers make the mistake all the time when they see us on your resume. They see the name and they are impressed. So it's the same prestige for nearly half the tuition."

I asked again how the schools actually differed. Ken looked me up and down. My hair was long. I was wearing jeans and a leather jacket. Then Ken said, "The Art Institute? That's just the rich kid's school. The Institute of Art will make sure you actually get a job after graduation."

Boy did he play me. He had my number. My dad and I were middle middle middle class. I didn't want to drain my hard working father of any more money than I already was. I would need to take out some substantial student loans myself to even pay the tuition for *this* school. As an accountant my dad worked twelve-hour days seven days a week at tax time. I didn't always agree with my father. He didn't always understand me, but he had been nothing but kind to me all my life. He bailed me out of jail enough for one lifetime because of drunken brawling and stupid teenage shit. I didn't want to be more of a burden on him than I already was. No, I didn't want to go to the rich kids school. I thought I would just make it as an artist regardless of any prestigious degree or connections that the famous Art Institute could offer. I was a kid. I thought I knew everything. I thought things would just work out.

A few minutes later we were signing papers and contacting student loan lenders, which decades later still have me by the balls. As I signed the papers TV kids shows from the eighties echoed in my head: If you simply believe in yourself you can do anything. It isn't that simple. Droves of daydreamers like myself happily climbed into the jaws of for-profit colleges. Without hesitation Ken roped me in, charmed me like a real street hustler, and then zeroed in for the kill. He was a headhunter.

The next fall when I arrived on campus I bumped into Ken in the hallway. His tone had changed. He seemed concerned about something. "Westley. I received a call from your father. He said that he may have filled out your application incorrectly."

"Oh yeah? What did he say?"

"He said that on the application where it asks if you had ever been convicted of a felony he said it should have said yes. What's the story there?"

"Well I was convicted of battery, which isn't a felony by the way. My dad is mistaken about that."

"Oh what happened?"

"My girlfriend back in high school told me that this guy had molested her when she was passed out. She had too much to drink. He took advantage of her. I took things into my own hands."

"You hit another student?"

"Hit him? Yes. Several times."

His brow furrowed. Then out of nowhere the heavy thoughts seemed to drift away from his face. Ken's tone softened, "Well I'm sure you were another person back then."

I thought: When? Last year? I really wasn't a different person. But he had seemed to rationalize the situation in his own mind so I didn't correct him. Four years later I graduated with honors. Most of the time I was on the Dean's list, though I really didn't pay attention to such things. I just wanted to create things.

Now here it is eight years later. Here's Ken the same college recruiter who told me tall-tales of the school guaranteeing job placement in a creative field after graduation. He recognizes me only because of my legal troubles.

Ken hands me his thousand-dollar suit. He acts surprised to see me behind the counter. It's awkward. But he pushes through the tension with a cheesy smile. Then he actually has the gall to ask me how I'm doing. The boss wanted me to make more chit chat with the customers so I tell him.

"Well I'm forty grand in debt. Lucky thing is the student loan people can't find me. I have no phone. I have no address. If I'm lucky I can find a job like this, but only if I leave my degree *off* the application. Otherwise I'm over qualified."

He plays dumb. "The school didn't find you a job after graduation?"

I feel my blood pressure rise, and it isn't just because of all the steam presses in the room. So I tell him, "No, no. The school got me *this* gig. You remember the fashion arts program at school? They said this is the best way to learn about the garment industry."

When the sarcasm dawns on him he purses his lips and nods solemnly.

Maybe he isn't playing dumb. I've come to find out that in corporate America most of the time the sales department doesn't even know what they're really selling. They sling around buzzwords pulled off a script. Sales people sell an image, a dream, smoke and mirrors, soap bubbles… It *is* an art. The best sales people lie to themselves first. Ken leaves the dry cleaners with a concerned look on his face like his bubble just got burst. Like anyone else Ken just wants to do his job and go home. Right now I just want to do my job and be left alone.

Chet comes up to me. "What did you say to that guy?" Herman must have been watching the exchange from afar.

"That guy? Don't worry about it. I know him. We were just reminiscing about old times."

When I was a kid I thought I knew everything. I thought I would be the next great artist. What a joke. How quickly the entitled become the disillusioned. The student loans seemed so far away. No one was on their guard. A for-profit college wasn't a household phrase yet. At that time the news wasn't filled with schools being sued by the students.

Job placement? Even a douchebag salesman like Ken couldn't be blamed for something like the great recession. Right now you'd be lucky to find an unpaid internship. It's true places like Chicago were saturated with a creative class. All the kids riding the glut of the nineteen-nineties economy went to college, many were the first in their family to do so. All the art nerds moved to the city and more than ever before. All the kids who hid in the art room to avoid the stress of high school, every stoner who tripped out on paints after burning one during lunch, every young dreamer with an ounce of talent and a little money might get roped into studying art in the Emerald City in the Land of Oz. Here we are.

Better bring your own heart, brain, and lots of courage. Throughout the decades artists living in the bowels of the cities were labeled as bohemians, beatniks, hipsters, then hippies, punks, and then hipsters again all because people need to reduce and degrade what they don't understand. People need to give it a name, a label, a way to encapsulate and move on. No one cares about these precious little dreamers because in passing it's impossible to distinguish the real artists from the trendy kids who can afford to dress in tight jeans, scarves, handlebar mustaches, and clear-rimmed glasses just to get laid.

John Adams told the French during the American Revolution: "I must study politics and war that my sons may have liberty to study mathematics and philosophy. My sons ought to study mathematics and philosophy, geography, natural history, naval architecture, navigation, commerce, and agriculture, in order to give their children a right to study painting, poetry, music, architecture, statuary, tapestry, and porcelain." Well here we are.

My folks fought their way into the middle class and proudly told me I could do anything I dared to dream. Sometimes I'm ashamed of how naive they were and in turn how naive I was. Perhaps the American Revolution isn't over yet. For some the war is still in progress.

Shortly after Ken's visit to the dry cleaners I get a tap on the shoulder. It's Chet. He says Herman told him to tell me I'm fired. No worries. I don't want to work for a racist like Herman anyway. Also between the part time gigs and writing songs in the street I now have four hundred bucks in my sock. I have finally made enough money for the security deposit needed for the practice space on the West Side.

Feeling bad that he has to be Herman's mouthpiece Chet lets me use his phone. He's a good kid. I go outside to make some calls. When Chet goes on a cigarette break I give him his phone back. He tells me he is thinking of going to college. I tell him what I know.

17

Nathan Xander picks me up in Chinatown. Nate is a folk singer. He has his girlfriend's little Ford pick-up truck. He said that he didn't recognize the number but figured I was the one calling. We are cruising west on Cermak Avenue listening to a cassette of *Henry's Dream* by Nick Cave and the Bad Seeds.

"Hey thanks for lending me your banjo," he tells me. "I used it on a new demo I made."

"Cool man. Let me hear it."

"Naw, I'm not in the mood to hear myself right now." Nate is tall with sly eyes and floppy long hair. He brushes his bangs out of his face as he regains his train of thought. "I have the banjo at my girlfriend's place. We can go pick it up for you."

"Awesome. Oh it isn't my banjo. Shanghai Mike said we could use it. You remember Mike?"

"Of course."

Using Nate's phone I call Bret the owner of the practice space. I'm in luck. The room I looked at is still available.

"I know that guy," says Nate. "My band used to have a room at his practice place at Kinzie and Ashland. That is, before SOLVE got killed."

"Goddamn. That's right. He was drumming for you wasn't he?" We still use the handle SOLVE he used as a graffiti tag when we speak of him.

"He was good too. SOLVE was just about the loudest drummer I ever had."

"He was a loud dude."

"The other practice space Bret has is where? Lake and Pulaski? You better be careful or you'll be the next one of us stabbed to death."

"The other day I was at the spot on Grand where SOLVE's graffiti buddies erected that shrine."

"It is still there?"

"Remnants. The building looks marked for demolition. They're putting up barriers and boarding up windows."

"Probably be a Starbucks in a month. I saw a thing in The Reader. Big companies are buying up all the vacant buildings in the city so they can flip them after the recession."

"Good times for some."

"Speaking of gentrification. My girlfriend just moved to a renovated building at California and Lake."

"Oh yeah?"

"That's where the hood begins now. Maybe it's my white guilt, but they say it's always the artists that move in first. You know looking for cheap rent and real culture. Then comes the cafes, condos, real-estate developers, and finally the yuppies move in until minorities and the artists can't afford to live there no more. Then the artists head further west and the cycle continues."

"I was just thinking about that. The other day I was writing a song for a guy who was hating on the Trump Tower. We got to talking about how the city is always changing. It's ironic that white artists who are willing to embrace and preserve culture are the ones that end up aiding in the destruction of it."

"Visiting my girlfriend I was walking my dog around there. You know Whalen, he's just a floppy little beagle. When this full-grown black dude saw my little dog he climbed up a chain link fence and said, 'Get your dog!'"

"Whalen ain't no German Shepard, but considering the cultural history with dogs…"

"Maybe that's it. Or the guy was just on drugs."

"Weren't you?"

"Little weed never made me that paranoid."

At the office at Kinzie and Ashland Bret is on the phone. We exchange the keys to the practice space for the cash with little ceremony. The keys are in an envelope with the code for the front door. We take Lake Avenue west under the endless El tracks. The sun stabs through the railroad ties above creating a tunnel of flickering shadows. Like an old film we fade into the West Side.

With my guitar on my back, my chair in one arm, and the banjo in the other I'm loaded for bear. Hopping on the Green Line at the California stop in a few minutes I'm at Lake and Pulaski. Self-consciously I lug my gear past the gauntlet of dudes on the corner. There's nothing like the look of hard eyes seeing a white guy with a fucking banjo entering the hood. Did I think I was there for a ho-down?

Passing the salvage yard I scurry towards the practice space. A kid about ten or twelve is on my heels. Once in earshot he goes, "Hey mister! Hey mister!"

"What?"

"You shoot?"

I slow my pace, "Sorry?"

"You shoot? Do you shoot? Do you shoot up?"

I stop. "Naw kid. I don't shoot."

He stops in his tracks. As he spins around back towards the corner he spouts, "Well fuck you then."

At the steel door of the practice space I punch in the security code. A tiny green light blinks and the lock clicks open. My eyes dilate in the darkness. The place has the aura of basements and crawl spaces. Musk. Dank. Water damage. Up the stairs I pass the graffiti on the crimson walls. Someone taped up a centerfold now faded and peeling. On the second floor I cross the common area and stick my key in the white wooden door to my room. It won't open. I jiggle it. Damn did Bret give me the wrong keys? I pull it out of the lock and examine it. I'm sweating from my trek. The key has those freshly serrated marks from being newly filed. He must have just had this key made. I put it back in the knob. I twist, shake, and push. Finally it gives. The knob turns and I enter the stale little cubbyhole.

The light creaks in. There is a reading lamp in one corner from a prior tenant. In the small back room there are some Christmas lights strewn along the floor. Plugging both in I close the door. I have light. I have space. I have all the time in the world. I have my own door. The world is on the other side of the door. It isn't much but I have a home. I've made it.

As I lock the door behind me it hits me. I've been running in circles for weeks. I've been hustling almost non-stop to get this key. A sense of relief floods my body. I sit down on the dirty carpet. I take my shirt off. It's hot in here. There's no window. But I don't care. It's mine. Tears start cracking through my eyes. To my surprise I'm crying. The shock sends a picture of myself to my mind's eye. Seeing myself from the outside I start laughing. Now I'm laughing and crying at the same time. I'm hysterical. I'm convulsing, snotting, surging. My ribs cave in and out.

All this time I've been telling myself I'm finally free. I've been telling myself I'm on an adventure. Was that just a survival mechanism? Was I free? I was free from one situation only to be dancing in the fire of another one. What's freedom anyway? I have questions, big questions. For the first time in a long time I have a chance to stop and think. All the questions come back like the tide. Maybe the human animal likes a cage as long as it holds the key to its own cage.

My eyes are dry. My brain is rung out like a sponge. Bunching up my shirt like a pillow I lay down my head peacefully. After passing out for a few minutes my mind is reset like a computer rebooting. Nothing is over. I have work to do. Using the subway trip by trip, load by load, I drag what things I had stashed in the attic in Pilsen crosstown to my new room. All night I'm lugging these big canvas bags that I once used to carry food when I was a deliveryman. They are big enough for catering orders. Months before I loaded them with some clothes, blankets, books, CDs, and even an old laptop. Unlike the attic I have electricity now. The screen on the laptop is shattered but I can still pop in a CD and hit the spacebar to listen to music. More importantly I can plug in the cheap coffeemaker I have wrapped in a towel.

It's exhausting hauling what's left of my possessions through the hood. I'm just a shadow that strobes between the streetlamps. I'm just a curious apparition. More concerning is how I might appear on Bret's security cameras. Hoping that it just looks like I'm bringing in gear to make music I stuff my burden in the small practice space. There's no point in worrying anyway. What choice do I have?

On the final trip to the attic I pinch a dusty box fan. I make it back before the Green Line stops for the night. I'm exhausted. I make a nest using a blue blanket my aunt Rachel made, an afghan my grandma knitted, and pad it with some clothes. Running the box fan over my sweaty body and sipping a cold beer from the vending machine the heat is almost tolerable.

I find a cooler where I can stash my blankets inside in case Bret ever enters my room to check if I'm living here. During the day I begin re-hiding everything in the bags and in the cooler and sliding them under the large shelves in the cubby between the two small square rooms. Any food I have I seal in the cooler right away. I'm already seeing mice scattering in the corner of my eye.

With no TV, no fridge, no shower, no phone, not even a window to look out I have zero distractions. Living in this cell I will be completely dedicated to my music. All I have is my cheap guitar, the banjo Shanghai Mike lent me, and my harmonicas. Propping up my folding chair and tuning up I can earnestly practice my songs. My voice reverberates off the tight walls.

Down the stairwell there's a yellow light at the end of the dark hall. A faucet drips guiding me forward. Here in the men's room the sink only runs at a trickle, but it is enough to take a bird-bath, comb my hair in the tarnished mirror, fill my cracked mug full of drinking water or pour the cup into my coffeemaker. Sometimes there's toilet paper, but I keep my own roll. At work or a diner the roll finds its way into my guitar case. The toilet here won't always flush, but I slip into the ladies room. Are you kidding? There aren't any ladies around anyway. To avoid having to get dressed just to use the bathroom at night sometimes I just aim into empty beer cans.

The place is lively in the evening. I can hear music all around me. There's a death metal band down below. They howl under my floor like demons in hell. A lone jazz drummer pops his skins and shatters his cymbals on the other side of the wall. Some folk singer down the hall nasally laments his lost love. A punk band thunders away hard and fast to my left. I am in the center of a hypercube made of music. However around midnight it's always quiet. Everyone goes home. It seems I am the only soul left on the premises. Though I can never be sure. Turning the corner at night I never know if someone will be standing there. The only sound is the slow-moving freight trains outside sliding by with the ominous clank and rattle of chains.

Remembering Bret said it's ok to crash on the couches if anyone in the band is too drunk to drive I decide to give it a try. After the noise has stopped from the bands I lay down on a ripped couch in the common area. But I can't close my eyes. Someone could be standing over me at any moment. Any little sound is like steps down the hall.

Preferring my little room I get up and take my chances sleeping behind the locked door. If Bret bothered to watch the security cameras he might notice that I always arrive at night and leave in the morning. But what's wrong with practicing music all night?

I can't sleep. Being off the grid for so long I thought I should write my mom to tell her I'm ok. I grab a legal pad from my bag and begin to write.

I'm letting her know that I am not coming home. I'm letting her know that I have made up my mind to stay in Chicago. I just want to play music. I tell her I feel like I have no choice. I tell her corny memories about growing up. Remember when I was a little kid and my favorite song was *Born to be Wild*? I'd get in trouble during sing-a-longs in kindergarten because I refused to sing the children songs. I would start singing Steppenwolf and be sent to stand in the corner.

I remind her that she was adventurous too when she was young. In the early 70's she lived in Southern California. She told me her idea of a fun weekend was to take acid and go hitchhiking just to see where she would end up. I remind her that my half-brother ran away with the carnival when he was sixteen. He still lives on the road somewhere in the South. Somehow this urge to be free was deeper than circumstance. Unable to find an envelope in my bags I fold the letter in my pocket.

Scratching my chin I wonder if I'm telling her the truth or just bullshitting my mom so she doesn't worry. Is it fate to be here? Is it nurture vs. nature and all that amateur psychology bullshit? No. It's free will. I've made a decision. I have decided to live this way. Subconsciously at first perhaps, but now fully aware this is what I want despite the drawbacks. Despite my aching back sleeping on the floor this is my choice.

I have decided from now on that I will do whatever I want. From now on I will not take any more crap. I will work when I can. I will play music when I feel like it. I will eat when I'm hungry. I will get drunk when I feel like getting drunk. I will float around the city. Suddenly the hard times seem easy because I don't give a shit. Do what thou wilt. Fate be damned.

99

For all my devil-may-care attitude as a squatter I can't quite shake the fear of getting found out. If Bret puts two and two together and sees I am living at the practice space the party will be over. My mind bubbles with paranoia but I take precautions. I hide my dirty clothes inside a trash bag in the room. Due to the cameras in the hall I made sure to wear the same outfit exiting as I do entering. This is easy because I have three identical pairs of work clothes: the required black slacks and button-up shirts. Many moons ago my mom bought me some nice white dress shirts as a present after graduating college. She wanted me to have decent button-ups for job interviews. Now the same shirts are tanned with chicken grease and full of burns from the oven at the deli. Every morning I dress in the same style of black pants and a stained shirt. There is no use being brazenly reckless under the gaze of the cameras. Yet each time I get back and all my stuff is still there I feel relieved.

Bringing beer or something to eat to a jam session is not atypical. So I don't worry about strutting in with a six-pack and a sack of take-out. Sneaking my dirty laundry in and out under the eye in the sky is a different story. Maybe no one is really watching. Maybe the cameras don't even work. Maybe it's all a bluff but I can't afford to be thrown out. So when my threads get so dirty that I can't stand it I stuff my guitar case full of clothes and hit the street.

A pair of middle-aged ladies coming off the Pulaski El tell me the local laundromat is on Madison Street. In Chicago Madison Street is where the numbers stop descending and begin to ascend in the other direction. Madison is zero north, zero south: all West Side. Along the way pit bulls snarl and chew chain link fences like dragons guarding the shotgun style homes. The streets are sparkled with broken glass like fallen stars. When I see a hard looking guy coming my way I worry about getting jacked for my guitar. I imagine that as the guitar case gets pulled away the joke would be on him as nothing but dirty laundry pops out like spring-snakes from a cartoon can.

Spying a post office on Madison I inquire about an envelope for the letter to my mom as well as renting one of the steel mailboxes installed in the wall of the lobby. The clerk gives me a look and explains I can't just buy one envelope only a whole box of envelopes. So I pass on the expense of renting a P.O. box. Only bad news comes in the mail anyway. After springing for the box of envelopes and postage I send my dispatch home to my mom.

At the laundromat I find a quiet corner. A dude with a mustache, shaved head, and a gold complexion notices that I don't need the quarter machines to make change for the washing machines. I have plenty of quarters in my guitar case that I pinched from that fountain in the park. Soon my threads are spinning in psychedelic swirls. As the stranger approaches he has a large tattoo of a rattlesnake coiling up his neck. I don't flinch. I just keep reading my book. He looks hard but be introduces himself as Washington the manager of the mat. We shake hands.

Mr. Washington props himself up on top of a washer nearby. The TV on the wall is on the weather channel. "Another hot one." He glances at the book I'm reading. "Is that the Bible?"

Letting out a chuckle I say, "No. No it's not the Bible. This one is called *Visions of Cody*." Mr. Washington nods. He's not really interested in my book. He asks about my guitar case. Soon he's talking about wild blues clubs in the South. He says he's from Jackson Mississippi and has been to all the juke joints. By the time my clothes are in the dryer we're exchanging dirty jokes and laughing out loud. When he helps himself to a cold can of Squirt from behind the counter he brings me one free of charge with natural Southern hospitality.

"Though I grew up in Mississippi I was actually born here in Chicago. My momma moved to Jackson in 1968. Look outside here at Madison Street. After Dr. King was killed in '68 this place was like a warzone. You ever see black and white newsreels from the sixties with those fire hoses, broken windows, buildings on fire and shit?"

"Sure."

"Well, this is what you were looking at. Dr. King had been here to help organize the community in the years leading up to '68. After he was taken away from us it just broke hearts. When the National Guard rolled in my momma scooped us up and took the first bus south. My Auntie stayed. She's in her eighties now. In the summer I always come up here and help her run the mat."

20

The pharmacy department at Dominick's put up a sign by the deli that the flu-shot will be available early this year. The managers are encouraging all the employees to get the shot. Joy and I are cleaning up the sandwich station or rather I'm cleaning and Joy is standing there with her nose dripping. She's withdrawing again. Bandi bustles by, "Wes you gonna get your flu shot?"

"Sure will. Look I have my vein hole all primed up from donating plasma."

"Oh you got jokes?"

"No look." I show her the little scar on my mainline from the plasma clinic.

"That ain't shit. Joy has a bunch of those. That's why she never rolls up her sleeves."

Joy sniffs back at Bandi.

"Joy you gonna get your flu shot?" Bandi prods.

Joy wipes her nose on her extended sleeve. "I ain't putting that shit in me. It makes you sick so you get used to having the flu. Why would I take something that will make me sick?"

"Wait a minute," Bandi stops. "You'll shoot up them drugs that make you sick, that are cut with who knows what, but you won't take the flu shot!"

"I don't take no drugs!"

Bandi and I laugh. Then Joy laughs too.

After work I usually buy a forty to sip on the train while riding back to the West Side. But just as often I go out. Nearly every night there is an open mic somewhere in the city. I keep my guitar under camera in the break room so after a tiresome shift I can go out and play.

Most nights I go to The Gallery Cabaret in Buck Town. On a quiet corner just north of Armitage and east of Western a lonely Leinenkugel's sign hangs over the sidewalk. It lights up with the image of an Indian princess. From the outside it looks like any sleepy neighborhood waterhole where old men might drink during the day and workers congregate in the evening. Looking closer at the hand painted sign above the door you'll notice strange colorful depictions of gypsies in head scarves and earrings shaking tambourines and the welcoming words: music, art, spirits, comedy. Cracking the heavy wooden door music pours out. Inside is a long narrow room with paintings on the left above a couple leather booths. The bar is on the right. Past the bathroom and the jukebox is a modest stage a mere single step up from the half a dozen tables where the audience waits and watches.

Kenny the owner insists on having free live music seven days a week with no cover charge. By eliminating the cover charge he has created an unofficial clubhouse for every thirsty musician in town. He is a cantankerous beer jockey in his late seventies and pale as a ghost due to his nocturnal lifestyle. Kenny's an old school Chicagoan. He mans the tapper himself as much as possible so he can save money on hired help. Under all his Chicago attitude he has a heart of gold. Kenny remembers Chicago in the late forties when he was a kid at the height of the big band era. When it's a slow night it's fun to get him talking about old times.

The place is not just a bar for musicians. The art on the walls features the work of new artists every month just like a regular art gallery, but one where a guy can rest his duff and get a cheap pitcher of suds while he eyeballs the paintings. If a piece speaks to Kenny he might buy it himself and give it a new life as one of the handful of pieces that live behind the bar. Surrounding the cruel mirror above the bar hangs a series of paintings depicting Edgar Allen Poe, Bernard Shaw, James Joyce, and Picasso done in black and white. There are two pieces Kenny created himself when he was young both nudes of ladies painted in neon green like wild lizard women topped off with bright orange hair.

Sometimes after bar time, as long as we still have money, Kenny locks the door and dims the lights and lets the regulars drink till dawn. Once the door is locked everyone busts out their smokes and lights up at the bar like the old days. Kenny barks, "I pay my taxes! I should be able to run my place anyway I want! No smoking? No beer after two? What the shit?" Naturally Kenny would have operated a speakeasy during prohibition.

On nights like this where we sing and drink after hours it isn't uncommon that Kenny will take my last dollar. But at the same time he will always spot me a few drinks if I bring in some tourists. I'd bait busking customers by telling them I know the only real bar left in Chicago. They'll order Patron and without missing a beat Kenny will say, "We don't got that shit! We have *Jose*!" The shots of Jose Cuervo are poured before the tourist has a chance to pout. Also, after a set us musicians get a free pitcher. Kenny is the best bartender in the world I say to myself as he looks both ways checking for cops before letting me slip out the side door at dawn.

Twice a week there is a free buffet at the Gallery with home cooked food during the open mic. I never miss it. I get seconds and stuff myself like I'm preparing for winter. The janitor Scottie cooks the chow. He's pint size, has a lazy eye, and sleeps on a cot in the basement.

The food is amazing: meatloaf, salad, baked chicken, potatoes, rice… All the starving artists come out of the woodwork. Scottie loves giving the musicians feedback, especially if he doesn't like them. "That song was fucking annoying… You've trying too hard…" Often I see Scottie on random corners in Buck Town perched on top of a mailbox happily reading a book like a literate gargoyle.

Tuesday is the Blues Jam hosted by Mr. Fish and the Blue Fins. Here I can meet guitar players, harmonica players, bassists, pianists, drummers… While keeping one eye open for guys to start a new band I focus on honing my own skills. I can't keep up with a lot of the hot shots on guitar. My folk-blues thing is less compatible with a live jam than Chicago blues. Mostly I just sign up to sing. I try to learn from the older musicians.

It's hard to make a living playing live music even when times are flush. Now when times are tough people don't go out so much. The result is that some of the best musicians in the world are just sitting around at the candle lit tables. Occasionally they will sign up for the jam to keep their chops up. There is all this talent just hanging out haloed behind the candle glow. When a jam is assembled pros are matched with novices. Sometimes you may be surprised who is the amateur and who is the forgotten legend. Rarely is it the dude in the pretentious fedora. Most of the audience is made up of other musicians nursing drinks waiting their turn to wail and moan on stage. Times are hard for live entertainment. So we play for each other.

A set will start with a basic blues riff, a shuffle, a boogie, and I'll sing some lyrics by John Lee Hooker or Howling Wolf. Then the guys take turns performing solos. By default it's the front man who gives the signal for who gives the next solo. While I'm taking a turn growling under the hot lights this responsibility falls at my feet. I feel a little shy pointing at a more seasoned musician to let him know it's his turn to let the notes fly. The scales flutter up the fretboard and up your spine. Music is its own language. It is a universal code. It speaks on a primal almost subatomic level. Like birds singing the guitars wail. No one knows what is being said in any literal sense. Emotions, stories, and feelings are conveyed intuitively through the vibrations.

At some point in college I realized all the great classic rock bands I grew up with are really blues-rock. From Zeppelin, the Stones, The Allman Brothers, The Yardbirds, The Animals, Cream, Ten Years After, Janis, Hendrix… it's all blues-rock. It dawned on me that maybe I was ready for the real thing. Even Black Sabbath started as a blues band before they invented heavy metal. The riff structure in metal that formed the basis for all the hard rock I grew up with in the nineties has more to do with the blues pentatonic scale than with three-chord rock-a-billy. All those British Invasion groups from the sixties were copying American rock and rollers who in turn were copying black songwriters. It's been a copy of a copy. I wanted to go to the source.

So at the Coconuts Record Store on the corner of Randolph and Wabash I bought an early John Lee Hooker record. The first track that did it for me was *I'm Bad Like Jesse James*. In the song Johnny describes how he's going to kill a guy for, "Going around town, telling everybody that he got my wife…" Musically the song is simple. It's stark. There are zero frills. The slower he plays the more menacing it sounds and the more I believe that he really means it. This isn't just a song. It's a genuine threat. It feels like he is really going to murder this motherfucker. There's no jumpy rhythm. There are no silly rhymes. Johnny isn't playing around. This isn't fun and games. This is the real thing. The song is devoid of art and artifice. The song has craft but no crafty little tricks. John Lee Hooker is the authentic voice I was looking for.

I know I'll never be able to pull off something like *I'm Bad Like Jesse James*. I'm no John Lee Hooker. My voice box is not the same instrument by any stretch. But what if like Hooker I write about what's really going on in my life and in the lives of people around me? Like all white rock and rollers I have no choice but to be inspired, add to the spring despite my distance to the source, and do my own thing. Like all folk music the basic structure of the blues is passed down generation to generation to be reinterpreted and added to. Simply to imitate would be bullshit. Just tell the truth. I'm not from Mississippi, but I've been around the block. If I can capture what is happening now, if I write about my own time, before too long it will be history. We're all just a link in the great jam session spanning the decades, a footnote in time, echoes in the abyss.

At first I was nervous when I sang with the older guys. But after the first set the crowd at the bar bought me drinks. The fact that a regular like Zeola, an old lady from Mississippi, asks me every night when I'm gonna sing is all the validation I need. Soon I'm asked to go to other jams including the Chicago Studio Club's Pro-Jam, which is invite only. Next I'm on the list to play the Gallery Cabaret on the weekends. I can set up a show pretty much whenever I want. I have graduated from the open mic to the weekend gigs where Kenny will pay me a cut of the bar receipts. My old band and I had hacked it through the popular clubs in Chicago last year, but it feels like the first time in my life people are truly relating to what I'm doing.

At the Gallery there's Burt the barfly who will open and close the place. With his girth it seems impossible to over serve the man. After a set he mutters to me, "West is the best."

There is Kay G a real live wire always hopped up from snorting something in the men's room. He's so confident he can make a pink ascot look masculine. Sometimes he sings strutting like Mick Jagger. Sometimes he plays bass for Fish and the Blue Fins.

Garret the soundman sports a bandana, pirate earring, and

a rattail. Sometimes he holds court in the back room rolling joints and telling old stories of being a roadie with The Rolling Stones, Ray Charles, and Guns N Roses. "All us on the crew called G N' R the Bums and Posers."

Mr. Fish is a big man with a long white beard and his hair tied back in a ponytail. Famous for his long crisp solos he runs the blues jam like a gentle giant not saying much until he begins singing where the words burst from his lips like bubbles popping to the beat.

Texas Fred is always around peering from behind grey locks and round red tinted shades. It's fun to get Fred talking about the sixties. "I went to the Village in New York because I was a folk singer. But I was a year late for that scene. Then I got drafted for 'Nam so I skipped the border and hitchhiked across Canada. Later I dipped down to San Francisco to see what the Haight and Ashbury thing was about, but again I was a year too late for that. I can't ever be a has-been because I'm a never-was… Finally, I found an Army base and turned myself in."

Little Joey wants to be called Buck Town Boy but no one ever does. He is always a mouth full of slurred words and mumbles. Dressed in cargo shorts and a plaid shirt he looks like a tourist, but the scar tissue over his unblinking right eye proves he is a real bar bum. When I'm broke Little Joey will give my glass a pour out of his pitcher. I return the favor when his pockets are inside out.

Nate Marsh, the one-man band, can somehow juggle finger picking, singing, whistling, snapping, toe tapping, harmonica blowing, tambourine stomping, kazoo zapping with ease. Whenever no one is around to play drums or bass we just call Nate's name.

Sometimes Tressa comes out from behind the bar and plays her accordion like a haunting gypsy in her headscarf.

There is also Dobro Joe, Izzy the Head, Sanjay Mehta, Miles Davis Minor, Michael McDowell, Cowboy Charlie, David Simms, Pat the Pocket, Shanghai Mike, Paul McGee, and draped in long white hair the master of blues harp Arthur the Grey Ghost.

Nate Marsh knows my situation. He's been there. In 2006 when he got back from serving overseas he hitchhiked to Chicago from Kansas. He slept under a pussy willow in Lincoln Park. My folk singer friend Nathan Xander found him playing on the street. Once he slept on my floor in Uptown when I was still in school. Like a drill sergeant he barks his advice from behind his thin mustache, "Out on the street you gotta be a soldier. You gotta know where the clean water is. You gotta know where the public bathrooms are. You gotta see a storm before it comes. You gotta remember Wes. You're a soldier."

Shanghai Mike is stout, has calculating eyes behind his spectacles, and curly hair. Mike got his handle because he lived in China for a spell playing his harmonica and belting out the blues in the clubs of Shanghai. "Funny thing is," he tells me, "In China they called me Chicago Mike. So I only know who I am by whatever town I just left."

Shanghai Mike asks about the banjo he lent me. I tell him I'm using it while I write songs for people on the street. People don't see a banjo too often. It catches their attention and I reel them in. His eyes narrow, "Just be careful with it out there. It's a family heirloom."

"Don't worry. I'm careful." This reminds me. The next patch of cash I can clear has got to go towards the Street Performer License. If I get busted and the cops leave Mike's banjo on the curb I'd be heartbroken.

21

After a long night singing the blues I am trying to sleep all day in my hiding spot. I awake to the sound of distant explosions. Getting dressed I open my door. With no windows in my lair it could be any time of day. A soft summer sunset glows red through the window above the front stairwell. The neighborhood sounds like a war zone. Guns mix with fireworks. Failing to realize it is already the Fourth of July I head to the men's room to throw some water on my face. The murder rate always spikes on America's birthday in a city that usually holds the number one spot for that statistic. The Second City has to be number one at something. On the Fourth a haze rises above the hood. Parts of Chicago seem more like the Iraq War. The setting sun hits the smoke like a bloody fog. The streetlamps are haloed in pink mist.

In rough parts of town, like all survival situations, people react either by becoming very hard or becoming very tender. There is an old couple that I see at the Pulaski train station every morning. The lady drags a walker, and the man drags his leg in a limp. They're on their way to panhandle downtown as I am on my way to busk with the banjo. We get to talking. They even call me by a nickname. The other day the man said, "Hey West Side-Wes. If you ever hear gunshots don't run. Just hit the ground... stay low. Stay low son. That's what I did last time when they were having a fight and I was in that alley."

By nature I'm a loner. I have no problem staying low. I poke around a bit but most of the time I keep to myself. Sometimes I pop into the Currency Exchange at Lake and Pulaski for a bus pass. Outside a dude in a white-tee under the El-station mumbles, "Loose squares. Loose squares." This is to let people know he has extra cigarettes for sale.

Sometimes I'll hit-up the Polish liquor store and get a six-pack of Old Milwaukee to help me sleep in my little hole. There's a small space for the customers to line up at the window. Otherwise all the bottles are behind the counter encased in two inches of bulletproof glass. We point at what we want through the blur and warp of the glycerin wall. Then the dude with the Polish accent wearing his red cap backwards fetches it. We tap on the glass like we're visiting someone in jail. "No not that one… That one! Yeah! Wait… How much is that?" Once rung up the cash goes first spun through a turn-style also made of bulletproof glass. Then the small revolving door spins back with the hooch and the change.

Some of the residential blocks off the avenues are green and people sit on their porches under the shade. They wave at each other and keep watch over things while sipping sweet tea. In other spots the area resembles a post-apocalyptic nightmare. There are dark blocks where the streetlights are shot out. There are closed factories and people sleeping in doorways. The unemployment office line at Ferdinand and Pulaski is long and brooding. The rail-yard knocks a maddening rhythm into the night. Grocery stores with fresh produce are out of reach. Families feed themselves at marked-up Bodegas or greasy diners.

Besides the cops or the Polish guy in his cage at the liquor store the only white people I ever see are obviously on heroin. When loaded they sag half asleep about to fall onto the subway tracks just before the train comes. As they withdraw they return to the neighborhood wide-awake riding on rolling heels in a blur of need.

The area is technically Garfield Park. Unofficially it's Vice Lord territory. The turf of a gang fueled by drug money. It's all over the papers how the Chicago Police have had to negotiate with them. Last week minding my own business an SUV full of cops rolled up. They eyed me curiously. When I didn't look loaded on smack they peeled away. All four of them wore bulletproof vests and had automatic rifles strapped to their seats. They looked scared. With their unblinking eyes and buzz-cuts they resembled fuzzy baby eaglets.

Likewise the dealers on the corner have come to realize I'm not there to buy their dope. They have made it clear I am not welcome. The twelve-year-old runners no longer approach me as I walk from the CTA station. Now the sentries cry, "Narc! Narc! 5-0!" as I pass. If I'm not there to bring drug money to the local economy then I symbolize the specter of something even darker approaching. They suspect I am the first hipster to get a foothold in the hood. Soon there will be underground rock shows in the warehouses. Then those warehouses will turn into legit clubs. Then the club will expand into a restaurant. Soon there will be cafes, condos, rents will go up, and everyone will have to move out.

The fact that I am unwashed, unshaven, and obviously poor does not keep some folks from putting up defenses. Sometimes when I cross the street an approaching car will speed up. The other day at a greasy spoon on Pulaski when I got up to get my food from the window I came back to my table only to find that my seat had been taken. The other night I was forced off the sidewalk. A gaggle of kids in their twenties decked out like they were coming home from a club shouldered me off the curb. "Watch your step white-boy!" one of the guys said with a grin. His teeth flashed in the night. Once upon a time I would have made the point that I'm not a white boy. I'm a white man. Obviously out of respect I would never call a black guy *boy* even if he was younger than me. But I don't say shit. This ain't my battle. I take the hint. I lay low and count my blessings.

This friendly Casper ghost is not welcome here. I'm no curious guest. It doesn't matter how poor I am. It doesn't matter how much I hate the rich just as much as anybody else. Can't they see I am a good little liberal? Can't they tell I love black music? Most of my heroes are black bluesmen. But how would people know? And if they did know why should they even care? What's that old man music have to do with them? So what if I am a pale face plucking a banjo? Don't you know the banjo originates from Africa? Only later was it co-opted by Dixieland jazz bands and borrowed by bluegrass. Shut up art nerd... What does Africa have to do with Chicago? Nothing.

Despite some of the friendly faces I've met in Garfield Park I have stopped exploring the blocks. I buy my food and drink and go straight to my practice space. There are some neighborhoods that will probably never get gentrified. That's ok with me.

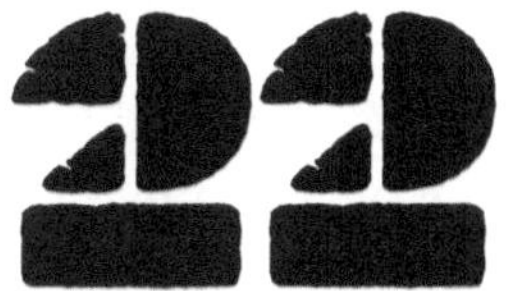

Besides food and the rent for the practice space my biggest living expense is a transit pass. Every payday I purchase a bus pass at the service desk at the grocery store for twenty-three bucks. From the moment the pass is activated at a turn-style or on a bus it's good for unlimited rides on the CTA for exactly one week down to the minute. To make it stretch I will usually sneak onto the train platform at least once before activating the pass. This can be done in a variety of ways.

Leaving work from Division Avenue I walk down to the Chicago Brown Line stop. There is a stairway coming down from the platform, which is exit-only. The turn-style at the top only turns one way: out. The rungs of the turn-style run from ankle height to above the head. However at this particular exit the space between the rungs and the glass wall is just wide enough to squeeze through. If I suck in my gut, turn my head, and scrape a few ribs I can slip in. Now I'm on the far end of the platform for free. The exit is far enough away from the booth where the attendant is stationed to go unnoticed. If the attendant does come my way the exit back to the street is right there. But I time my squeeze just as I hear the train coming. It has to be just right. Too soon the conductor on the train will see me sneaking in. Too late the exit will be flooded with passengers exiting the correct direction through the turn-style.

The most common way of getting on the platform for free is

when approaching the turn-styles head for the handicap door. There is a broad gate for folks in wheelchairs to use. When loaded with my music gear it makes sense to use the gate rather than fumble through the vertical turn-style even when I am paying the fare. If you reach over the gate to the exiting side and hit the blue button with the universal symbol for the handicapped the gate unlocks and you can push right through. This move only works if the turn-styles are crowded with people and blocking the view of the attendant. It's still important to pretend to swipe a transit pass through the scanner before reaching for the blue button. This pantomime prevents fellow passengers from becoming busybodies and informing the attendant. Did the card beep when it was swiped? Or not? I don't know… Did it?

When I do get assigned hours at the deli I am usually scheduled for evening shift. This is fine with me. It allows me to play out at night and sleep in during the day. But last night I was asked to come in early to help with the morning shift. This threw off what little routine I have. But it's nice to be done for the day early in the afternoon. I stand in the parking lot staring up at the skyline yawning when I hear a voice.

"Hey mister. Hey! You want a bike?"

Turning around I see three small black children holding a mountain bike. They have to be about eight or nine.

I look at the bike. It's a little small but it appears to be fairly new. I tell them, "Well sure. I could use a bike. Nobody's missing it are they? I mean, is someone going to come looking for it?"

"No," they reply in eerie unison.

"Well ok, how much you want for it?"

"You can just take it mister."

They look up at me with these big eyes. Like mysterious angels they have appeared like a vision. They hand over the bike and then they run off towards the projects. POOF. They're gone.

So now I have a bike. I no longer need to spend money on a transit pass. Saving twenty-three-bucks is a lot when you have to eat on five or ten a day. I forgot how much fun riding a bike is. It's been years. I'm moving fast and free. Getting anywhere on the CTA means heading one direction, then stopping to transfer just to turn in the next direction. On a bike I can zigzag through the Chicago grid.

Now I bike home to the West Side every night singing along with the lone hum of the wheels. Usually I zip down Halsted and then head west through the meatpacking district. This is where Skip James wrote *Hard Times on the Killing Floor*. Working in the slaughterhouses in the West Loop was so bad in the nineteen thirties it was enough to send him back to Mississippi.

Pumping along Fulton Market I fly all the way to Karlov and Kenzie where my fortress lies. I pass factories and bump across pot-holed side streets. I whistle and talk to myself flashing between streetlights. My spokes spin and ping pong like children's songs. Broken dreams sleep in abandoned cars. Pools of oil pocket the bombed surface of the moon. Spools of razor wire fall off freight trains like tumbleweeds. Overpasses crisscross above like electric salad. Dogs howl at police sirens until they harmonize. In the summer rain I hide under a train bridge as the droplets plunk puddles like piano keys.

Now if Bret is watching on the security cameras he is seeing me heft a bike up the stairs and stuffing it in my room. I am all set. The only creature comfort I really miss is a mattress. Always sleeping on the floor is like camping. My muscles ache constantly. No matter how late I stay up I wake up early from sleeping on my sore back. I live on will alone. I push forward like a moronic shark.

Ironically there is a mattress recycling plant directly across the street from my little crash pad. It mocks me. There are palettes full of box springs stacked to the sky. There are beds right there! But there is no way I could sneak one in. Pulling a bike up the stairs is one thing but a mattress would be too much. It would be obvious that I live inside.

As I burst out the steel door in the morning I practically collide with a homeless man dressed in a stocking cap and rags. He's standing on the sidewalk smoking a cigarette, grinning, and burning a mattress. Between drags he explains he's gonna turn in the metal springs for scrap once he burns away the fluff. I start laughing. Then he starts laughing. I want a bed so bad. But I just stand there and watch him burn the mattress. Ash and cotton float away like dandelion seeds. He and I laugh out loud. We laugh in spite of ourselves. Our laughter vibrates with the licking flames.

23

Meanwhile it's July in Chicago. During the winter the city goes into hibernation. But in the summer Chicago can be one of the most exciting cities in the world. Rent at the practice space isn't due for another few weeks. So I begin to take it easy. I am going to do whatever I feel like. I'm going to follow my nose. Consequences be damned.

On my days off I strap my guitar case on my back and bring my bike on the train and slide downtown. Here I sneak into my old college and check my email. My student ID has been expired for years but I give a confident wave to the doorman and soon I'm stealing toilet paper and sitting in the computer lab. I check the teacher's lounge for donuts. Next I play music on Michigan Ave, Millennium Park, or Navy Pier till I have some pocket money.

From there I take the bike trail along the lake heading to the North Side. Living in the industrial side of town you forget how soft and beautiful Chicago can be. At sunset the buildings and the water turn a warm flesh-tone along the lake. The glass and the water melt together. After the summer rain the air is warm and everyone seems to be enjoying life, but they are too cool to admit it.

Sometimes I begin to laugh out loud because the lakefront is so beautiful it's ridiculous. But my dirty neck is itching beneath the sun. So I pull up to North Avenue Beach and hop in the lake. Dunking my pageboy cap in the water it stays wet and cool on my head for the next few hours. I have a two-dollar bottle of shampoo in my guitar case and begin washing my hair in front of all the yuppies, swimmers, sunbathers, and volleyball freaks. Everyone is out-to-be-in. I'm down and out.

First stop heading north is the building where my ex-professor Mr. Blue stays. We call him Blue because he only wears blue. Even his furniture is blue. His toilet paper is blue. I still don't have a phone so I have his doorman announce me. If he's at home suddenly I'm sitting poolside on the 44th floor in Lincoln Park staring down at the city and pointing out the places that punctuate my journey.

If Blue isn't home I keep heading north ringing doorbells and knocking on wood of friends and mild acquaintances. Some have moved out and strangers give me the eye and slam doors. In a row I knock on doors up the Gold Coast offering jokes and jive in exchange for a couch to crash. If no one is home the end of the line is the Heartland Café up in Rogers Park. Here I can sign up for the open mic and play some songs. If the kitchen is open the hippies in the back will serve up plates of happy health food before the long trek south again.

This cool summer morning I am on my bike spiraling along the path that wraps around Montrose Harbor like the Yellow Brick Road. South of the lily pond I discover a dirt road that runs between Lake Michigan and the Golf Course. Hopping the dangling chain that blocks entry to the service road soon I am on a quiet path crumpling into the rocks and surf. I am the only soul around besides the rare homeless person peeking up from under the rocks where they duck from the golf-balls falling like sparse pieces of hail. Suddenly I have my own private lakefront. I pull up a rock and stare into the void. Boats slide across the glass. The air is alive with seaweed and foam. The waves whisper. Clouds reflect the whitecaps. The seagulls yelp, "Help. Help. Help."

Euphoria pours over me. The air is laced with déjà vu. Here where the land falls into the lake I stare at the point where the sky meets the water. I feel like I can see out the back of my head. Like a duck-eye scene in a David Lynch film I have the sensation of seeing two directions at once. The past is nothing but fading memories. The future is a mystery. I feel like anything can happen. I feel like this moment is the exact center point of my life.

On the North Side I usually end up at Matt Jensen's place. Due to the heat in my windowless cell I try to crash anywhere other than the practice space as much as possible. I rotate my doorbell rings among a handful of friends, but I prefer Matt's company. After a shower and a shave we scoop up something to drink at the corner. We talk about every little thing, smoke out on the fire escape, and laugh ourselves silly. First I update him on my adventures. As I vent Matt sits in an office chair rolling back and forth stroking his beard as I lay horizontal on the recliner looking like I am in psychoanalysis. He should charge by the hour.

Matt used to do impromptu video projections while my band would play a set. It was always great stuff like mixing Betty Boop cartoons with fluorescent fractals. His apartment is a place where I can watch movies and check my email. It makes me feel normal. At the end of a chatter session I set up camp on his floor using cushions and blankets. Matt is one of the good ones. He has a warm and laidback presence, which is calming to someone like me who has an intense anxious personality. In college we used to call him Jesus to spoof his beard, but it was more than just that. He has the aura. He is one of the Buddhas.

"Did you write any new songs about people lately?" he asks.

"I think I might have accidently wrote one about myself."

"Let's hear it."

To a swing beat I pound on my guitar in manic fervor and I chant out a bug-eyed rendition of a new song.

I'm the Village Idiot.
I have no bed.
I'll convince you I'm a genius then
ask you for bread.
I have stars in my eyes and
freedom in my shoes.
I have nothing to worry because
I have nothing left to lose.

I knew a girl, equally injured.
Everyone said that's cute.
She rang away, home they say, and
I'm not looking for any substitute.

Yes, I'm the Village Idiot and
I'm there for you.
I'm the Village Idiot.
I'm everybody's fool.
I do things on a dare.
I get paid in beer.
I'm the Village Idiot and
I have nothing left to fear.

Matt is making faces at me from behind his beard as I belt it out. When I'm done he lets out a laugh. "That one's great! It's funny, but in a disturbing way." He begins fishing around in his closet rattling junk around. He emerges with a trombone. The slide is dented. "I used to play this in the fucking marching band in high school. That song could use a wacky trombone."

We start jamming and hamming it up. I yodel, chant, and cackle. I repeat the sparse verses ad-nausea faster and faster until the rhythm crescendos and crashes into chaotic madness. When the song settles and the chords clear Matt burps out a long sad *whomp, whomp, whaaaaa* with the slide like the sound effect in a Vaudeville radio show. We bust up laughing.

"Man, you gotta play on this track if I ever record it."

"For sure."

Matt tells me he's about to leave the city next week to visit his family back in Ohio. He asks me to house-sit and take care of his cat. He asks as if I'd be doing him a favor, but we both know he's doing me the favor. He knows my answer is yes, yes, yes. He says I can even sleep in his bed. His cat hates me. It's a stray that only trusts Matt, but we'll survive living in this studio apartment together for a week. We're both alley cats.

My new mantra is yes. Anything that comes along I say yes. I go for the ride. I blow with the wind. After a long relationship having to account to my ex for all my comings and goings I begin to say yes to every new experience that comes by. As a bit of a lone-wolf I've spent years avoiding eye contact, putting up a wall, looking within, knowing thyself. No news was good news. No rolling dice, no drama. Less friends, less problems. But now the whole city is my friend. I am out in the open. I am skinless in the street.

When the bars close after a jam session I'll tag along with some friendly faces to share a bottle and crash on a random couch. In the morning I clean up a bit for my host, wash the dirty tumblers in the sink, leave a thank you note in the form of a poem on the fridge, and slip out the door checking the green street signs on the corner for my whereabouts. I am receptive to all energies. Sometimes I wear out my welcome. But just as often people latch onto me when I make eye contact. They can see my heart is open.

The other day this older couple claimed to have read my aura from behind the deli counter. As I was punching out for lunch they offered to take me to a café and pick up the bill for a few minutes of my time. My answer was: yes. I chowed a sandwich and washed it down with coffee as they explained a pyramid scheme hocking New Age wares. They sold healing bracelets, mood rings, orthopedic shoes, space-age textiles, and most importantly the promise of getting rich quick. They didn't seem rich to me. They didn't even join me for lunch. After I was done with my free chow I sipped my coffee and explained to them I have no car to carry the wares, no clean shirts, no savings, and have zero money to invest. I might be friendly and smiling while I am at work, but I am not going to be their salesman, especially if I have to buy what I am selling first. They suddenly transformed from whispering little spiritual hippies to zealous snapping demons.

I have another customer at Dominick's who has nicknamed me Kentucky. She comes in today in a sundress and dangling earnings. She asks me if I am from the South. "No ma'am," I answer in my dumb farm boy voice, which is a customer service tactic more than any literal accent.

"Well, you sound like you're from Kentucky."

"Nope Wisconsin. The drawl on certain words likely has more to do with hanging out in the hood than being a country bumpkin. You know the Southern accent surged in Chicago ever since the Great Migration when black folks left the South for the factory jobs in the North. Due to all the economic segregation in this town it's been preserved. But you know if a guy is open to it the vernacular rubs off."

She isn't interested in a history lesson. She introduces herself as Tammy. She looks like she is in her forties with a honey complexion and hair up in a bun dyed dark red.

Bandi whizzes by and sees me lollygagging. "Hey, Parkside! You going to hop on dishes?"

"I'm helping a customer Bandi."

Tammy asks, "Why she call you Parkside?"

"Oh there's that fancy condo called Parkside that just went up across the street that everyone is salty about. She jokes that since I went to college I must be able to afford to live there."

"Huh, that's where I live. I'm at Parkside."

"Truth is I can't afford my own place. I squat in a warehouse out west."

"I can only afford Parkside because of my disability payments through the military. I joined the army, but hurt my knee in training."

"Huh."

She goes on. "People assume things about me too. Because I'm African American they think I agree with whatever Obama does. They think I like hip-hop. Not this girl. I like southern rock like Lynyrd Skynyrd. I like Patsy Cline."

"I prefer black music. Blues. Jazz. I'm trying to play the blues myself."

"Really? I know some people in the music industry."

"Oh yeah?" I light up when she says this.

She smiles. "Ah ha. Yes. I know a copyright lawyer and a manager."

"Oh cool." She has my attention.

"Maybe I could help you."

"That'd sure be nice of you. You should come to The Gallery Cabaret and hear me do my thing at the blues jam."

When I tell her where the Gallery is she stops smiling.

"I'm more of a downtown lady. Normally I don't cross Halsted Street."

"Halsted? Really? Buck Town is safe as anywhere in town."

"No, I like the Loop. I like Lincoln Park or Lakeview."

"Sure. Let's get a drink. You name the place."

"Oh I don't drink."

"Let's get coffee then."

"Ok."

"Tell you what. I'm staying at my friends place up in Lakeview or the Boys Town area. I'm off next Thursday. Let's get coffee on the corner of Clark and Belmont."

"Alright. Seven?"

"That'll work."

She smiles and rolls her shopping cart away.

Normally I would never do this. We don't seem to have anything in common. But what if the music industry connections are genuine? I feel a bit like one of my customers on Michigan Avenue after I've waved them in offering to write a song about them. If you make the song all about them they love it. Maybe she was telling me what I wanted to hear. I feel like a mark. But my new mantra is yes. When an opportunity presents itself I'm going to go with it and see where it leads.

25

It's fascinating how things work out. Everything comes together if you look for the signs. The city is like a matrix. Traffic moves like grooves in a slot machine. Being out on the street so much I am beginning to get superstitious. I am beginning to get a tactile feel for my own luck. I will bump into just the right person at just the right time. Or I'll be hungry and will sneak into my old school where they'll have free sandwiches for doing a survey. I begin to notice streaks of green lights lining up as I bike down an avenue. I make the bus just in time three times in a row, or likewise miss the train by a few seconds and always three times in a row. Something tells me to turn this way or that. I say yes to this whispering voice. I begin to call these signs "psychic bites."

My instincts feel sharp to where I am able to anticipate things just before they happen. There will be a bus pulling up just around the next corner. There might be free samples in this café. The phone at work will ring and by the subconscious tone of the ring I know which regular customer it is. If someone pops into my mind more than once I will probably see that person that day. I am surfing karma. I am spinning in the golden ratio. I can see it now that I am unplugged from the TV world. The streets click along in a deterministic rhythm. You can get a feel for the flow if you simply pay attention. The universe gives you everything you need and only when you need it. Maybe I am going crazy but I feel like my life is charmed. To keep from going off the deep end I tell myself: It's not magic or synchronicity. Life is just repetitive. Either way: pay attention.

Beach Poets for example. This is a poetry reading on Loyola Beach that has been going on since 1992. Cathleen Schandelmeier is the host. While I am housesitting for Matt I am scheduled to do a featured set on the beach. I get some chuckles from the poets when I show up wearing black slacks and a long sleeve shirt at the beach, but they listen up when I sing my songs. There are stories in the songs.

Afterwards Cathleen tells me about a company that is doing a focus group. For a hundred bucks you can give your opinion on a spray that decorates your home carpet. The catch is you have to be a homeowner, which I am the opposite. But right here on the beach she hands me her phone and I call them up. I lie about being a homeowner. The lady who's doing the screening for the survey asks me about my occupation. A grocery store clerk cannot afford a house so I crunch some wits and blurt out: I own a butcher shop. She promptly informs me that she is a vegetarian. But it makes no difference. In a few days I am sitting with all these pleasant Baby Boomers in a conference room in Lincoln Park hemming and hawing about the product. There are stencils to shape the spray on carpet samples. I bend a spiraled stencil this way and that and soon my carpet sample has a cartoon devil on it. Rad. After an hour of bullshit I have a hundred dollars in my pocket. Thanks Cathleen.

At Beach Poets I meet Janet Kuypers who runs a small press and publishes underground lit. She invites me to feature at her open mic at a place called The Café in Lincoln Square. One gig leads to another. After they pass the hat at The Café I have gathered another thirty bucks. These things happen in streaks. I've been living on luck. I've been pushing it pretty hard. Eventually the streak is bound to run out. I tell myself: pay attention.

26

As agreed I am standing at the corner of Clark and Belmont waiting to get coffee with Tammy and talk about the music business. The Clark bus rolls up and Tammy steps off. I can see her limp now. She told me last week that she hurt her knee in the Army. She walks slowly towards me.

"Hi Kentucky," she greets me.

"Hey there," I respond trying not to roll my eyes at the nickname.

In slow motion we stroll through the Dunkin Donuts parking lot. Under the fluorescent lights the pastel pastries glow. An androgynous teenager is sleeping on one of the tables. For years this corner in Boys Town has been a meet up spot for runaways and castaways in the LBGT community. In the suburbs and throughout the Midwest so many of these kids are not welcome at home just for being who they are. Many of them end up in Boys Town. At Dunkin the transgender folks can use the only unisex bathroom around. I know the spot from freshman year. Us kids would score designer drugs for our cheesy rave parties. At the door Tammy's pace slows to a crawl.

"I'm more of a Starbucks kinda girl."

Sure as death and taxes there's a Starbucks across the street. There is plenty of room inside Dunkin and the plain coffee is just over a buck. Inside Starbucks it's shoulder to shoulder. People are crunching on computers and talking at full volume on phones. There's only room at the little stools lined up in the front window. Tammy has trouble getting on the stool. When she does I have trouble hearing her over the din. So we take our coffees to go. We stroll down Belmont towards the lake.

"What kinda coffee did you get Kentucky?"

"Black."

"Just like a cowboy."

"I just want the caffeine. I'm not looking for dessert. Those Starbucks drinks are like milkshakes."

There's a lull in the conversation.

"Do you mind," she starts, "can you stand on the left side facing the street?"

"Sure whatever you say." I step around her. "Why? What's the difference?"

"A woman walking with a man when she is on the left side towards the street is a signal that the woman is for sale."

"What? I've never heard of that."

"It's true. It's a code."

"Well no one is going to roll up on you in this neighborhood. In the unlikely event that they do I'll tell them where to stick it."

"You'd be surprised. Hey I think the school I used to work at is around here." Tammy brings us to an elementary school off a side street just north of Belmont. "I used to be a teachers assistant here part time." Tammy pushes on the front door. It opens and we go inside. It's quiet inside. All the kids have gone home after summer school. There's little lockers decorated with finger paintings. I feel like a giant. She inches up some stairs. In the teacher's lounge she finds some people she used to work with. They seem surprised to see her. They seem more surprised to see me. But small talk is made.

The small talk is small. I'm bored. I'm caffeinated. I'm pacing.

Finally I say, "Let's swing by my friend's place. My guitar is there. I could play you a song."

On the way out taking the steps one by one Tammy says, "You should give my son guitar lessons." I begin to explain how I am self-taught. I only use open tunings for slide guitar. Open tunings are only used in Delta blues from Mississippi or in Death Metal from Scandinavia. Unless her son is into that stuff he might want to go to a traditional guitar teacher. She doesn't respond. She doesn't seem to be listening to my long pretentious explanation. She just hears: no.

Eventually we make it to the door of Matt's building. "This is it."

"Oh, is your friend up there too?"

"He's in Cleveland seeing his folks, but my guitar is upstairs. Also I have demos on CD from my old band in my guitar case. You could take one to your friend in the music business."

"I don't think I know you well enough to go into a strange building alone."

"Alright. That's fine. Do you want to wait here while I go upstairs and get my guitar case?"

"It's getting dark. I don't know about standing out here by myself."

We are at an impasse. Tammy seems too afraid of life to live it. Maybe something happened to her. Maybe she's traumatized. She was in the Army. But didn't she say she hurt her knee before she even got out of training? Whatever is actually bothering her she doesn't seem willing to tell me. Somehow I want to let her know that I am not going to hurt her. Maybe it would help if I assure her that I don't have any sexual feelings towards her. This way it would be clear that as a man she's safe with me. But I can't think of any way of saying that which doesn't sound insulting.

After standing frozen under the yellow light above the door for a long minute I offer to walk her to the train. We limp to the Belmont El stop with me walking on the left against the street the whole way so no one will mistake me for a pimp. As if anyone would. Maybe I'm the one for sale? At the CTA station she pauses by the turn-style. "Well goodnight Kentucky." She inches her chin up and her eyes go dewy. Is she waiting for a kiss goodnight? Did she assume we were on a date this whole time?

"Hey," I start. "Could you please stop calling me Kentucky? I said I wasn't from Kentucky."

"Yeah ok."

With that I give her a friendly wave and shoot off at my natural rapid pace down the sidewalk. Back there over my shoulder something is off. Under all Tammy's pleasant posturing there is sadness. Under pretending to be too good for Dunkin Donuts or too fancy to leave downtown there is fear. Whatever it is I'm not going to find out. I have living to do. I can't be slowed down now. I have enough sadness of my own.

I dip into 1000 Liquors on Sheffield and circle back to Matt's apartment. In the night I toast my four walls, the soft bed, and the air-conditioner hanging in the window. Putting my guitar down now and then I get up to take a leak. I don't even have to get dressed to use the bathroom. At the moment I have a pot to piss in. Life is good.

Matt's cat is sitting in the bathtub as it has been the whole time I've been here. Occasionally he slinks out to eat or use the cat box. As I answer natures' call the cat hisses at me. With my one free hand I reach over and try to pet him. He swipes a claw in my direction. He seems afraid of everything just like Tammy. He doesn't trust anyone. He's been traumatized too. I fill the little guy's bowl with cat food and lay down in the big soft bed. The world is so full of sadness. I don't know what more I can do.

27

Immediately after Matt gets back into town and I hand off his keys I see my old English professor JT in the window of a café. He invites me to stay with him for a few days. His wife and daughter are visiting his in-laws in France. Meanwhile he's enjoying a stint of bachelorhood. "I found myself drinking a beer in the shower the other night," he says rubbing his chin. "I've been smoking cigars, staying up late, and playing my guitar."

"Sounds like my life minus the shower."

JT is a soft-spoken clean-cut guy. His eyes are always lit up and curious. He is all elbow patches and shrugging shoulders. He has an unassuming manner but with a wild streak lurking just under his good breeding. He was the first teacher who ever encouraged my writing. Long after his class he would edit my work and meet up with me to talk shop. He gave me notes on my first novel, which was very compassionate of him because that first book was a cesspool of pretension. Back in high school my English teachers would only comment on the alarming content in my writing. I would get graded according to morality not the mechanics of writing. They never bothered to encourage me despite my obvious enthusiasm for the language.

JT's place is on the second floor of a brown brick walk-up at Montrose and Racine. The large windows overlook Graceland Cemetery.

We stay up plucking guitars, blowing harp, and drinking exotic liquors he has brought back from Europe. He cracks open an ornate wooden cabinet and we sample rare extracts, absinthe, and digestives. Like mad scientists we mix this with that. We taste combinations no one has ever tasted before. The music plays. For a couple days the sun goes up and down without a care.

Suddenly the party is reaching an end. The next morning JT is going to drive to Iowa to visit his Alma Mater. To put a cherry on the top of the lost nights we decide to bike up Clark Street and go to Carols, the only country bar in Chicago.

Inside Carols the hillbilly band is busting a gut. The pedal steel is shedding tears. The drums are knocking on the barn door. The singer is snorting sawdust. We order a bucket of Lone Stars and grab a table. After the first set the band invites anyone in the audience who can sing to sit in, basically karaoke with a live band. I sing the George Thorogood number *I Drink Alone*. JT does some early Elvis when the King was still a rock-a billy bastard.

The hands on the clock drop. It's bar time. After shaking down the crowd for their tabs the bartender kicks everyone out. The bodies stumble onto the sidewalk. Some aging raver is mumbling past his lip ring about everyone going to his apartment for meth and open sex. Polite smiles and lack of eye contact is all he gets as a reply. "Man, back in the nineties everyone was much more down to party."

JT is unlocking the bikes. I find myself making out with a leathery lady with sandy blonde hair. JT taps me on the shoulder. He's got to be up in the morning. He's going to Iowa tomorrow, back to his old college, back to literary heaven. As we leave the country bar I feel as cool as a cowboy. I'm fucking Clint Eastwood. I'm just another nameless stranger in Chicago. I'm the good, the bad, and the ugly. Slowly I saddle up on my bike. Over my shoulder I give the blonde lass a cool wave. I spur my bike pedal. I'm ready to set off into the sunset.

As I shove off my foot slips. I fall off the bike. The ground rushes up. The Earth swells. I face plant on the hard pavement. I land eye first. My luck has run out.

There is a flash of light where before there was only darkness. The universe expands and contracts. All the traffic lights in Chicago turn red at once. "Stop!" the silence screams. Rolling blackouts. Blue tornadoes. Cracking ice. The power is cut. All the El-trains screech to a halt. The third rail is out. All the cabs get hailed and pull to the curb in unison. All the luck and light bleeds down the gutter into Lake Michigan. My skull is made of cement. My head is connected to the sidewalk. Sounds from under the ocean moan in my ears as my mind drifts through space. Slowly I float until I hit the edge of the universe.

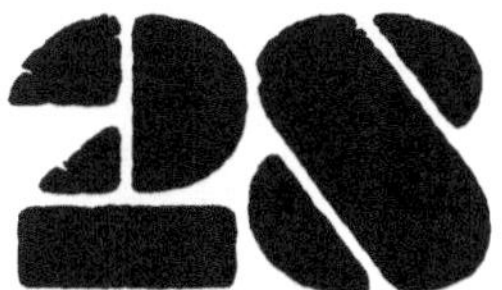

Bouncing back from oblivion my eyes open. My head is in a pool of blood. The sound is muffled but people are excited saying things like, "Oh my god…" and "Are you ok?"

Then one of the voices says, "We should call 9-11."

However well meaning this is calling 9-11 means cops. The cops might help me at first, but I'll still get charged with public drunkenness while operating a bike or whatever they can think up. I don't have a real address. Due to my shallow pockets JT was the one paying for the buckets of beer all night. He's my former teacher. It's against the rules at my college to fraternize with the students. No. Help from the authorities would only create more problems than it would solve. These are my thoughts as the adrenaline runs through my head.

JT helps me up. The shock has sobered me up instantly.

"Let's get out of here," I say to JT.

We walk the bikes down a dark side street. After a few blocks we hear sirens in the distance. I straddle my bike and begin to coast down the sidewalk. JT mounts up as well. At a corner JT stops his bike, reaches in his pocket and stuffs something inside a bush. The police are not the kind of help we need.

Weaving through the quiet blocks behind Truman College we're back at JT's apartment in just a few minutes. JT hands me a towel.

"Why don't you wash the blood off and then we'll take a look and see how bad it is."

In the shower the pain starts. I wash the blood off my face and out of my hair. It spirals down the drain like Hitchcock. My thoughts are echoing. I can hear them in my skull. I realize I'm talking to myself out loud. My voice is reverberating in the shower.

Under the kitchen lights we assess the damage. I have road-burn from my forehead to my chin. The first layer of skin is scraped off. The point of impact is above my right eye. Half the hair from my eyebrow is scraped off. There is a cut above the eye that won't stop bleeding. I have to get it stitched up.

JT emerges with a first aid kit. We bandage my face as best we can. As for stitches I insist that we go to St. Josephs. I've been told that the ER there is free. Turns out I'm wrong. It means more debt, but that's the plan. At Montrose and Broadway we hail a cab.

On the way to the hospital JT tells me he heard me in the shower moaning. "You said: Why do I keep doing this? Why do I keep doing this to myself?"

As the city lights blur by I think: I'm at the bottom of a binge. Sometimes it seems like there's nothing better to do on this planet than lube the brain with booze. This chemical has become part of the human genetic code. On this rock the race is blurred in the haze and malaise of ethanol like a bacterium saturated in a petri dish. From Russia to America we are under a god who has passed out. We stare through a mandala of double vision. We peer up at stars smeared across the sky like dead fireflies. As the planet turns at five-o-clock every night my stomach opens expecting alcohol like some twilight flower unfolding its' soft jaws.

Where do the sober get the love to go on? Is it like fasting? That burning light in the empty pit of the stomach? Is it like the runners high? No pain no gain? I think about how religion seems to substitute that soft spot on the top of the crown that alcohol usually occupies. There's something missing. Perhaps at some point we'll evolve to where the void is filled. Evolution or revelation will come someday. Something is going on upstairs, but for now I stagger on. Even at rock bottom I can't make the leap of faith. I can't give up the hole in my soul. It's the lack of answers, the mystery that makes everything so beautiful. I can't pretend to know what's going on. Once you make up your mind about the universe you stop thinking and start telling others what to do. The wonder is gone. While I'm still on Earth I'm going to indulge in Earthly pleasures. The poetic triumvirate: wine, women, and song. Perhaps I should sing songs more than I slug and slurp. Perhaps I just need a good woman. It's all about balance. My scales have tipped. These are the thoughts that loop in my head as I stare out the taxi window.

It's a slow night at the emergency room on the North Side. There's an empty bed next to mine so JT curls up and takes a nap. The excitement is over. A tiny nurse stitches up my brow. Twelve stitches. "Do you work at the plasma clinic?" I ask her. "I think I know you." Nurses are like angels.

After I'm sewn up I'm ready to go. I wanna leave. The nurse asks me if I lost consciousness. I tell her no. I'm lying. Regardless they ask me to stick around for observation. They ask that I stay awake in case I have a concussion. I try to entertain myself. As morning shift comes in I point at JT sleeping in the bed next to me. "Hey, I don't think that guys breathing!" The nurses pounce on JT like a flock of pixies. He wakes up giggling. Their exam must have tickled.

Still they make us wait. I'm about to make a break for the door when they ask me to come into the backroom for a cat scan. Afterward they say my skull has a hairline fracture. There's not much that can be done about that besides just let it heal. Back in the front I tell JT I'm officially a crackhead. He nods to acknowledge my stubborn wit, but he's laughed out.

Finally the angels get sick of me and I'm discharged. We're free.

The discharge nurse calls after me. "Make an appointment in six weeks to get the stitches out!"

It's bright outside. Our eyes burn in the sunlight. In the cab back I'm playing with my jaw. It pops when I move it back and forth. "Hey. This could be a new instrument." JT yawns. He is beyond weary. My welcome is worn out. Slumming with me is no longer amusing. The novelty has dissolved with the dawn.

After a few hours sleep on his couch I wake up to the sound of JT packing for Iowa. He's off to visit his old school. When he sees I'm awake he pulls a bike helmet out of the closet. He hands it to me. I put it on. It makes me look like a dork, but I strap the helmet on tight. I thank him, sling my guitar on my back, and head out the door.

JT is a kind man. I would have dreaded it if I had caused him any more trouble. Unlike myself he has a lot to lose.

29

Back on my bike I'm heading west on Montrose Avenue. I'm not sure where I am going. It's hot. The humidity weighs on my shoulders. My eye is swelling shut. Sweat mixes with the puss coming out of the road burn. My vision is limited. I have to be more careful than ever jostling with the cars. Things seem bad. I have to admit it now.

Riding slowly, carefully, I feel too tired to pump all the way back to my hole at Lake and Pulaski. I'm not sure I can make it. With the helmet on I look like a bloody mushroom. My handlebars turn like a dowsing rod. Right and left I weave not knowing why.

In Lincoln Square I ring Shanghai Mike's buzzer. When he answers the door he stares at me in horror. Pink sweat drips down my chin. I'm a gory mess. He hands me a bottle of water and I move on in silence.

When I cross the Chicago River I head south through Horner Park to avoid traffic. At Logan Boulevard I lay in the grass in the median for a few hours. I remember an old friend had moved into the area. I haven't seen Nicolai in about a year. Not since a housewarming party where his bike messenger friends partied long into the night. I wonder if I can remember where it is. It was a two story flat just off the boulevard.

Bike Messengers are a very militant subculture. This elitism is well deserved. Pedaling at high speeds through the madness of downtown they have a high mortality rate. Even in the digital age there are files, mostly legal documents needing physical signatures, which have to go from building to building as fast as possible. Often decorated with tribal piercings and dreadlocked manes they scour the buzzing lanes like the pirates of the Loop.

On Wrightwood I see a stoop full of torn sleeves, beards, tattoos, and hanging bike chains. One of the guys Bjorn recognizes me and hands me a cold PBR. Nicolai isn't home yet. The rest of the messengers are deep into the after work ritual converging on the porch cooling down in sync with the setting sun.

As I place the cold can of PBR on my swollen eye Bjorn inspects my injuries. "Ahhhh that shit will heal," he tells me. "That's nothing man. I've lost teeth twice!"

He pulls out a plate of false teeth and waves them under my one good eye. "See? No big deal." He steps inside for a minute and comes back with a T-shirt displaying the names of dozens of bike-messengers who died in traffic. These guys are fast, brave, and tough. Mostly their suffering goes unsung.

"The difference is," I tell'em, "these aren't war wounds. This is just my drunken dumb ass."

"Yeah that happens too."

"I'm twenty-seven. I'm getting too old for this shit."

"Twenty-seven ain't old."

The shadows grow long until they turn into the night. Soon I'm feeling a bit better despite looking like the Hunchback of Notre Dame. I pull out my guitar and the guys are digging it. Now it's a cool summer night. There is a party forming around me. As the sun drops my eye seals completely shut.

As I sit strumming on the steps a little brunette catches my one good eye. She has jet-black hair, pale skin, and big eyes. She looks too good to be true. She probably is. I blink, or rather I wink. Maybe I do have a concussion? Her ruby lips peel away from her drink as she suddenly turns to me, "What's your name?" I tell her. She takes me by the hand and leads me inside. In the dark room bike parts and tools come into focus. In the kitchen she makes me an ice pack with cubes from the tray wrapped in a towel. Is she real?

She begins icing my face. She is very close. I am sweaty. I am bloody. I probably smell bad. But we begin to kiss. She takes me by the hand and leads me to the sofa in the living room. Everybody else is out on the stoop just on the other side of the blinds. She plops down on a cushion. She pulls up her blouse and down her bra. She pinches her areolas as if to activate them. She pulls my face into her chest. Soon my bloody face mixes with her milky skin.

Suddenly Nicolai walks in the door. The girl jumps up, puts away her scoops, and disappears into the shadows. When Nicolai's eyes adjust to the dark room he embraces me. "Wes! How've you been?" Now my face is being pushed into Nicolai's hairy chest. I'm in a daze. Where did the girl go? Was she a figment of my imagination?

"Who was that?" I ask. Nicolai's too excited to answer. We used to be roommates in Rogers Park one lost summer. That seems long ago. He lands another beer in my hand and leads me back to the porch.

The ruckus gathers momentum. There is another party under the Blue Line tracks at Sacramento and Fullerton. I'm beat but I tag along with Bjorn, Nicolai, and the gang. I just want to get the brunettes' name. She's at the second shindig too but acting cool like nothing had happened. Bjorn tells me her name is Trudy.

A few hours ago I felt really down. Then this girl picked me out from every guy at the party: the most haggard gory mess of a man. Something about that excited me. She didn't give a shit. It was punk rock. It was reckless. But down deep it was caring.

She mingles with other clumps of people. When I catch up with her I ask her why she kissed me? "Well, at least half your face is cute." I ask her for her number. As I write it down on the back of a receipt she asks for mine. I don't have a number. I don't have a phone, but now I want to get one. I ask her if she would come see me play some time? No she says, but maybe in a few months when she turns twenty-one.

I should be thinking: she is too young for me. I've just gotten out of a long relationship. I have no money. I have no phone. She can't go out to the bars with me. My mug is a mess. But she didn't seem to give a damn. Maybe if she didn't care about my face she wouldn't care about all that other bullshit. The fact that she is giving me any attention gives me hope. But maybe my smashed face isn't the only open wound.

All the noise has attracted the cops. The crowd moves to the middle of the boulevard drinking and singing picnic style. The cops come again. The gang keeps hopping on their bikes and moving further west. Soon I fall behind. With my one eye I can't keep up any longer. I veer off unnoticed. I head back to Nicolai's place. No one is there but the door is open. I lay my sore head down on the couch where I had been seduced. Exhausted I pass out.

30

As I walk into Dominick's Bandi sees my injured face. Like seeing a man carrying flowers she asks, "What you do Wes? You piss off your woman? You two get into it?"

"No Bandi. I told you we broke up months ago."

"I've heard that before."

Roxy actually listens to me but also assumes, "You get beat up on the West Side?"

"No. No, I'm just a fool."

Mr. Sunshine is nicer. "You gotta get yourself some of that Cocoa Butter. It will help you bet your color back."

"What color?" Bandi snaps. She waves a deli knife at him. "Sunshine I can cut you to till the white meat shows. As for uncle Wes I don't think so."

She makes everyone laugh and the mood is light again.

But now Moe sees me. "Westley. What happened to your face? You can't work around food until that heals up."

Oh great I think. Now I'm going to lose what hours I do get. I might even lose my job. I throw my apron on the floor and head to the pharmacy department. There I get some hydrogen peroxide and some extra large Band-Aids. Also I find an eye-patch for three dollars.

At the men's room sink I pour the peroxide down my cheek. The flesh sizzles. The eye-patch has a male model on the little cardboard box. The model has his hair slicked back and that pinched scowl all models seem to make. With the black patch over his eye he looks like some sort of international man of mystery. When I strap the thing on I look like a fucking pirate. Yaaargh.

There is no time to cry into the mirror. I am living day to day. I do not reflect on the situation. There is no time. There is only time to react. There is only moving forward. Regardless things are being documented. My old friend Daniel Stine busses in from Michigan. We do a set at the Gallery. We moan till dawn. Somebody taped the show. The next time I am at Matt's I see it on YouTube. My gory eye is on display. Shanghai Mike is at the gig. He sits in. We just yell out the key of the song and he honks along on harp. At the bar after the set Mike leans over, "How's your eye?"

Flipping the eye-patch up I give him a peak. "I'll live. You know I think this eye is cursed. This isn't the first time I had to wear an eye patch on this eye."

"Oh Yeah? What do you mean?"

"This is one of those stories that your parents repeat over and over at family gatherings until you get sick of hearing it. I was just a baby. The memory I have is probably not even a memory at all just images of what they were telling me years later. Apparently my older brother was taking me for a walk in a stroller. As he walked down the country road he was bouncing a stick in one hand and pushing me in a stroller with another. You know like a walking stick, but it was pointed at the end so when the tip would hit the pavement it would bounce back and he would catch it. When telling the story my mom would make a throwing motion flicking her fingers like releasing a spear. But then, as the story goes, the stick bounced back and went into my eye. So my brother started running home with me. Just then my dad came around the corner on his motorcycle. When he saw the blood on my face he loaded me into the car and took me to the hospital. My tear duct was damaged and they slapped an eye patch on me. My folks always talk about the waiting room when going for check-ups where I would crawl from stranger to stranger stand up and grin at each person with a patch over my eye."

Mike nods, "A cursed eye."

"I took it for granted that it was all true because I got so bored of hearing this fucking baby story. But lately it's dawned on me that my mom wasn't even there when I was hurt. She was just taking my brother's word for it. How do you bounce a pointed stick while walking down a road? Really who bounces sticks? Is that even physically possible? He probably just stabbed me straight in the eye with the pointed end. When I came along my brother wasn't the youngest one in the family anymore. It's the age-old story. The fact that he stabbed me was too horrible for my parents to consider. So it became a cute baby story instead."

Shanghai Mike tips his beer. Wiping the foam from his lips he brings the topic back to the task at hand: the blues. "You know, Robert Johnson had a cursed eye. He had a cataract over one eye. It gave him an unsettling appearance. Down in the Delta where Voodoo and Christian superstitions would reinforce each other people saw it as an evil eye. This added to the myth that he had made a deal with the devil to sell his soul in exchange for his chops on guitar."

"I've tried to sell my soul, but no one's buying."

"All that meet the devil at the crossroads stuff was typically rumors that bluesmen would start themselves. It's a kind of insurance policy. Imagine going from town to town and playing juke joints, gambling halls, and barns on plantations. The local workers, gamblers, and drunkards see a musician in a nice suit rambling through town with a wad of cash in their shoe and singing songs to their women. To keep from getting clobbered it's a good thing to have people afraid of you.

Who's more scary than the devil?"

"I don't know. Maybe a real person?" I laugh.

"The whole myth where the hero makes a deal with a malevolent being exchanging the soul for talent, fame, fortune, or immortality actually predates Christianity. It's in Gilgamesh the oldest surviving piece of literature in the world traced back to ancient Mesopotamia."

"Sign me up. Where do I make the deal?"

Mike ignores my jive. "But the moral of these stories usually is that the devil's bargain is a sucker's bet. The deal backfires. Even when the hero gets what is promised it is short lived. The devil always comes to collect. There are no shortcuts. There are no easy answers."

"I know. When I said sign me up I would have winked if I had an extra eye available."

Leaving philosophy for the future I keep living in the present. I just keep moving forward. I live in the moment. I have to pose for my street performers license right now. Since I can't work around food with an open wound I have to hit the street in a big way to make up for losing hours at work. I can't put it off any longer. I wonder if my wounds will give me a sympathy factor while busking or if my mug will just scare people away? I have been running a big risk playing on the street without the license. I'm no Robert Johnson. I don't know if I have any crossroads phantom watching over me. The bike accident has taken some of the wind out of my sails. Yet thanks to the survey I scammed a few weeks back I have finally cleared the hundred dollars to pay the fee to the city for the license.

On my way to City Hall my bike falls apart under me. I'm six foot and the bike is a size too small. The frame has been creaking and moaning for days. Finally the back wheel flies off at the corner of Damen and Division. My butt lands with a thud on the cement. Leaving the damn thing on the curb I spit and chase down a bus. So much for the free bike. Nothing is free.

At City Hall the bureau that handles the ID photos is about to close. In one of those musky old rooms with the big wooden beams from another era I'm filling out the paperwork as fast as I can. The young man in the photo booth doesn't say so much as hello. He's ready to go home. "You only get one take," he sneers. So I take off my eye patch, sit in front of the white background, and tilt my pageboy cap. At the last second I smirk. At who or what I'm not sure. He's packing up the equipment as soon as it snaps. A crude government badge drops through a slot. Now I have a license to beg. It looks extra pathetic with my face all red and full of scabs. I start laughing as he closes the door behind me. Despite the rush just to survive things are being documented. Slowly I'm returning to civilization.

The next step is to get a phone so I can call that wild girl I met in Logan Square. A bodega at the corner of Sedgwick and North has a Cricket stand that hooks me up. I'm back on the grid. I wish Trudy could come to one of my shows. In the meantime, I'm in the computer lab at the Harold Washington Library and I find her on Facebook. She's on break between quarters at Columbia. Right now she's in St. Louis visiting some fling. He looks like a trendy hipster. He has all the accessories: hair gel, ironic glasses, piercings, oh so carefully tasteful tattoos. But I don't get discouraged.

Quickly I find out I have to learn how to text message. I'm only a few years older than Trudy, but there's already a generation gap. I always found texting to be too time-consuming. Why type up what could be conveyed in a few seconds talking on the phone? All the subtlety and tone is lost with texting. The way things are said is often much more important than what is said. But when I call her she doesn't answer. A few seconds after my missed call there is a text that says: What's up? It turns out the only way to engage with her is texting. So I begin training my thumbs between practicing guitar.

Instead of meeting up with Trudy I have Tammy showing up at the Gallery. Somehow she's gotten up the courage to venture west of Halsted Street. Shanghai Mike is sitting at the bar minding his own business. Trying to get my attention she plucks a curl of Mike's hair, pulls it straight, and then releases it letting it curl back. He looks over his shoulder wondering if he's about to be in a bar fight. When he sees it's a lady he smiles politely and turns back towards the stage. She laughs. Then when I'm singing she gets up and waves her arms around. The rest of the room was sitting listening to the music, but now they are looking at her.

After my set I'm at the bar. Kenny pours my free beer for performing. Tammy has me cornered. "So what's the story with living in a warehouse?"

"It's not a warehouse exactly. It was a YMCA in the 1800s. It's a strange looking building so it's easier just to say warehouse." To show what I mean I give her the address so she can look it up on Google Maps when she has access to the street-view feature.

When I get a chance I look up the history of these old red brick buildings. YMCA housing in Chicago began in the 1860s. Besides the small rooms the amenities included gyms and auditoriums. According to the YMCA website the original intent was to give young men from rural areas safe and affordable places to stay in the city. Funny thing is here I am over a hundred years later using the place illegally for its original purpose.

"So," Tammy begins, "is that where you go and like pass out on drugs like Jim Morrison? Something like that?"

"Something like that…" I finish off my beer. Without fail one the guys at the jam will coax me into doing a cover of The Doors. We'd do *Been Down So Long, Five to One, LA Woman* once, but mostly

Roadhouse Blues over and over. Tonight was no different. Despite my battered face there's a certain Irish resemblance to Morrison in the jawline. Perhaps Jim would have ended up looking like *me* if he survived past twenty-seven?

"Do you want another beer?"

"Sure."

Tammy buys me a beer and gets herself another Sprite.

"One of the blues bums here at the Gallery talked about starting a Doors cover band. I told him no thanks. Sure you can make some quick cash doing songs people actually know. And yeah I love that music, but I don't want to be another Elvis Impersonator. Singing original songs at gigs is a much longer and harder road. But it's the long shots in life that are worth taking."

Tammy baits me with a couple more leading questions. I dive into a few more self-indulgent soliloquies. Suddenly Kenny barks, "Last call! Last call!"

The lights go up and everyone gasps at the mirror behind the bar. Kenny plays the swing music he loves from the forties on the jukebox. This clears out the crowd. It doesn't appear that he's going to hold an illegal afterhours session tonight.

Walking Tammy to the Blue Line as usual I keep to her left so no one thinks she's a working girl. The Blue Line runs 24/7. The trouble is in order to get to my crash pad I'd have to transfer to the Green Line downtown. All the buses heading west are done. The Green Line doesn't run again until four am. That means I have two hours to kill before I can even head towards Garfield Park. Tammy offers that I can crash at her place. I agree. My mantra is still yes. Also, Dominick's is across the street from her condo at Parkside. Tomorrow before work I could just stroll across the parking lot. Easy commute.

The slow pace that she walks I begin to think that it would have been quicker to wait for the Green Line. By the time we get on the platform we just miss the first Blue Line. The train pulls away as we wait for the elevator. In the Loop we slowly shuffle through the tunnel connecting the Blue Line to the Red Line. By the time we emerge from the Clark and Division stop in Old Town I am sobering up.

As we approach the Parkside Building I am getting tired. Finally we're almost to the door when she turns to me, "You've been drinking a lot of beer. Why don't you go get some gum from Dominick's?"

"Gum? I don't want no gum."

It finally dawns on me that she isn't offering me a place to crash because I need one. She wants my breath to be fresh.

"Here, I'll even pay for the gum." She starts digging in her purse.

"Put your money away. I'm tired. Let's just go to sleep."

"Get some Neosporin for your face too."

"Man, stop mothering me."

We go back and forth like this. Out of frustration I stop walking, bend over, and flip my arms down on the sidewalk. I prop myself up and stick my legs in the air. "Hey mom! Look at me. I'm doing a handstand!"

Her eyes pop out. As I topple back on my feet I start laughing. "I'll go get some gum if it will make you happy. Then can we go to sleep?" Dominick's is 24/7. Still it's a ghost town inside. I've never seen it so quiet. Dale the security guard gives me a nod.

Returning with the gum Tammy and I go inside Parkside. I'm chewing Juicy Fruit like a ballplayer but we're not settling down just yet. She wants to show me the gym in the basement. She gets on one of the machines and shows me how she exercises her sore knee. I try to be nice but the sun is coming up. Obviously she has suffered in her life, but she is really enjoying telling me about it.

Still chewing Juicy Fruit she says to me, "I thought you would get peppermint to freshen your breath."

Inside her apartment she asks that I try to be quiet because her son and daughter are asleep in one of the bedrooms. Yet she begins showing me pictures and telling me stories. Here is a picture of her husband Vlad. "He went back to Russia a few years ago." I wonder to myself if he was a mail order husband. Here's a Polaroid of Tammy in a black burqa. "I was into Islam for awhile. I'm no longer religious now." There's a story here but I'm too tired to ask any follow up questions.

A yawn escapes me. Tammy finally relents. In her bedroom there is a divan at the foot of her bed. She gets in her bed and pulls up the covers. I flip off my shoes and make myself comfortable on the divan. I'm curled up like a dog at her feet. After a few minutes she asks, "Are you sure you wouldn't rather get in the bed? There's plenty of room."

My mantra isn't always yes. I pretend I'm asleep. Soon I am.

A couple hours later I'm awoke by blaring Southern Rock. Tammy is Playing *Sweet Home Alabama* in the living room. I emerge rubbing my eyes. There's coffee.

"Do you like my music?"

"Do you have any Neal Young?" I ask because of the beef between Young and Skynyrd.

"Um. I don't know. I don't think so."

She offers cream and sugar. I decline.

"That's right. You like your coffee black like a cowboy."

As I chug the coffee Tammy's teenage daughter enters the living room. When she sees me her lip curls and her eyes pop. Tammy grins like the cat that got the canary. The telepathy in the room is palatable. I'm thinking: we didn't even do anything. Saying as much would be hurtful to Tammy and would only serve to enforce the daughter's assumptions. And what do I really care what she thinks? She gathers her things and places them in her backpack and leaves in a huff without saying anything.

But she makes it clear she doesn't like her mom bringing random dudes into the house. I can't blame her.

Tammy offers to make me breakfast. I decline. After coffee I'm out the door free as the bird in that damn song *Free Bird* Tammy has blasting. I can hear it echoing down the hall. I never did one show without some asshole in the back sarcastically requesting, "Free Bird! Play Free Bird!" The best response is to flip the bird and say here's your free bird. At the deli I get my own breakfast: French toast sticks, a cup of fruit, and a slice of ham. It costs seven bucks but seems free compared to accepting any more hospitality.

Southern Rock? Calling me Kentucky? Jim Morrison? Saying I drink my coffee like a cowboy? There's no polite way to say it. Tammy has a white-guy fetish. She doesn't like me for me.

31

Everyone knows the Preacher. Everyday he's perched downtown on State Street. Clad in his black suit and red bow tie he stands stiffly like a sundial as the hours spin shadows around his ankles. Motionless he spouts the word from under his overbite and over his microphone. The gospel and whatever he makes up as he goes along reverberates from a small amplifier on the pavement. He's been a fixture for decades. This is his spot. For the first time I notice his street performer's license like a flag clipped to his microphone.

High heels click down the pavement. A lady in large sunglasses puffs a Virginia Slim. The Preacher sniffs and says, "Heaven has no place for no cigarette smoker."

Wait, what?

I stop to watch the Preacher.

Preach Preacher preach.

Another shopper passes. "Your skirt is too faaaaar too short. You are exposed to the devil and all his sinful desire."

As I get closer I notice the blank look on his face. His eyes are glassy. He has no twinkle. No curiosity. He only has his faith. His mind is made up. He knows everything. He *is* the truth. The Preacher is here to teach not to learn.

The Preacher wipes the smog from his brow with a silk

handkerchief. "Global Warming is not the result of cars in the air, but hell below growing closer to the surface of the world."

Cringing at his nonsense I unfold my chair and tune up my guitar a few feet away. I'm in earshot of his fire and brimstone. Having a street performers license myself we're free to have public discourse.

As loud as I can I sing *Come in my Kitchen* by Robert Johnson.

The Preacher gives me the side eye. "Blues is the devil's music. The sin of a Saturday night has no place on Sunday morning."

That's too much. I smirk. The average passerby takes no notice. But the Preacher and I are in a duel. In response to his judgmental wrath I start moaning a new song I've been working on.

So you've seen suffering.
It's all messed up, all levels corrupt.
> *But you ain't seen nothing*
> *till you've seen the world with a little compassion.*

You've been high. You've been low.
You've tasted and touched, and felt so much in this life.
> *But you ain't seen nothing*
> *till you've opened your heart with a little compassion*

You ate up drama, humanity tragedy,
and twisted it around into dark comedy.
> *But you ain't felt nothing*
> *till you've opened your heart with a little sympathy.*

Man is cursed. Man is damned.
It's all based on lies, and you think you know why.

But you ain't seen nothing
till you've seen the world through a woman's eyes.

The world is crying, weeping at the seams.
It decays as it grows like a delicate dream.
You'll really see something
when you open your heart with compassion.

After I have my say I pack up my guitar and float along the river of foot traffic. I'm no match for the sound of cars on State Street. I'm no match for the Preacher's little amplifier. There is no use arguing with someone who already knows everything. It's like protesting against Earthquakes. It's like trying to domesticate a saber-tooth-tiger. It's like trying to keep the world from spinning. The world remains dizzy as it turns. The world rotates in circles of contradiction. If it didn't we would all be stuck in the same place. It's a balance. The Preacher is always at the same spot. Like a sentry he is always at his post. He is inflexible. He is unmoved. He will always be there. He will never change.

52

I'm in a fix. I'm broke again. The last few weeks have been a blur of playing out and crashing around. Between the street performer license, losing hours at the deli due to my open wounds, getting the flip-phone, and honestly soothing myself with beer rather than hustling, my money roll has thinned. It dawns on me that I have to make rent in three days. I have to hit the streets.

Out of the blue Trudy texts me. She says that she is back in Chicago. She invites me over to her place at Armitage and Humboldt. I should get a good night's sleep and start busking like mad in the morning. Instead I find myself saying I'm on my way.

Walking through Humboldt Park I remember there's a gang-war taking place here. I'm cutting through with the banjo on my back like an idiot. Finally I'm in Logan Square. We're sitting in the grass on the median of the boulevard sipping PBR tallboys. Trudy's roommate Chloe is there as a buffer. The three of us make small talk. Trudy's big eyes blink behind her vintage glasses. She bites her lip nervously. When she shifts in the grass her curves sway.

She tells me about her trip. She says she isn't seeing the guy in St. Louis anymore. He bores her. I don't want to be boring so I say, "Well I'm a crazy person. I live in my practice space on the West Side. First thing tomorrow I have to be back downtown writing songs for people."

Tossing a few anecdotes about my comings and goings Chloe and Trudy smile at each other.

"Well, you can stay here if you want."

"Yeah," says Chloe. "Let's go inside."

It seems decided that I'm just crazy enough not to be boring, but not too crazy to be left out in the cold. They have a spacious three-bedroom loft with a kitchen, den, living room, and a screen porch. Chloe announces she is going to bed. She has class in the morning. Sitting on the couch Trudy picks out a movie. "This is my favorite. It's called *Freeway*." Her and I share a blanket as the film flickers away.

As the credits roll she says she is going to bed. I stretch out on the couch thanking her again for the place to crash. She disappears down the hall into her bedroom. It's late but I can't sleep. My phone stashed on the coffee table lights up.

It's Trudy. She texts: Is the couch ok?

Sure. It's ok. I text back: I'd rather be in bed with you.

She texts again: Then come sleep with me. Second door on the left.

The floorboards creak forward. An hour later we fall asleep.

In the morning I am in a warm bed with a soft girl. For a moment everything seems animated. Her Victorian silk pillows glow in the dusty beams of sunlight cutting through the blinds. The dawn hits her velvet hair. It shines like obsidian. As she gently drools on her pillow lipstick meets her mascara in a pool next to her lower lip where it flies out like a ribbon down the avenue to the horizon.

Sliding out from under the dewy covers I pull my slacks up quietly. Feeling like a lucky bum I hoist my case on my back and tiptoe out the front door, wishing I could stay. I have to get luckier. I'm broke.

The Armitage bus takes me from Logan Square straight to the Lincoln Park Zoo. I play by the polar bears for a few minutes. A mother and her tot come up to me. I fake my way through a rendition of *Wheels on the Bus* as she bounces her baby on her knee. Out of her bottle bag I get a good tip. Next, who do I see by the camels but my buddy from the blues jam: Dobro Joe. He's balancing his steel National guitar on his lap sliding into notes that send shivers up my spine. Now that's a beautiful piece of equipment.

"How you making out?"

"Slow so far. You?"

"A couple bucks."

Joe asks, "You have a street performer license for the Zoo too?"

I show him my new license.

"There's a different one for the Zoo."

"Wait a minute. This isn't good for the whole city?"

"No." Joe shows me the one he has. "The Zoo has their own policy and their own performers license. Same with playing down in the subway there's a separate license to busk on CTA grounds."

"What the…? No one told me that."

Joe and I do a couple numbers together. I leave before I get my license checked by the Zoo security guards. I have my work cut out for me. After I split I play the beach, Lincoln Park, in front of Second City, Navy Pier, downtown, everywhere. Three days to piece together a hundred and seventy-five bucks. Anywhere there're out-of-towners is good for busking. College areas are good too. These are gonna be long days in Chicago.

Around noon I take the Blue Line up to Milwaukee, North, and Damen in Wicker Park where the hipsters hangout. Artists support each other. The five points are bustling. My face has healed a great deal. The scabs had proved to scare people away rather than pull heartstrings.

No longer using my cap to gather bills I'm using a can that I found in the practice space. It's the bottom half of a cylinder used to package a Champaign bottle. One of the past bands must have been celebrating a milestone and left it after popping a cork.

Set-up between the club Subterraneans and the Damen stop a young man in a suit, a silk scarf trailing out behind him, and wild curly hair gets off the train. Rushing along and staring at his phone he accidently kicks over my can. Coins fly into the air. I stomp on the bills before they scatter like leaves. The young guy feels so bad he fishes out a twenty and hands it to me. Once absolved he scurries down the sidewalk and back on his phone. I'm left thinking to myself: I wish more people would kick the can over. So I push the can further out into the sidewalk so it's really in the way.

There's a lull. I change spots on the intersection. Now I'm in front of the Flatiron Building. A young lady with seventies shades and tattoos spots my sign. She asks for a song. Smiling warm and friendly I begin asking her questions. I need things to write about. But she says she doesn't have any problems. Desperate I begin pulling things from her tattoos.

"What does that one say?"

She flips her elbow up. The ink reads: Carpe Diem.

"Oh cool. Live for today? Like live life to the fullest right? So, do you like to party?" She doesn't respond. She spins on her heels and marches off the opposite way. Maybe that came out wrong? I must have offended her.

A crusty punk in dreadlocks is camped out in front of the Double Door with his mangy mutt bound in a bandana. He's begging too. He's just looking for food not shelter. Shaking a dirty Big Gulp cup full of change he sidles up to me.

"Hey brother," out comes a gruff voice. "You know *Big Rock Candy Mountains* on that banjo?"

"Naw dude. I just tune it like I would a guitar and play what I know. It has a good tone though." Obviously he's not gonna give me any of his coin. To kill time I start playing *Chocolate Jesus* by Tom Waits.

He barks, "What do you mean? You play banjo but don't know *Candy Rock Mountains*?" He drifts away.

It's not adding up. My luck has to change.

It's getting hot. I'm thirsty. I'm losing face. My voice is cracking. I feel pale, white, worn out. I ask myself: if I was flush and I saw myself singing on the corner would I pay myself a tip? Probably not...

The banjo is a little louder than my dusty old classical guitar but it's still no match for the traffic. I wish I could be like Robert Johnson and go down to the crossroads and get a decent instrument that would magically rise over the din. The crossroads of North and Damen have not yielded any such deals.

I pack up and get back on the Blue Line. On the ride downtown I begin entertaining back-up plans. What if I don't make rent? What if I get thrown out of the practice space? It would be too much to ask Matt to let me move in. There's barely enough room for him, his cat, and the cat box. Could I ask Trudy if I could stay with her for a while? It's too soon. We just met. I'm not even sure if she likes me that much. There's no back-up plan. I need my own place. I need to make the rent.

Doubt is setting in. I'm tapping my forehead against the glass on the train doors. People move away. I had all the brains but I wasted them. I flushed everything down the toilet. I'm useless. All I think about is abstractions, philosophy, poetry, blues, wannabe beatnik bullshit, hopes, dreams, ghosts, hallucinations...

Only a fucking genius would be dumb enough to go to art school. Live the dream for a discount! Step right up! See the one and only wonder of the world! See the geek, the freak, the tender little soul! Step right up folks! See the one-eyed hipster pirate! Come on in! Pay your tuition and POOF! When the smoke clears it's a funhouse mirror and you're staring at yourself distorted and thin. Sign here! Sellout! Buy in! Stare at yourself. Stare into the void. Stare into a myopic mirror maze of contradictions…

So now you're on the street? So you're young and white in America? What's the problem? On top of everything else you think the world should accept you as a blues musician? You think you're that entitled? Come one! Come all! Step right up folks! See the precious little artist. The prince of all dying art forms! Right this way. Listen to the truth that you didn't want to hear. Hear the answer to the question no one asked. Jesus not working for you? Try existential loop-de-loops! A cosmic roller coaster round and round from the sky to the ground. The Big Bang created evolution and we'll evolve into god! POOF! BANG! We blow ourselves up again. What fun!

Back downtown I get off at the Monroe stop. The tunnel echoes with intense drumming. A black dude over six feet tall with a long face is pounding a set of white plastic buckets. Sometimes he flips the switch to the boom box he has strapped to a little cart. A familiar song fills the platform and he drums along. When he turns on the tunes the break-dancers down by the exit adjust their routines spinning on their shoulders and gyrating on sheets of cardboard. As I enter the scene the drummer sees me carrying the banjo. Without hesitation he says, "Let's Jam."

He plays fast. I pluck along as best I can.

After the first improvised number he smiles and offers me his hand. We shake.

"My name's David. David Russell. I've been playing this spot for years."

As I've learned the license to play on the street is different than the one to play in the tunnels. The buskers down below are tough and territorial. The lady with the castanets who whistles over the Spanish violin chased me away once. Usually I don't mess with the mole people. But David is warm and friendly. He has his subway credentials proudly displayed on his cart. When he really gets rolling on the buckets he closes his eyes and nods. In no time the place is rocking. People are taking off their headphones. Kids are bobbing their heads. Businessmen are taking pictures of us with their phones. A white kid playing banjo and a middle aged black dude jamming out. God bless America.

After about an hour David stops, leans over, and gathers all the money that has landed in his can since I sat down. He promptly counts it and hands me half the take.

"I'm born to drum son. I've been doing this since I was nine. Sometimes I'm down here all day. Sometimes all night. It's the only way to live."

David tells me busking is all he does. He's made me a list of every open-mic in the city that has free food for musicians. "This is a way of life. One time at about four in the morning there were three drunk businessmen that just came from the airport. I was the only one down here. They gave me five-hundred dollars!"

He asks me to watch his stuff while he pops up top for a minute. David just met me but already he trusts me to watch his gear. When you play music with someone a bond immediately forms. He disappears to the surface. When he comes back he has a bucket of warm pea soup. "I know a cook at one of the restaurants above. I just wish I had a big piece of bread to dip in this." Instead he raises the bucket to his lips and pours. I do the same.

Trains come. Trains go. The platform clears. The tips slow.

In the middle of a song David cuts the beat. "I think the magic moment has passed young blood."

"I believe so. You notice things like that too?"

"Sure-nough. Some trains bring sweet people. Others sour.

When things slow down best thing to do is mix it up."

"Yeah, my fingers are bleeding from trying to keep up with you."

"Thanks for mixing it up with me during that last rush. That was something different. For now I'm going back to beating with my boom box."

"Cool David. Thanks so much man."

"Yeah let's do it again sometime."

As I return to the light at the top of the stairs I give him a wave. Between beats he salutes with his drumstick. What a guy. The world is turning.

At night I take the short bus ride into the West Loop and ring the buzzer of my buddy Will Leland. He lets me sleep on the roof of his building on a lawn chair. From there I overlook the skyline. I look at my kingdom. With a little hard work and some luck I will conquer. Even in the summer it gets cold up there late at night, but this guarantees I awake early and get back to hustling. It's a short trip back to the war zone where I smile, strum, and sing, sing, sing. Time is ticking.

These are long days. I run into forgotten friends and I make new ones. Fifty percent of my customers are couples out on dates. The man always steps up and asks for a romantic song. I beg a few details from them: where they met, what they do, where they are going... Then I spin the words into a tender ballad using the same three chords. The guy always gives me a generous tip. This makes him look like a man of the people in front of his date.

Reading a customer is a delicate thing. Like with the lady in Wicker Park sometimes I miscalculate and the fish is off the hook. Some people don't want romantic songs, or they don't present any serious problems. Here it's best to make the song as funny as possible. Try to channel Frank Zappa.

A joker with his baseball cap on backwards, cargo shorts, and colorful glasses is showing off for his friends. Grinning, faces glowing red, and shifty eyed they look stoned. When he sees my sign he comes up to me and says, "My problem is that I just learned that the interest rate on my trust fund just went down from 2.2 to 1.6. I'm living in hell! My money isn't making *as* much money as it used to."

He laughs showing his choppers. I have to admit that he has a wit to him. He's spoofing the blues with his first world problems. So I play along. "I feel you man. I have a song for you."

> *My interest rate, baby*
> *Went from two point two*
> > *Down to one point six*
> *My interest rate, mamma*
> *Went from two point two*
> > *to one point six*
> *Soon I'll be out on the street sucking dicks!*

He busts a gut. His buddies double over. Their red eyes were squinting. Now they are popping out. Straight out of the trust fund the joker plants a ten in my open palm. This is the strange psychology of self-deprecating humor. The more you insult someone the more they like you, the more they laugh, and the more they tip. It's a little masochistic. As a white guy from the Midwest with my share of privilege I'm familiar with this flagellation. But before I write something like this I have to be careful that whoever I'm singing for has a good sense of humor.

After asking so many people their problems to write songs about I can clearly see we all have the same worries. From every walk of life we all want love, to have purpose, to feel like we belong but also feel somehow unique. Writing a blues based on what they tell me the music acts as a mirror. No one wants a solution to their problem. They don't want the answers. No one wants the meaning of life. People simply want to feel alive.

Nickel by dime, quarter by buck, I make my rent money on the third day. Just in the nick of time the last bill folds into my hand at Navy Pier. A wave of relief fills me. Somehow I am prouder at this moment than any other moment I can remember. More proud than when my band played the Green Mill or the Double Door last year. I hustled more in the last three days than I ever did. I breathe easy. For a minute there I thought I would finally go crazy. For a minute I thought I was going to be truly homeless not just squatting.

The people of Chicago helped me. David Russell in the subway helped me. All my happy customers helped me. I feel like I got paid for just for being myself joking and crooning and making stuff up. Now that I hit my goal I stroll into the small park between Navy Pier and the water purification plant. Despite the fact that it is right next to the biggest tourist trap in the city no one seems to know about it. Probably because Milton Lee Park is in the shadow of all the madness at the pier is why the place is a quiet little patch of green. I lie down in the grass. I cloud watch. I watch the people on the Navy Pier Ferris Wheel spin through the sky. I can see the buildings along the gold coast rising out of the lake like a coral reef of crystals. I call my mom. We talk a long time. I am vague about how things are going. All that matters is that the tone of my voice is positive. She is glad to hear from me.

By nightfall I'm back at the practice space. As instructed I put my hard earned rent into the provided envelope and drop it through the mail slot in the office door. As all my money drops into the darkness I wonder how often does Bret really come to collect the envelopes? How often does he really visit this location? Was I rushing for no reason? How much money is lying behind this wooden door right now? These thoughts pass as quickly as they come.

With my remaining scratch I get a cold beer from the vending machine. I stagger upstairs to my hard earned hole and lay down. Thank you Chicago. Thank you busking gods. For now I am only hippie homeless. There is still a big difference between being a hustler and a squatter and truly being one of the many uncared for, unloved, and unwanted people left out in the cold street.

33

It's strange to watch people die. Sometimes you don't notice: the alcoholic brother, or the father who's been working himself to death slowly. Because you see them everyday and they fade slowly like a mountain eroding in slow motion. But in the city you might notice it more because the people on the street are seen in chapters. It isn't frame by frame. It's a montage. The decay leaps ahead.

I remember this man on the subway who did a convincing rap. He said he was freshly living on the street. He said he wasn't really homeless, and if he could only make a certain amount of change he could get back on his feet something about how he was saving up for a train ticket to a city in the South where some relatives lived. He wore glasses and spoke well. The next time I saw him was about a year later: no glasses, just squinting, and desperately mumbling under his breath half-words, which dolled out the gist and ghostly approximations of still being there like bat squeaks in the night. He needed food to live but wasn't sure if he wanted to be alive. Yet he didn't want to die slowly which was what he was doing.

You know you can't do anything. Sure you could take them to a shelter, but they've been there. You could at least give them a blanket. That might help. You could give them change and they might spend it on booze. But what are you going to spend your money on?

When I was in art school I wrote a poem called *On Mescaline talking to a Street Girl.* The girl in the poem used to hang around in a merry band of druggie teens on the corner of Sheridan and Wilson. I would watch them from the roof of my building where I'd hang out sometimes to get some air. She wore neon candy-kid accessories popular with rave culture at the time. I never knew her. I got an abstract poem out of bumping into her one winter night. I was experimenting with drugs myself like a good little art student hoping to bend my head with surrealism like a melting clock. Rushing home in the cold as the sun went down she asked me for change. Twisted on mescaline I was confused and made up the words in my head.

Do you have any change?
do you change?
do change
Change your mind?
Do you mind?
Begging the question.
Questioning the begging?
You get what you ask for.
Fifty cents, there you got what you asked for.
Is that what you asked for?
Surfing karma.
Deal decked out.
Decked out and knocked out.
Left out in the cold, right out there.
Never mean to, even when I mean to.
I didn't mean to be mean to you. I mean it.
I'd rather be there for you to lean to.
To know that we don't know, you know?

The real words were more like:

"Hey, do you have two quarters?" she asked.

I emptied my pockets high, passive, uncharacteristically open. "There you go," I told her.

"I have this cigar…" her young voice cracked as she held up an unlit Black & Mild. I knew this awkward gesture was street code for a proposition. More seasoned prostitutes would strongly insinuate, "I have a *cigarette*… but no *light*." They would hit the notes harder until there was nothing left between the lines.

"No thanks. I don't smoke," is all I said to her as if I didn't understand she was cold and desperate to get inside somewhere, anywhere. Meanwhile I went upstairs where it was warm. Like a hippie stereotype I put on a Ravi Shankar record. I watched my blanket turn into a portal. I laughed into tape recorders and wrote a surrealistic poem like a good little art student, which didn't help her at all. I watched everything grow and decay like God breathing. Outside people were just decaying.

That was a long time ago. The other day I saw the same girl on the train while I was on my way downtown to busk. She was wrapped in dirty blankets with just her little round face protruding. She had surrounded herself in rancid trash bags. She seemed to recognize me from Uptown. "Aren't you my cousin?" she asked.

"No, I don't think so."

"Oh… I thought you were my cousin…" She stuck out her lower lip and nodded, scrunching her face like a bullfrog, an expression that was far beyond her years.

The train rattled on. I never paid her for the poem she inspired. Even if it was just a bad art school poem it was worth something. Just another surreal poem meanwhile she lived something so real most of us refuse to imagine it. Maybe we all live in our own fantasies. Perhaps making our fantasies become the truth is the trick. For our own protection we keep blinders on pretending to be normal, which is something that doesn't really exist. Normal is the ultimate fantasy. Normal is the agreed delusion. I have decided to write as close to reality as possible. Whatever that is.

When writing what would be considered gritty realism it is important to remember that even gritty realism is as subjective as anything else. It's a sliding scale. Humans have such different perceptions of reality. This accounts for the vastly different tastes in art and entertainment. What seems more poetic? The fantastic images from our dreams? Or the stark truth of the street that few are brave enough to acknowledge, but when someone does it rings true? Usually it is a mix of both. Like a mad scientist an artist will take a dab of truth and sweeten it with a hint of beauty so the medicine goes down easy. If you just say bleakly what happened is it art or reporting the news? Is journalism or documentary an art or is it not? If the work is pure fantasy does it do anyone any good in the real world? Does art have to have a moral? Or is it better to have some moral ambiguity? Or an open question that forces people to question themselves or double down on who they are? Does it have to contain some satire? Are there rules? Or is it just a matter of taste? Are there exceptions to every rule? How much in fiction is actually fiction and how much is inspired by memory? How much of our memories are actually fiction? According to studies on eyewitness testimony much of our daily memory is distorted. If our memories are actually confabulation, then is life a work of art that we create? Is reality itself a work of art? Are we all artists fighting over the interpretation of reality? Or are we just instruments of nature, the one artist?

These are the kinds of questions my friend SOLVE and I would discuss usually while walking the back alleys sharing a forty as he pasted up street art. Street art is a strange juxtaposition in itself. His goal seemed to be to put some magic into the streets, but also put some of the streets into his art. The ratio would fluctuate. The images he put up on the Chicago streets were often dreamlike. You turn a corner and there is a cutout of an eerie schoolgirl, a mad scientist, or some mystical clouds. At one of his gallery shows it was more about bringing the streets to the art world: graffiti, tags, gritty images, some photos of the process.

Despite his hard street-smart stance SOLVE could be very kind. When the whole gang was going out for Thai Food I said I had to cut out. I was broke as usual. SOLVE said he'd pay for me. So over Pad Thai we kept talking about life, art, rules in art, art without rules, outlaw artists, and the war of images and ideas out there: all the advertisements that lie, the few that sell it to you straight, laws that man has made up, and laws of nature that govern us all. I never had Thai Food before. Quickly it became a favorite sweetened by the fact that my friend had turned me on to it.

So it was all the more terrible when I heard he was murdered. Of all places he was at a fucking art show. He got into an argument with some punk from the 77 Gang who liked to carry a knife and use it. In an alley he was stabbed a dozen times.

At the funeral Nathan Xander sang some songs. Later he asked out loud, "How do you go from riding your bike to an art show like a happy kid to pulling out a knife and stabbing someone?"

My friend Nicolai and I drove together, for the funeral, to Madison where SOLVE grew up. On the way he said, "When I first heard about it I thought this couldn't be real. I thought maybe he was faking his death like some kind of performance art. It took awhile before it sunk in."

At the wake a tape recorder was passed around. His parents intended it to be used for anyone who wished to share some of their memories about SOLVE with the family. When the tape recorder came to me I told the story about how SOLVE kindly bought me the Thai Food. It seemed trite. I began telling another story one that meant more to me.

Once SOLVE invited Israel, Nicolai, and all our mutual friends to a housewarming party at his place off Lawrence and Sheridan in Uptown. In the unit below his new neighbors were also having a friendly get together. As the night wore on people came and went and mingled in the hallway and on the stairs. Soon the two shindigs were combining into one big party. However the two units had different ideas of a party. Upstairs in SOLVE's place there was intense underground electronic music playing on a turntable, live painting, people passing joints, and a messy BYOB policy with people drinking out of paper bags. Just below the floor in the unit below was a nice older gay couple who were well dressed, playing smooth jazz on an expensive stereo, and had tasteful art framed neatly on the wall. One of the gentlemen, Sven, was very intrigued by our chaotic art party, "Oh, this reminds me of my college days! I love this. It's like staring into my past!"

Downstairs perhaps some of us wished we were staring into our future. At their party there was food! What a strange thing to have at a party. There were cheese platters, sausages, pickles, salsa, little club sandwiches, dips unpronounceable. More and more of the starving artists began gravitating to the downstairs unit. Sven and his partner even had a full bar with every kind of liquor and mixer one could imagine. SOLVE and I began bartending for the crowd. As the party thinned out we found ourselves merely mixing for ourselves. As two Wisconsin natives we both had a false belief that our alcohol tolerances were supernatural. We began mixing and matching liquors.

Soon it was *Fight Club* time. SOLVE and I had stumbled onto the subject of back alley boxing. From the back porch the gentle middle-aged neighbors watched in horror as SOLVE and I squared off in the alley. Those left at the party gathered around us. They formed a circle. They called out their favorites. SOLVE was the home team and highly favored.

Someone yelled, "Action!" like it was all just a movie. As he charged SOLVE reared his fist back and scrunched his face. I pivoted. He came again. I ducked. We danced in circles. He landed some good punches. I got mine in. The blows made us laugh because the booze had numbed us to the pain. It was like thumping a leg that had fallen asleep.

Like any fight remotely serious we ended up on the ground. It was all too fast to know who did the trip or the tackle. We probably just fell over. Now we were rolling on the ground. As we wrestled our bones clicked against the pavement. Once on the cement I had the weight advantage. SOLVE was much taller than I, but skinnier. He was built like Abraham Lincoln: slender, taunt muscle, and long gangly arms. On top of the slim frame SOLVE had a pronounced Irish head and a jaw of steel haloed by a shock of blond curls he wore in a cropped pomp. He might have had the reach on me but on the ground I could shift my weight and pin him down. Soon I was sitting on his chest. I held his arms down with mine.

Now it was time for my friend to yell uncle. SOLVE refused to relent. He kicked and squirmed. "I'm gonna get you man!" he said still fighting.

"Alright, next I'm gonna head-butt you unless you call it."

Over my shoulder I could hear Sven say, "Oh myyyyyyyy," as his clove cigarette dangled off the back porch.

"Just do it!" SOLVE yelled back at me. "Do it man! I'm not quitting!"

"Ok, hear it comes." I drew my head back.

Jeremiah, one of SOLVE's roommates, stepped in to break it up. He pulled at my shoulder. "Don't do it Wes."

SOLVE screamed at him. "No! No! Just do it. This is real! This is real!"

Jeremiah backed off. SOLVE wanted to go all the way.

I brought my skull down. My head hit his head. Once, twice against the pavement... I stopped and looked at him. He was still defiant. He was still squirming. "Come on you fucker! Come on! This is real!"

I bowed to him once more. Hard.

"Alright, alright, you win man. You win."

I stood up. I offered him my hand. He took it. I helped him up. Then we embraced. Each one of us had bloody third eyes. We laughed. Sobered by all the adrenaline SOLVE cried out, "Shows over! More drinks!" Arm in arm we headed back inside.

It was important for him to keep it real. It was part of his integrity as an artist and as a person even if that meant getting his skull knocked. As I recited this story into his parent's tape recorder at the wake I hoped to get this point across. But the reception hall was crowded. I was sitting at a table with friends who were carrying on, getting loud, over indulging to cover their sadness. I rambled long and hard into the tape recorder about SOLVE and I fighting in the alley growing self-conscious that he had died in a similar alley. I repeated lines when I thought the background noise might have overcome my words. I tried to explain that sometimes such brute force brings two boys closer together. It's a way brothers bond. It's a way to show each other our strength and help each other grow stronger. We couldn't go around hugging each other. So we did the next best thing: wrestle, box, even head-butt. After the fight we hugged all we wanted.

As I rambled into the tape I hoped that when his parents heard this that they would understand. I hoped it wasn't taken wrong. I hoped it wasn't lost in the ruckus of the crowd around me. I hoped it wasn't lost in my slurred words wetted with drink and mourning. I wanted it understood that when SOLVE and I fought it was for fun. It came from a completely different place than the fight that ultimately took him from us. It was to feel alive not to extinguish life. I over explained. I shivered in horror thinking that I would be misunderstood. I didn't want to hurt him. I didn't want to hurt the old couple that will listen to the tape. Here my friend, their baby, laid there slain by another form of macho bullshit... Here I am babbling about boxing and brotherhood hoping that it means to them what it meant to SOLVE and I. I tried to make it clear when SOLVE yelled, "Do it! Do it! This is real!" it was because he wanted to go all the way. He didn't want to just pretend. He didn't fake his way through life. He didn't deserve what happened to him, but he didn't back down for anyone even some murderous punk... He didn't relent to bullies. Some asshole who didn't even fight fair, but cheats with a knife against someone who only brought his fists.

My other friend from college Israel Alpizar arrived at the scene of the crime shortly after the ambulance arrived too late. He said, "It looked like a horror movie." Again the only frame of reference any person would have for something so painfully real is a phony piece of art like a slasher flick.

When SOLVE yelled to me, "This is real! This is real!" how real was it? I hit him hard, but not as hard as I could. As I brought down my head-butt I hurt my head as much as I hurt his. We just wanted to feel something... but not too much. We didn't want to really hurt each other. We didn't want to kill each other. We just wanted to feel like men, whatever that is. Now, he's no longer a man. He isn't anything anymore. He's gone. He'll never become the man he would have been. He went all the way, past the pain on the surface, past boxing like brothers, to a place of pain and anguish so horrible no one ever returns to describe. There will be no art that captures what he went through as he breathed his last breath. There will be no art that will ever make us understand what he felt as he lay their bleeding. It was real. It was too real… so real that the dream is gone. The light is gone. The life is gone.

There are limits to words. There are limits to art. There are some things people can't know and don't want to know. There are things that if the experience was really captured the effect would probably take us away with it. There are answers just on the other side of that pain that no one comes back from. The people lost in the streets of Chicago die slowly in chapters. My friend SOLVE died in a flash. His life was cut short. It wasn't fair. It wasn't romantic. He didn't live a full life first, though he tried his damnedest. There is no substitute for life. Art reflects, inspires, and enhances life. But art is no substitute for living. There is no art better than surviving and going on to live a long passionate existence despite all the horrors in the world. My friend SOLVE's life was just starting. He never got a chance to truly go all the way.

34

With a phone in my pocket I'm back on the grid. Friends who were not responsive to my random ding-dongs on doors have begun responding to my calls. Sid Yiddish is a poet and performance artist. Every other Wednesday I take the Red Line to the end of the line. At the Howard stop he picks me up in his little baby-blue Saturn. He bumps up to the curb with his long full beard draped over the window-sill. He's wearing a novelty fisherman's hat where a stuffed mackerel appears to be impaled through his forehead. The cap is encrusted with buttons from punk bands. The jalopy is riding on a donut spare. I have to shove newspapers and first drafts of poems off the seat to make room for my ass. But once inside he's all smiles and hugs.

Updating him on my life these past months he strokes his beard and nods. As I spin my yarn he drives defensively. We take turns venting. Beats therapy. Our sad sack stories unravel and sound rehearsed like the second drafts to poems. I slow my roll when I come to my old band breaking up. Truth be told the whole band thing started when Sid and I teamed up reading our poems at open mics, slams, coffee shops, and art galleries. I kept inviting more and more musicians to back up our spoken word pieces until it was a band rather than poetry accompaniment. Once I stopped reciting poems and started singing there was little room for Sid in the group. Knowing Sid will have little sympathy for my losing the band since I nudged him out first I skip the topic all together. But here we are again: just two down and out artists. After everything we're still good friends.

We wheel through Evanston to a church that runs a food bank out of the basement. We line up with everyone at the door mostly working class people from the North Side. Some have their kids with them. I feel lucky to only have to worry about taking care of myself. Looking around Sid comments again that he wishes he had a family. He's about to turn fifty. He just never met the right woman.

As we reach the front of the line the pastor is a handsome middle age lady close to Sid's age. He swipes his mustache aside until his lips show. When she can see him he puffs his lower lip out and stands there forlorn.

"What's wrong Sid?"

Sid unravels a litany of laments loaded into his cheek. He spits it out like the third draft to a poem.

She's sweet and places a hand on his shoulder. "It's ok Sid. You just keep the faith." He lights up and watches her as she walks away. Nudging him with my elbow he snaps out of it and turns red.

From where we stand we can see volunteers in the back bagging up the small care packages in brown paper bags. One of the little angels asks if we have any dietary restrictions?

"Could I get mine Kosher please?" Sid asks.

"Extra meat for me," I say. "Just kidding. Whatever is easy for you guys is fine."

We are handed tickets with numbers printed on them. Back in the car we get in the line of brake lights streaming towards the exit. At the gate kids are handing the care packages through the car windows that correspond to the tickets.

I think to myself so these are what real Christians are like? Even those of us in this baby blue Saturn are welcome. The rosy cheeked teens hand us our groceries. One for the Jewish mensch behind the beard. One for myself who remains religiously unaffiliated.

As I get out at the Howard stop Sid says to me, "You can take my bag Wes."

"You sure?"

"Yeah I'm sure. Think next time I should ask her out?"

"Who? You're going to try and date the priest or pastor or whatever?"

"Yeah."

I smile, but then I scratch my chin. "Why not? Couldn't hurt."

"Oh it can always hurt."

With the last word Sid pulls away into the Indian summer twilight. The days are getting shorter. It reminds me winter is on the horizon.

Sid isn't the only one feeling lonely. We text but I don't see Trudy much in September. She says she is busy at school. I think school has just begun. It's far from finals. Maybe she found someone else.

Grabbing a Strohls from the vending machine downstairs I ask myself what I have to be jealous of? She spent one night with me. I'm only six years older but I'm acting like a dirty old man in a mid-life crisis. So I don't question her in fear of pushing her away. In fact I'm a bit embarrassed that I have any feelings at all. I didn't realize how raw my emotions were after three long years in a bad relationship.

It's best to keep busy and not dwell on it. If I keep my brain occupied and my stomach full my heart will find its way. Rather than hound Trudy I try to play it cool. I have decided to record a demo of my new songs. It seems absurd that someone who is on the edge of homelessness can home record. But these days it's entirely possible. I have the practice space. It has zero airflow but this means it's quiet enough to record once the loud bands go home. I still have my laptop. It has an internal microphone. The same software the kids at the plasma clinic were jawing about came factory installed on this Mac. As if they were waiting for me I found a pair of headphones left on a shelf in the practice space abandoned by some previous tenant.

The only problem is that the screen on my laptop is shattered. Hoping that the screen is the only thing wrong with it I take the pathetic thing to Micro Center on Elston Avenue. If all the connections still work I could run an external monitor through the line out and see what I am doing despite the broken screen. The clerk behind the counter recognizes me from college. I recognize him too. We went to the same school but we don't say anything. We're both thinking how's your degree working out for you?

There's a small external plasma screen monitor just under a hundred bucks. Luckily I have it in my roll. I kept hitting the streets after making rent so I won't cut it close again. My eye has been healing and the patch is off. So I've got my hours back at the deli. Things will be slim for a few weeks but I have the scratch.

Yet before putting cash on the barrel I ask my ex-school chum if I can take it out of the box to make sure my laptop still works when using the monitor. Showing him my smashed screen he looks me in the eye, looks both ways, and says ok. He shows me where to connect the cords and bingo the monitor lights up and when I squiggle the mouse the cursor dances on the monitor screen.

However the small monitor comes in a pretty big box. So here I am heading home through the hood lugging a box that advertises in big letters: plasma screen. This ain't no banjo. This looks like something in demand at the pawnshop.

Back in my hole I unfold a Chicago Reader. There's an article saying Eddie Kramer is going to give a lecture at the Harold Washington

Library. It says he was the sound engineer for Hendrix. All three albums that Jimi made before his death Mr. Kramer was there setting up mics, mixing, and adding the famous psychedelic effects to meet the vision of the most untouchable musician of all time. Man, I'd sure like to hear what he has to say before I start recording my modest project. The ticket price to the lecture is kind of steep, but I decide to check it out anyway. Maybe I'll mill around. Down by the library is a good place to busk.

My plan is to record a new acoustic demo using simple software. Nothing fancy. It will be a very low-fi demo in the tradition of early Delta blues records. Using only the internal mic on my Mac it will be basically singing into the yonder can like it was in the nineteen thirties but with the basic technology of 2010. This means limited over-dubs. The mix is going to be simple. You either do it or you do a retake. Having a good demo is like having a business card. It might lead to better gigs. It's the best way to document your art. What are you going to do when you're gone? Leave behind the sheet music?

Unless they are delusional none of the local bands, singer song-writers, or the blues bums at the Gallery are holding their breath waiting to be signed by a big record label anymore. Starting with Napster the big labels have been crumbling just like the rest of us. Because of this it is less and less likely for their to be another Led Zeppelin, Yes, or Nirvana. Downloading has taken down the big boys and you get what you pay for. Even if a great band is recorded properly it is less likely to have the means to be hyped-up and distributed. Companies are no longer looking to produce great albums. They are looking for that one club single full of loops and auto-tune. It is back to a market of singles just like the 45s in the fifties. Only in the psychedelic era did album sales first outsell singles. The time of great albums lasted a few decades. This is only a fraction of the entire history of recorded music.

No matter who you are few people are willing to buy your album when they can stream it or just download the hit. Even the biggest pop-stars are back to relying on live performance to pay their bills. The luxury of taking the time to write complicated albums in a studio is over for most artists. Even living legends have to get out on the road like carpet-baggers and shake that ass. Still making a good album is its own reward.

Ironically the same technology that has brought down the music industry has made home recording possible for everyone, even squatter bums who can't afford much else. This has made homespun music thrive in a handful of genres. Music that can be made properly while outside a studio includes techno, rap, or raw acoustic songs. Anything that involves a drum set requires extra mics and a decent studio space. Complicated music involving multiple live instruments like jazz or progressive-rock is out of the question recording from a couch. Only the primordial beat of dance, industrial, and rap can cheat with a drum machine and a pair of headphones. Since folk music and Delta blues doesn't require drums or any overdubs ironically roots music has survived in the "future." Going forward has sent some of us back in time.

Living in this fragile cube my guitar is sounding better than ever. There is music inside of me. With nothing but time to practice my fingers have finally bridged that gap between what's playing in my head and what's actually coming out the hole in the guitar. It's a liberating feeling. I'm flying. I'm free. After all the loud modern bands in this old YMCA have left for the night there is only the faint sound of country blues coming from behind my door. The ghostly hum of the blues lingers like the root to all the genres to come, reverberating in the background like some aquifer waiting for rock and rap and the rest to be plucked from the air. Like a curvy woman the guitar sleeps next to me.

In the early hours I hear a different sound. Almost like a chant there is a voice going, "Hup! Ready… Hup! Ready…" There is a thud after each phrase. As always I'm lying on the ground with my ear to the floor. Just bumps in the night I think. I roll over. Next I hear, "One and two and three and four…" Now I am awake. Throwing on a shirt and pulling up my pants I creak my door open. As the hinges squeak I think I hear, "Careful with that medicine ball."

In my socks I shuffle downstairs to the men's room. The whole place is quiet as Christmas Eve. Yawning I think perhaps I was just dreaming. Perhaps there's more than just music inside of me. Once the pressure is off my bladder I turn back down the dark hallway. My heart jumps as I see a figure at the end of the hall. A man in white shorts, white undershirt, and cropped hair is briskly walking away. To cover the jolt of fear I casually say, "Oh, hey there." He's shrinking down the hallway but as he looks over his shoulder I swear he has a handlebar mustache. As I rapidly rub the sleep out of my eyes something far away clicks like a door being closed. Tempted to follow I wonder if he is another squatter, but I just scurry up the stairs to my room where I lock the door. The north hallway on the ground floor is where he vanished. Most of the lights in that part of the building are broken. Either that guy in the handlebar mustache is a black-belt level hipster or I'm seeing phantoms.

55

Here I am set up at State and Van Buren. It's been a slow day. Three college kids stop when they see the banjo. They want to hear me play it. I offer to write them a song, but they don't have time for that. As they inch out of my web I ask, "Well, what kind of music do you like?"

One guy lingers with a wisp of green hair over one eye. He says, "I like folk music." In his skinny jeans and tank top he doesn't look like a folky. He probably says this just because he sees the banjo. After a corny version of *Sweet Home Chicago* by Robert Johnson he squeezes a five out of his tight jeans. A little Chicago pride always works.

His friends are calling to him from the crosswalk. The light has changed. They are two beefy bros in name brand uniforms and baseball caps. "Just go! I'll meet you there!" he yells after them.

He turns back to me, "You have a band?"

"I did. I play solo now."

"I play guitar in a three piece punk band. We've played some parties, some of the clubs around town."

"You play the Mutiny yet?"

"Yeah we played there. All these club owners want to know upfront how many people will come and see us. And we're like how many people frequent your club bitch? One place even told us we had to pay *them* to play there."

"Don't do that. It's a scam."

"Shit it's like we're just starting out. We get our friends to come out a couple times. After that it thins out. But our shit is good."

"Even when it's good people don't want to see the same band over and over. You network with other bands that are like yours? It helps if you get each other shows and pool your people together. Start a little scene. Then there's new music for everyone."

"Yeah we've tried that. We promote on Facebook and MySpace. We even hang fliers up at school and around the club."

"It's hard man. It takes so long to break through. Do you mix in a few covers to, you know, please the crowd?"

"We do covers but we get creative with them. We change the tempo or the key and mix up which genre it's in."

"That's really cool. But if you get so creative that the song isn't instantly recognizable then you might as well be doing originals."

"True."

"It takes a while for people to absorb your songs."

"Man we're still trying to get people to listen to the songs in the first place."

"I hear that. I almost miss playing bowling alleys and VFWs back in Wisconsin. At least back home there was always a crowd just because there was nothing else to do on the weekend. Even people that hated our little metal band would show up because it was a small town and there was nothing better going on."

"In Chicago there's a million things to do. They're always like we'll catch you next time. Man I don't know if there will be a next time. We played Reggies on like a Wednesday. It was like we were at band practice. It was us, the other bands, and the bartender."

"I've been there man. Here I have a little song for you. It's called *Local Band Blues*. I wrote this one after our drummer's visa ran out and had to go back to Australia."

My new friend smiles as I whip up a little two-chord country lick on the banjo and begin my sarcastic bitching.

Bring a smile, bring a grin,
five bucks to get in.
We look pretty good
when the lights are dim.
Buy yourself a drink
tonic w/ a hint of gin.
We'll play the rock star
flaying limb from limb.

The audience is made up of the other bands
& few of their lovely girlfriends.
Singing into space, just like a star.
Is it just an excuse to close the bar?
During the day we mop up shit,
some are punk rockers who work for corporate.
The kids request hip-hop, & wave good-bye.
We sell our souls, but no one buys.

At the chorus I slow things down and strum a cheesy chord that hangs in the air before each phrase.

But…
Someday we'll all be famous,
everyone at the same time.
We'll pat each other on the back
in a great big conga-line.

We'll all have our own
reality TV show.
 But there won't be any audience
because no one will be left at home.
 So buy me a drink,
 add me as a friend.
 No matter how big you get
 it's all forgotten in the end.

They call the kids hipsters
just like in the 50's.
Every decade a different name
sometimes on repeat.
But everyone has talent
everywhere you go.
Speaking the truth
that you already know.

You know you're different
just like everybody else.
You really inspire me
because you remind me of myself.
It's hard to become famous
when mankind doubles every year.
Billions of voices,
a chorus of tears.

 So…
 So buy me a drink,
 add me as a friend.

> *However big the following*
> *it's all forgotten in eternity.*
> *These local band blues*
> *have got a hold of me.*

My skinny punk rocker friend has been staring at the ground nodding and tapping his foot with his arms crossed. When I'm done he asks, "You ever play that one live?"

"No. I wouldn't dare."

We both laugh. "Yeah," he says, "That's an inside joke."

"I should though. Maybe next time I find myself playing to a room filled with other musicians just waiting for their turn to play I'll share that one."

He cracks his fingers into his tight jeans and slides another five out for me. With that he's on his way.

It's almost time for the lecture I wanted to see at the Library. Playing live is great and all but I want to learn about making records. In the end I want to make art. I want to leave something behind. Even if it's just a few burnt CDs. Playing shows are fun, but looking out beyond the stage lights sometimes I wonder if it clicks. Can you hear my words over the drums? Is the PA as loud as this monitor? Will everyone at the bar swilling beer even remember this night?

The Harold Washington library is one of my favorite places in Chicago. It's a beautiful building painted burgundy. Massive metal sculptures of wise bookish owls sprawl over the corners of the roof like rusted green gargoyles. When I first moved to the city the library was a peaceful place for me. I didn't know anyone. I didn't have any friends. The kids from school were not very adventurous. The first like minded people I met were writers entombed in the books inside the Harold Washington Library. Misfits, introverts, extroverts, drunks, dreamers, poets, these writers became my imaginary friends. They still are.

In the bowels of the Library is an auditorium. I mill around with the crowd as they flap programs in their hands. It's hard to blend in with a banjo on your back. But with a little intuitive timing I slip in with a party of five after they handed over their tickets. The ushers are too busy to notice. Or they just don't care.

After finding a place in the back the lights are dimmed. The lecture starts. A slight but buoyant Englishman in a grey goatee comes out on stage. Everyone applauds. He talks about the music industry, recording techniques, and rock star antidotes. He clicks a remote to a massive screen that shows a slideshow of photos he took himself at various sessions. Eddie Kramer was there. He's one of the most respected producers and engineers in rock and roll history. He was at the helm when the Kinks first used distortion in pop music. He recorded the sessions for the *All You Need is Love* and *Baby You're a Rich Man* for the Beatles. Not only did he work on every Hendrix album, but with the Rolling Stones, Led Zeppelin, Frank Zappa, the live albums for The Allman Brothers... the list goes on and on.

The lecture is interesting. He plays audio clips of tracks he helped create. His photos are from the most fertile period of rock experimentation. He explains the end of *A Whole Lotta Love* by Led Zeppelin. There's a section where Robert Plant's vocals echo before he even sings. It sounds cool but it turns out this wasn't intentional. It was a mistake. One of the vocal takes leaked onto the master track. To make it sound like they were just being creative they cranked up the reverb. This gave it an eerie psychedelic effect. This is the same track Willie Dixon sued Zeppelin over. I was at the Blues Heaven Foundation in the South Loop when Dixon's surviving wife and daughter explained that the riff for *A Whole Lotta Love* is one of Willie Dixon's compositions. But he didn't mind British bands ripping him off too much. He won the lawsuit and pocketed a cool million.

There is a Q and A session after the lecture. I float down the steps and get in line to ask a question. I have half a dozen questions in my mind. As I wait in line I percolate on a multiple part question. The line inches up. Finally my turn arrives. I'm handed the microphone.

What I really wanted to ask is, "Could you please record me and make me famous so I don't have to work bullshit jobs anymore?"

But I chicken out. I phrase it more constructively. I ask Mr. Kramer, "As the record companies are signing less and less people because of illegal downloading, and home recording is more readily available; how likely do you see a struggling musician like myself ever finding themselves working with a talented producer like yourself?"

For an Englishman he is taken aback by the number of syllables I had loaded into my mouth. He responds, "Wow do you have three hours? I don't know. The three big record companies are in trouble. They are merging and trying to save their losses. I don't know how good that is for artistic freedom and distributing good music. Can you make a great record with a laptop in a room, in a bathroom, or in a closet? I don't know."

"What I do know is that nothing beats getting great musicians in the SAME room so they can look each other in the face and play. I mean Plant and Page HATE each other! Mick and Keith HATE each other! I don't mean that literally, but they're not best friends. They play well together because they look at one another and say I'm going to blow you away just because you think I can't. They feed off that energy in the studio. One thing I notice when I hear newer recordings is how sterile it is. It sounds like nothing was recorded at the same time. I don't know if it's good that every person with Pro-Tools is able to clip every little buzz and clip from the mix. It's rock and roll. It's supposed to be HAIRY!" When he says this the room explodes with applause.

Later I'm scratching my head on the train as the Green Line chases the sun back to the West Side. Mr. Kramer is right. Recording a rock band on a laptop lacks energy, but I think for my purposes it could still work. I could record acoustic blues with all the vigor I could get at an expensive studio.

Back in my room I find myself learning how to mix pretty fast. I find myself inviting musicians I meet at jams to come record. Eduardo White is an amazing harmonica player from Brazil. I meet him at the Gallery and he agrees to drive over to the practice space to record. He's a virtuoso. He makes the harp sound like a swampy saxophone. After the session I never see him again. I'm unable to ever find him on social media. Who was that mystery man? I visit Dobro Joe in Jefferson Park and he lays down some pedal steel. Afterwards I find myself lugging the laptop and the monitor on the Pulaski bus and back through the alley behind the practice space.

The only other artist besides Eduardo who has the balls to record with me in the hood is my old friend poet Sid Yiddish. On the surface he's middle-aged and nervous. He looks like a mad Rabbi. Yet he's a brave soul. In the eighties when he was a reporter he snuck into a Klu Klux Klan rally with a tape recorder in his jacket to expose their hate speech. He's no fool though. After he records some spoken word for my demo he asks me to walk him to the train. In his rainbow skullcap and classic I Love New York t-shirt the entrepreneurs on the corner slinging dust are eyeing him thinking there's another one. The fucking artists are moving in.

I realize most of my musician friends are older than I am. They never met that special lady who said those magic words: I'm not hanging out all night in some sleazy club anymore.

Around this time I ding-dong on south Dearborn Avenue where my old songwriting partner lives. Guitar Mike is home for once. He buzzes me in. The place is cleaned up. There's no more wet socks hanging on the radiator. I see the new girlfriend has kept Mike calibrated. He says as much. I update him on things with me. I bitch a bit about not having a proper guitar for the demo I'm working on. After catching up we get in his van, which used to be the old band van. We used to pile in with equipment on the way to gigs good and bad. This time we load the van with the odds and ends he let me store at his place after my breakup. There are the rest of my books, spools of CDs, and a suitcase full of some clothes. Some old PA speakers I've had since a band in high school. He throws in a used Les Paul Electric Guitar and a small practice amp. "Here man," he says out the side of his mouth, "Borrow this to record your new songs."

"Thanks Mike."

As we haul the last of my loose ends into the practice space I can sense he feels a little guilty. Not that anything is his fault. He doesn't owe me anything. But he can see that I'm giving everything to the music. He's ten times more talented than I will ever be but he's going the safe route, the smart route. He's become a music teacher. He has children clapping along at an elementary school. He has them forming a rock band for the talent show. In the summer he tutors students on guitar and piano. He's a master musician. Any instrument you throw at him he can play it. Any song he hears Mike leans in, listens, and starts playing along.

He's the one who came up with the name of our band. Once upon a time Mike, Justin on bass, Nathan Vining on drums, and I hopped on a Metra Train. To brainstorm names the four of us sipped pints of whisky all the way to the end of the line. These commuter trains allow drinking. It's a fringe benefit for suburban commuters. On the CTA here in town you still have to hide it. When we reached the Wisconsin border Guitar Mike thought of the name Cousin Bones. It sounded like a character from an old blues song. Maybe someone who hopped freight trains. Maybe a migrant worker from the dustbowl during the Great Depression. Maybe an alias for an outlaw on the run. Maybe a bootlegger in Appalachia during Prohibition. Maybe a stage name for a musician adrift in Chicago. We'd write songs using these blues archetypes as if we were writing stories for a character.

Now as we unload at the practice space I thank him again for letting me use his guitar. I walk him back to the van. Under the lone streetlamp at the end of the block I asked him for one more favor. "Hey remember when the band would play a show and inevitably someone would ask if I was Cousin Bones since I was the lead singer?"

"Right."

"And we'd be like no this is the name of the band. All for one and one for all."

"Yeah I remember."

"Well since the band ain't no more I wanted to ask if it's cool with you if I can use the name for my solo stuff. I've been signing up for open mics under my birth name, and I've come to realize it's not very catchy. Cousin Bones is easy to remember, and after all that's happened… well I feel like I've become the character we created."

"Go for it brother. Do what you gotta do."

With that he tips his flat cap and pulls the old van away. After Guitar Mike's blessing I go back upstairs and begin working on the demo in earnest. Inside one of the bags he was storing for me is an old pair of overalls. I slip them on. Looks like something Cousin Bones would wear. There is no giving up the ghost. What's in a name? Hard times are happening. It's not my fault. It's not bad choices. It's just life. Right? Listen to these songs from the nineteen thirties: Skip James, Robert Johnson, Charlie Patton. This has all happened before. This is art. This isn't happening to Westley. This is happening to Cousin Bones.

Amongst my old things I find a toenail clippers. In the men's room I stare into the tarnished mirror and use the clippers to take out the stitches from my eyebrow.

Later in the night I'm recording the Les Paul and using the computer to replicate that fifties reverb like early John Lee Hooker, but I keep hearing thuds and voices in my headphones. I rip the phones off my skull and put an ear to the wall. There is noise out in the hallway. Popping my head out the door there are about thirty high school kids in the common area drinking, smoking, skateboarding down the hall, and playing beer-pong. It's too loud to record. What can I do but grab my guitar and go out and join them? At first I think one of the bands must have been hosting a party. But I begin to suspect that there is no band. Someone probably rented a room just to be free to do whatever they wanted. It's not too different than why I'm here. It ain't much but we're free. They just want to party. I was the same when I was their age. I'm not too much different now.

What can I do but play a song for them? They have bags of ice, plastic cups, and bottles of rum. The drinks are strong and sweet. We're living the dream. Never rock stars but forever living like rock stars. How long can the dream last? William Blake said, "Excess leads to the palace of wisdom." How long can you tour the palace until you reach the dungeon? After a few drinks the rum goes to my head. I dig my eye patch out of my wallet and do a Captain Morgan impression. Some of the kids laugh. Some roll their eyes. Feeling like their elder I warn them that they might end up like me in ten years.

36

At the corner of Division and Ashland is where Milwaukee Avenue cuts diagonally creating a pavement triangle like a small island. Here under the trees and above the subway stop a pleasant fountain inhales and exhales water in silent meditation. Local street urchins line up their grocery carts like a dystopian cabstand. Some sit on the edge of the fountain smoking discarded butts. Every so often a new cart rolls up and the weary scavenger steps up to the waters and dips hands stained with exhaust and alley silt. Once the grease drips away the hands now wash a worn face covered in tar and soot from last night's dirty pillow stuffed with decades of broken dreams.

Just outside the subway exit I've positioned myself with the banjo and my sign as I eye commuters for a dime. Here I am in plain view for those emerging from the stairs underground as well as those rolling off the buses.

The Division Bus squeaks to a halt. The doors are forced open by a tall impatient brute with sandy blond hair and a red face. As he steps off the bus he lifts an open bottle of Bud from the chest pocket of his flannel and chugs it as if he *wants* the driver to see he has an open container. Without taking a beat he spots me with the banjo and blurts out, "Hey man! Can you play the blues?"

I point to my sign: Tell Me Your Problem. I'll Write You a Blues

Song.

"Oh wow! Yeah! I'm a bluesman myself." The words spill from his twisted jowls.

He leans over to listen and puts his hand on my shoulder as I play the first verse of Skip James's *Hard Times on the Killing Floor,* which sounds nice and crisp on the banjo. My new friend doesn't have the patience for the whole song. He flips out as I start the second verse. "Oh wow. You like the *real* blues too. I'm not yelling am I?"

"Little bit."

"Sorry I have some hearing loss from Nam and playing in bands all my life. Say, let me have a turn at that banjo."

The way he's staggering around I'm sure I could catch him if he took off with Shanghai Mike's banjo. He seems a little manic but harmless. So I hand him the ancient axe and he plucks around adjusting the tunings. "Don't remember if I have ever played a banjo before…"

As he delves into a lecture about the blues it doesn't take me long to realize that this man is not going to give me a tip. He doesn't see my hustle as a novelty. He doesn't see me as entertainment. He sees me as a peer or perhaps a pupil. That's ok with me. The blues are a way of life. I enjoy talking with him, or rather listening to him. Even among Chicago musicians it's rare to find those that prefer Delta blues over the electric blues that our fair city is known for. Despite his long monologues and spitting as he talks it's refreshing to find someone with a similar interest. It sounds like he really knows his stuff.

He claims he knows all of Charlie Patton's picking secrets and some of Robert Johnson's. He tells me he brought a pair of opera glasses to the Lyric Opera House when "Honey-boy" Edwards played there so he could spy on his picking techniques. Likewise he says when he performs he turns away so no one can steal *his* secrets. In fact one of his band mates was peeking at his fingers during a show and it came to blows on stage. He got kicked out of the band. Yet despite all this, and despite the fact that he doesn't even know my name, after just a few minutes he offers to teach me everything he knows.

Smiling and nodding I have the man's life story before the next bus pulls up. "I can't drink no more you see." He lifts up his shirt revealing a long jagged scar. "I have no large intestine. It was blasted out my belly by a shotgun in L.A. I got shot by my best friend! Shit, we were choirboys together. You see he had some videotape of me playing guitar. He wouldn't give me the tape back! I didn't want my picking secrets getting out you see? Well, we got into it… After the surgery I just sat in a chair drinking whisky until the pain went away."

Wait a minute? He's not supposed to drink, but next he's drinking bottles of whisky? Didn't he just chug a beer when he got off the bus?

He says that he spends his time between the VA Hospital and his apartment above the Blue Star Lounge at the corner of Grand & Ashland. "I haven't paid rent in a year! I know they have some mold in the walls. It's been making me cough. I'm gonna sue them for a million dollars! Hell, I might end up owning the Blue Star Lounge! When that day comes you should come play. My neighbors don't say shit to me cause they'll know I'll beat them up cause I'm a real Blues Man!" I make a mental note to beat up my neighbors from now on or I'll never be a real Blues Man…

As he spits out his stories he wipes the sandy blonde hair out of his eyes. His hair is more sand than blonde. When he does this he reveals a face cut with wrinkles but bright blue eyes full of light as if there's a much younger man trapped inside his leathery exterior who is just aching to escape. "I parachuted into Vietnam playing guitar behind my back," he laughs out loud.

"Slow down soldier. What's your name?"

"I'm Tommy. Tommy James. But I've gone by half a dozen stage names. TJ Jamal. Timmy John. Jimmy James…"

We get back on the subject of Charlie Patton the elder of all bluesman. Though Patton didn't record till the late nineteen twenties he's the oldest Bluesman ever caught on record. His songs are the oldest audible traces of blues we have. His style comes from an era that predates when W.C. Handy first wrote down the blues in musical notes in the nineteen teens. Before Charlie Patton things evaporate into a speculative mix of folk standards, field hollers, and primordial soup passed down by ear. Patton's style, though acoustic, is polyrhythmic having both a bass line and a slide line on the same guitar neck. He was a true one-man band: stomping, strumming, and singing. People used to actually dance to his music without the aide of drums. People in Mississippi used to come from miles around to dance to a single man stomping on the floor.

Tommy proceeds to show me Patton's picking style telling me, "Don't show anyone else." I nod along but I can't keep up with him. He's talking a mile a minute. I'm a songwriter. I was never interested in showing off on guitar. Those types of players will bore you about their equipment for hours, but speak little about what the music actually means to them. It is unlikely that I will ever attempt to do the things Tommy is trying to teach me. But according to him the elaborate pickings of Charlie Patton could be done with a hooked claw motion, which Tommy could do using a system of protective Band-aides strategically placed on certain points of his fingers.

Eventually he tires himself out. The sun is diving towards the western suburbs. "I better catch the next Ashland bus down to my place. I have some jiffy pop left for dinner." We exchange numbers. I tell him I'd like to do a gig with him. Not just because I want to help a fellow country-blues artist, but because I am curious if he can do half the things he says he can.

As he turns to go Tommy says something strange. "Yeah lets do some gigs. If you're not careful you'll end up like me in ten years." This is almost exactly what I told the high school kids partying in my practice space the other night… word for word. With that he gives me a hard salute and dives into traffic in front of the oncoming Ashland bus. Tommy has both hands up now like he's trying to scare away a bear. The bus hits the brakes almost mowing him down. He just smiles at the driver and gets on.

A few days later I see him sitting quietly on the Milwaukee bus reading a book. I have learned not to ignore coincidence so I get his attention. He's sober now. I remind him of our first conversation. "Oh yeah, hey. The young bluesman right?"

"Right." I give him my number again. Soon he's calling me in the middle of the night.

"Hello, Tommy?"

"Hey yeah, I'm in this caaaab! … *No! Go around that car!* … Hey Wes, buddy I'm spending my last dollar on this cab to chase down this bus because I left a Howling Wolf book on it... *Faster man…* It's an expensive full-size photo book!"

"Oh. Ok. Hope you catch it."

"They're telling me that I might have had Tuberculosis lying dormant in my body! Yeah shit, is that the bus? … Anyway, I've got the rocking-pneumonia."

Next he tells me about trying to set up a gig at Buddy Guys. Tommy says he is planning a big comeback show. He had been a side-man in the early nineties playing lead guitar. Now he says he's ready for his solo acoustic debut. After years of study he believes he is ready. His time has come. Tommy says that not only does he practice during the day, but he plays Delta blues records while he sleeps so the songs will soak in.

"I like the real stuff, the acoustic stuff. I thought about what I really liked about the blues, and I remembered fishing back in Iowa when I was a kid. So I started taking my acoustic to Garfield Park and go fishing."

"Man," I said. "I hang out down there too. Last week they fished a dead junkie out of that pond. It can be kind of rough down there."

"I'm rough!"

"I believe it."

"Hey Wes. You know how I told you I used opera glasses to see what Honey-boy Edwards does on his axe?"

"Yeah."

"Well, here's the verdict. I don't think Robert Johnson ever showed Honey-boy how he played those songs. I might be the only one who figured it out! There ain't nobody doing what I'm doing."

For this reason Tommy keeps turning me down when I invite him to play at the Gallery or the other little bars around town. He says he's too afraid someone will steal his techniques. He only wants to debut downtown at Buddy's.

Buddy Guy's is the most famous blues club in the world. You can't just waltz in there and demand a show. You have to be on the top in the first place. So I tell him, "As a pro I'm sure you know it's different practicing alone than it is playing in front of lots of people. How long has it been? You have to get used to performing again Tommy. You can't just play the material. You have to make eye contact and ham it up. Before you play Buddy's you need some warm-up gigs."

He finally concedes, "Alright, alright, you're wise beyond your years. Maybe I'll pawn something so I have enough cash for a beer."

Once he agrees I invite him to my next set at the Gallery Cabaret. Tommy shows up wearing dark shades even though the sun has long since ducked under the horizon. Behind the black glasses he's nervous but he's keeping his cool.

After I play a couple songs I set my guitar down and wave Tommy up. It's the peak of the evening when those who have to work in the morning keep saying one more, and the hardcore bar closers are just getting warmed up. I lean into the mic, "Alright people you're in for a treat. We have with us Tommy James a master of the real folk-blues. Let him know you're here."

As the room applauds Tommy leans in and whispers to me, "Maybe I'll do like one song, maybe two songs."

"Just do what you feel."

The energy dips as Tommy gets the microphone where he wants it. Someone in the back coughs. He finally takes off the sunglasses and squints at the crowd. The first number starts slow. He fumbles a bit. One of his weird Band-aides that he claims helps with the finger picking is dangling from a thumb. The first verse starts. His voice is faint. I shuffle over to the mixer, find the dial for his mic, and turn it up.

He sticks the ending with a crunching chord. The room claps. I let out an encouraging *Whoo*. Tommy sits up a little straighter. He coughs. He clears his throat again. He whips out a handkerchief and spits. I start to feel bad. Maybe he was telling the truth about the pneumonia, or the lawsuit with his landlord because of the mold in his apartment. Maybe he caught Agent Orange in Vietnam. Or maybe it is just years of drinking, smoking, and living fast.

But the next song Tommy's voice is twice as strong. His eyes close. As he chops his axe I can tell he's getting there. He's getting lost in the music. All the prying eyes in the Gallery have faded out far beyond the stage lights.

By the third song he's moaning hard, stomping, the licks are rollicking, rumbustious, raw, subtle but strong. Tommy said he'd only play two songs, but his guitar is chugging along like a freight train. He does *If I Had Possession Over Judgement Day* by Robert Johnson, which is almost impossible. He does some original songs full of tall tales but after getting to know Tommy I almost believe they are true. Before he reluctantly surrenders the stage to the next act he does a total of eight songs. To massive applause he comes off the stage sweating and grinning ear to ear.

I tell him, "It doesn't matter if anyone saw your picking secrets. No one can play that stuff but you."

Like any good storyteller it's hard to tell how much of what Tommy says is real and how much is exaggeration. It makes me wonder how distorted my own stories will sound given another thirty years. But one thing is for real: Tommy can play the blues. Amazingly he can play the bass line and the slide on guitar simultaneously. When he played *I Shall Not Be Moved* the way Charlie Patton recorded it I had a tear in my eye. Underneath the manic, neurotic, but ever smiling persona is an authentic voice. Tucked under his frantic bobbing Adam's apple Tommy had swallowed a world of pain. It has brewed in his scarred belly where it rose up and cried out with angst and jubilation. Maybe he really is ready to play at Buddy's.

Not only does his talent turn out to be true, but also what he said about being sick appears to be real. Despite all the smiles he leans on his guitar case like a crutch as we walk to the bar. When I introduce him to Kenny who offers him a free beer Tommy says, "No. No beer tonight. Say, I think I better take a cab home."

Tommy sips some water as the other musicians and barflies pat him on the back. Next I walk with him to Armitage to flag a cab. "I just hope this credit card I got in the mail works. Otherwise I'll have to fight a cab driver."

A Checker Cab pulls up and I hand the driver fifteen bucks. "This should get him to Ashland and Grand right?" The cabbie nods.

"Hey thanks, Wes man. Thanks for everything."

The cab pulls off with a puff of purple smoke.

Back inside the Gallery I get a whisky on ice. I take a sip. Rumination begins. Things have finally started to slow down long enough to think. There are funny shapes in my glass. As the ice melts the shapes change. I think about the past. I think about the future. I think about death. I think about life and love. I wonder if another woman will ever touch me again. I stare through the glass like a crystal ball. My vision telescopes back and forth…

I'll never see Tommy again. In the morning I will call his number but his phone will be disconnected. A few days later I will call the VA hospital to see if they have any record of him. The operator is nice. She indulges me. She checks all the locations with me for twenty minutes. She has all the data from all the VA locations in Chicago. But there is no match for TJ Jamal, Tommy James, or any of the other odd stage names he gave me. Eventually I will play the Blue Star Lounge, which was the club he said he lived above. Only now it's called Grandbar. During my set I play a song based on Tommy's tall tales and ask the crowd if anybody has seen him. Crickets.

He had mentioned that he was going to move to a flophouse in Uptown until his lawsuit went through. Uptown is full of halfway houses, veteran's programs, sanitariums, methadone clinics, and housing for the elderly. One hospital had famously forced out a legion of mental patients into the street years ago when some law changed and funding went down the gutter. Some of the lost souls are still milling around, noses stuck in corners, their eyeballs flashing in the headlights.

Shaking the ice in my glass I see I will take the Red Line to Uptown and ask around. The bartender at the Green Mill hasn't seen him. Rick the owner of the Shake Rattle & Read record store hasn't seen him. If he'd been around they'd know. He would visit these haunts.

How can you miss a six-foot guy who rants and raves about Delta blues? I leave notes with my contact info with the doormen at all the public housing joints. One lady at the front desk says, "Oh yeah, the guy that's always talking about his music. I haven't seen him for a long time."

When I first met Tommy I bumped into him twice. It seemed it was meant to be that we'd be friends. In my experience chance encounters always happen in threes. I'm still waiting for the third time. Maybe I will get more serious about my guitar technique and let him teach me his picking secrets. I'll still look for Tommy, but slowly I will start to sense that he's gone. Smiling I think that Tommy doesn't mind. He lived hard and never compromised.

As I sit at the bar at the Gallery staring through my glass Kenny has locked the doors and dimmed the lights again. He's up for making some extra bucks after bar time. It's quiet now. The jukebox plays Miles Davis. The trumpet moans the like a lonely foghorn. Mr. Fish the host of the blues jam and leader of The Blue Fins lights up a Newport at the end of the bar. Most of the other regulars have petered out. I bum a cigarette from him. I don't even smoke. I just want to feel like we're two flies in the same ointment.

I begin to wonder what kind of an old man I might become? I wonder if I am the only person who will ever remember how good Tommy played tonight? He didn't have any family. He was just another ghost walking the grid in Chicago. Just another face reflected in the windows. It seems like a sad end to be alone in a big cold town. To fight your whole life trying to perfect a style of music no one cares about anymore. Just treading water in an ocean of obscurity trying not to let your head go under.

I ask Kenny for another drink. As he pours I look at him. He's seventy something. I can see through his pale skin. His blue veins flow like rivers as he tops me off. For a second it seems like he's pouring his blood into my glass. I think about all my older friends. It seems all my friends are old. Just like the blues. They might not be in style, but they are classic. Things don't need to be new to be cool. Things that are hip will soon become hype.

I wonder if this is going to be my future? Am I going to be like Tommy still inches from living on the street, just older and better at guitar? Am I gonna be like my friend Sid Yiddish waiting endlessly for his big break and still dating at fifty? Or like Mr. Blue my professor who'd rather be making art than teaching it to brats who are only there because they wanted to leave their parent's house? Like JT who has a beautiful wife, a kid, a house, a career, and enough love inside him to make time for it all? Dobro Joe, Shanghai Mike, Little Joey, Texas Fred, Cowboy Charlie, Art the Grey Ghost all my friends are older. They never let on that they're lonely. That is, until the music starts.

Soon it's just Mr. Fish, Kenny, and I sitting in the dim lights. No one is waiting for us to come home. I reach for my phone. I text Trudy again. I wish she would text me back. It would be so much nicer to walk down Armitage and sleep in a big soft bed with a young woman. To feel smooth skin against mine, to smell a women's hair would be so much nicer than waiting for the Green Line to start up again so I can go crash on the floor at dawn.

Suddenly I realize I'm talking out loud. Mr. Fish and Kenny are listening. "She never answers the phone." My voice is raw from singing. "Man, women are there and then they're gone… Does it ever get easier?"

The two men twice my age answer in stereo: "No." They don't even have to think about it.

Mr. Fish sips his smoke coolly. He blows little rings in the air. When he sings he bellows from a beer-belly as I do. The three of us sit in this dank room with nothing better to do. But what's better to do? The music is still ringing in our ears. Everyone else in Chicago is being kicked out of bars or is fast asleep. We are the lost souls that have found each other. The blues bums put up with me because I'm the youngest person at the jam that cares about this music. With a little practice I could be the future of the scene long after they are gone. When I first started hanging out here I wanted to be like these old guys. In the mirror behind the bar I see my face outlined in wrinkles and my hair fade grey.

"What if I never find someone who loves me?" I ask out loud.

Kenny says, "Wes, why don't you go home?"

"I don't have a home!" I snap.

Kenny doesn't balk. He just smiles.

"Sorry Kenny. It's just… I've been running in circles just trying not to go crazy. When I stop and think about it I get all fucking dramatic. Sorry."

"Want another drink?"

"Sure."

I reach in my pocket.

"Put your money away."

Kenny pours me another round on the house. The whisky cracks through the ice. "So what? I live the way I want to live and if I can't find someone to love me for who I really am… then the hell with them… the hell with the world. It's better than compromising. It's better to live alone than to live a lie… in a cage. Isn't music enough? Music is like platonic love or some shit right? It's everywhere and nowhere… like god. Isn't that enough?"

"You might have a song there," Mr. Fish quips.

I stay quiet as we wait for the sun. The shapes in my glass are moving again. There are faces refracted in the ice. The following year Mr. Fish will pass away from stomach cancer. The news comes out of nowhere. None of us will know he's sick until he's gone. He will play music steadily to the end. There will be no funeral. He cannot afford one. He will donate his body to science. Medical students will operate on him as a cadaver. He will be a practice dummy for future surgeons. He won't even have a pauper's grave. He will become medical waste. There will be a wake at the Gallery where everyone tells old stories and we finally tell Mr. Fish how much we love him now that he's no longer around to hear it. I will always remember the night we played *Boogie Chillin* by John Lee Hooker together. He nailed the swampy riff.

Giving the glass a shake the shapes reform. There's more. Kenny will live to be almost ninety. He will die in 2020 almost ten years to this very day. After complications from a new strain of the flu he passes away. The new virus has sent the whole planet into quarantine. After the global pandemic is over the Gallery Cabaret reopens, but without Kenny it's never the same again.

37

My phone wakes me early in the morning.

Eyes closed I open my mouth. "Hello?"

"Hey Kentucky."

"Who? Oh this must be Tammy? Tammy I asked you nicely to stop calling me that."

"I'm outside. Come on. Come let me in."

"Outside? Outside where?"

"Outside your place."

"You're outside my place?"

"Remember you showed me on Goggle where you hide out. Are you really like Jim Morrison? Passed out in there? Now come on and let me inside."

I pull the phone away from my face. Son of a bitch… I don't need this. Fuck this shit and fuck Jim Morrison. I sit up, rub my eyes, and clear my throat. "Tammy, you mean to say that you don't like to go west of Halsted, but now you're standing outside at Karlov and Kinzie?"

"Yes I'm here. Come open this door boy."

"Look this is my place. This is all I have. I was sleeping. Now you call… You keep telling me what to do. I don't like that."

"Why you being mean? Don't you like surprises?"

"Listen to me. I did not invite you here. I did not ask you to do this. This place is mine. This is mine."

I hang up. I lay my head back down, but I can't get back to sleep. My back is sore. Might as well begin my routine. I roll up my bedding and hide it in the cooler. I slid the cooler into the shadows under the shelf. I pull up my pants. Fuck there's new mouse droppings in here. I need to buy a damn whiskbroom now. As the weather cools more mice have been sneaking in. I see them darting in the corner of my eye as I stumble down to the first floor and enter the men's room.

The faucet trickles into my palms until I have enough to throw on my face. Then I place my mug under the drip. By the time I drain my bladder the mug is brimming. I take it upstairs and pour it in the cof-feemaker. After a stiff cup my headache subsides. Kenny was serving up complimentary whisky last night. I hope I didn't say anything too weird. I hope Tommy got home ok… I throw on my work shirt, reach into a bag under the shelf and grab a can of fruit cocktail for the commute.

Cracking open the steel door of the practice space I look both ways. No Tammy. What was that about? Marching across the neighbor-hood I reach the Pulaski station. The loose squares man is there hustling at his usual spot. On the platform there's an open bench. I sit and crack my can of fruit cocktail pinching peaches and pears and the one cherry. Down below I can hear the chanting, "Loose squares! Loose squares!"

When who do I see coming down the platform but Tammy. Figures it took her longer to get here than it took me. She doesn't look happy.

"I took a cab all the way out here. You gonna pay for my cab?"

"No. Why should I?"

"There ain't no cabs on Pulaski to go back."

"Ain't that the truth…"

She's indignant. "I have to pass all these yards… dogs jumping at me. I don't like seeing no pit, no pit-bull."

"Sorry, but I didn't invite you over."

"I thought I could help you. I thought I could help you clean up. I thought…"

"Help me? Look, I don't want any help."

"What you got there?"

"You mean my breakfast?"

"Yeah."

"Just fruit cocktail."

"Why you eat it with your hands? That's nasty."

"My god. If I wanted to be mothered I would go back to Wisconsin."

As the train approaches she says, "You know I'd go to jail a lot longer for hitting a white guy than for hitting a black guy."

"Wait, what? Well, you're probably right but why…" The train roars up.

On the train there's only one seat left. I walk with Tammy. She sits down in the empty seat and starts rubbing her knee. Standing, I grip a handlebar as the train pulls forward. I stare out the window. In the reflection I see her rubbing her knee and looking up at me. Next she begins digging in her purse. "Kentucky, I wrote a song about you."

I try not to roll my eyes, "Oh yeah?"

"Here I have it." Tammy pulls out some eight by eleven sheets. "It's called *Handstand*. Remember when we were having our first fight that night and you did a handstand?"

"First fight? What is this? Sure I remember doing a handstand."

"Here let me read you the song."

She reads the song. The verses are a jumble of lines with no meter and no rhymes. The chorus is a chant that merely goes: Handstand, handstand, handstand…

"That's nice of you," I tell her. "Good to see you being creative."

"I got it copyrighted. I saw a lawyer. I don't want anyone to steal my ideas."

Oh sure, I think, she's been dangling music industry connections under my nose since day one. It all turned out to be smoke, mist, funhouse mirrors without the fun. Now she writes a song and pays to have it copy-written? What for? She played me. She played to my ego. She played to my desires to be a musician. What a fool I've been. What a mark. This is what happens when you hustle with your heart on your sleeve. Just when you think you're the one hustling really you're the mark.

"Do you think you will write some music for my song? Do you think you could sing it?"

"I don't think so. I like to do my own material."

At Clark & Lake I walk with her over the bridge to the other platform where the Brown Line will take us to Old Town. She's dragging her feet. I'm not sure but I think she's doing it on purpose. Up on the bridge the next Brown Line rolls in underneath us. We're going to miss it. For an instant I'm temped to jump off the bridge on top of the train like a train robber in some forgotten Western. That would blow her fucking mind. But no, I try to be a gentleman. I walk her to the platform.

Just as she likes I walk her from the Sedgwick stop to Division careful to stand to her left so no one thinks she's for sale. I bid her farewell at Dominick's. Then Tammy walks quite naturally and swiftly towards the Park Side Complex.

We have a lot of regulars at the deli. It seems the crazier they are, the more regular they are. There is this ex-cop who has warmed up to me. Living off his pension he comes in for meat and cheese to make sandwiches every week. He asks me what neighborhood I stay in.

"Round Lake and Pulaski."

He freaks out. "My beat was down there for twenty years! Pardon me, but what the hell are you doing down there?"

I smile and shrug.

From the pocket of his trench coat he pulls out a pistol and lays it on the deli counter. "Do you know what this is?"

"Looks like a 38."

"You gotta protect yourself. I've seen people kill each other for little over five bucks. By my dead Irish mother get the fuck out of there."

I never trusted cops. But back home in Wisconsin I came from a place swarming with bored and stupid country cops. Cops whose peak of excitement was giving tickets for jaywalking. This man, a Chicago cop, has seen real crime. Still it's pretty weird to pull out a piece in the middle of a grocery store.

He asks, "How many times have you been a victim of crime?"

"Really I've had no trouble. There's some obvious drug traffic activity. But it seems pretty much live and let live."

"Well my advice is to exercise your 2nd Amendment rights." He puts the gun away and pushes his cart towards the butcher counter. He's right about one thing. I can't stay in Garfield Park forever. Not because of crime so much as winter is coming. Next on my list I need to save for a space heater.

Bandi sidles up, "What was that about?"

"Who the guy in the trench coat?"

"Yeah."

"Just some perve who wanted to show me his big gun."

"You crazy. Prep those pizzas Wes. It's pizza Friday."

On five-dollar pizza day we clean out the inventory of dough, sauce, and cheese. Around diner time the line will be out the door, the pizza oven will be at capacity, and the phone will be ringing off the hook as the whole neighborhood will be calling ahead to place their order. It's best to prep the pizzas early. I have multiple pies laid out on the prepping counter. I add the sauce and the cheese, place a paper sheet on top of each one, and then stack them on a cart. Once the cart is full I wheel it back into the cooler. This will save time during the rush. All I'll need to do is throw on the toppings, which is the only thing that varies from order to order.

On my break I call Tommy James the bluesman. I wonder if he's feeling better? When I call his number it gives me the disconnected signal. I have a flash of déjà vu. Somehow I didn't think he would answer in the first place.

As always around six-o-clock all our regulars are lined up. Bandi is at the register and I'm working the oven. My sleeves are rolled up. I'm sweating. In the middle of the rush Bandi calls me over her shoulder, "Hey Wes. You have a customer."

It's Tammy. I think: now what? Mocking me with schoolyard baby talk Bandi says, "She says she wants *you* to take her *order...*"

playfully insinuating we're in love. Bandi steps aside, grips a pizza cutter, and starts slicing a pie. "I'm sick of that register any-hoo. Hey! This one? They want it cut in squares or triangle slices?"

"They want it cut in circles," I lip back.

At the register I ask Tammy what she wants on her pizza?

"I'm not sure. So I was wondering about my song. Are you going to use it?"

"I already told you. No. No I'm not going to sing your song."

Tammy is holding up the show. The line is growing behind her.

"Well let me get one pizza, pepperoni, and please make sure it's well done. I don't like it when the pizza is doughy."

"No problem. Come back in fifteen minutes and it will be ready."

She pays her five dollars and then disappears into the produce section.

In fifteen minutes I pull out Tammy's pizza. It's perfect. It has a nice amber-brown finish on the top. It's not doughy at all.

She's on time. "You want this cut in slices or little squares."

"Squares I guess."

I grab the pizza cutter and slice a grid across the pie like a map of Chicago.

"Loose squares! Loose squares!" I call out.

Bandi laughs, "Wes you crazy."

I box up the pizza and slide it over the counter to Tammy.

Once she's out of earshot Bandi asks, "Is she your giiiiiiiirlfriend?"

"No. But she thinks so."

A minute later Tammy is back. She has the store manager Mr. Peterson with her.

Mr. Peterson waves me over, "Westley. This customer says you burnt her pizza." I look at Tammy. She's standing there holding the pizza box with her head down with a look on her face like someone just shot her favorite pet pony.

"Let me take a look at it?"

Mr. Peterson takes possession of the pizza in question and passes it over to me. "Please make this customer a new pizza right away."

I pop another pepperoni in the oven. Then I open up Tammy's pizza box. Yep, it is still perfectly cooked. I slide the unwanted pizza onto the free sample tray and place it on top of the counter next to the register.

"Loose squares! Loose squares!" I call out as I prop up the sign that says: Free Sample.

All the hungry customers who have been waiting patiently to pick up their order grab a napkin and a slice. Mr. Peterson sees all the customers chewing happily.

Tammy asks him, "Could I please get a refund since I have to wait for a new one?"

Mr. Peterson rubs his chin thoughtfully. "It appears that your pizza is perfectly fine. Everyone is enjoying it. Westley how's that replacement pizza coming?"

"I think it's ready Mr. Peterson."

The oven is super hot, but even so the pie has only been inside a few minutes. I pull it out, slice it, and box it up. It's doughy. I run around the counter and deliver it personally.

"Here you go ma'am," I say to Tammy in my most cheesy customer service voice.

She takes the box. "I'm gonna tell the po-po where you live."

"Have a good night ma'am."

Tammy turns and pouts out the door. When I turn around Mr. Peterson is having a free sample. Things are slowing down. I grab one myself.

After nine the oven is off. The counters have been washed. The slicers have been cleaned. I'm in the back doing the dishes. Bandi comes back to my sink and drops off the last of the hot food trays.

"Wes I saw how you handled that lady. She was out to get you!"

"Yeah that was some quick thinking."

"That was some stone cold gangster shit Wes."

"Think so?"

"You're a reverse Oreo. You're black inside."

We laugh. As she turns to go I ask, "Do you think I could get that in writing? You know in case someone ever gives me trouble. I could pull out a certificate that says: Bandi is black and she says I'm cool."

"You mean like when you got beat up and your eye was all fucked up?"

"I told you. I got drunk. I had a bike accident. No one beat me up."

"Well if you do get cornered and you pull out a reverse Oreo certificate then you'd really get your ass beat." We laugh again.

"Yeah suppose so."

I finish up and head back to the West Side.

Every couple months Bret changes the code on the steel door at the front of the practice space. Bands come. Bands go. Bands break up. Band members lend equipment and then change their minds. There's no way around it band-mates fight. Being in a band is like being in a relationship with three or four people at once. It's all brotherhood while you're making beautiful music together. But one bad gig, or someone is writing too much of the material or not enough, or someone takes too many solos, suddenly there's a rift in the dynamic of the group. Jealousy, alliances, creative differences are all the things that are avoided when you're a lone guitar slinger like myself. To protect the equipment inside from anyone who isn't suppose to be there anymore Bret changes the code on the lock. Every month each unit gets an envelope under their door to use for the rent drop. Before he changes the code he writes the new one on the envelope.

It's almost ten when the Green Line arrives at Lake and Pulaski. I'm tired. After all that business with Tammy at work and staying out until dawn the night before I just want to lay down on the floor and pass out.

When I get to the steel door I punch in the code. The little light on the lock usually blinks green and the door snaps open. Now it blinks red. I remember there's a new code for the door. I wrote it down on the back of a receipt. I search my wallet. No dice. It was just here.

After fumbling through my wallet self-consciously at the end of the dark street I give up. Maybe I could call Bret for the new code. It's late but maybe he'll answer. I pull out my phone. It's dead. Damn I didn't charge the fucking thing.

Putting my ear to the door I listen for music. Silence. Checking the street there's no cars or conspicuous vans. Fat chance any of the bands will be coming in or out anytime soon.

The new code on the envelope was like 1001 or 0110. It was something binary and symmetrical. After trying different combinations for twenty minutes I give up. I'm out of luck. Son of a bitch.

Cursing at myself I head down Kinzie Street where the massive stadium size lights line the Metra tracks. My shadow grows long and short as I walk between the industrial haloes. At Pulaski I head south back towards the EL station. I have no choice but to get back on the train. Maybe I'll ride the train all night.

Pulaski is pretty well lit. There's a small row of houses before the CTA stop.

I hear a noise.

Just ahead I can see three guys about seventeen or eighteen. They're laughing and pulling at a screen door of a darkened house. I get the feeling that it isn't their house. As they leave the home they don't bother to shut the door. They fall backwards toward the sidewalk. The leader of the pack is a tall skinny kid with hate in his eyes. Next is a husky guy squinting and smiling. The third guy holds back basically in the shadow of the other two.

As I pass the tall one steps in front of me blocking my way.

Instinctively I step off the sidewalk and into the street continuing to move at the same pace. They follow me along the curb.

"He wants ta dance," laughs the husky one.

Flashing him a look over my shoulder I start to dance as I walk. I do a little jig. I dance like a psychotic chicken as I continue toward the train. My philosophy has always been if you're in a situation keep the other side guessing. Let them think you're a little crazy, which is the truth anyway.

"He thinks we're sweet," says the husky one.

"No sir, we're Vice Lords!" barks the leader.

If it comes to blows I know I am going to lose. I've been in enough fights when I was kid to know that fistfights are nothing like the movies. It's simple physics: three against one… I lose. It's not a fair fight. I should run. But at the same time this is bullshit. I've done nothing to these guys. At the very least I am not going to give them the satisfaction of acting scared, but I stop dancing. I kept moving at the same pace.

"Alright white boy," yells the skinny one. "You have five seconds to run before we kick the dog shit out of you!"

Over my shoulder I ask, "Why?" I'm not trying to fence with him. I *really* want to know why. Why am I an enemy? Why does a group of guys think they are tough when they gang up on one person? If they want to fight why not do it like men: one on one, man to man? I really want to know.

"That's just what we do!" is the only answer I get.

I continue to walk at the same pace.

"You got any bread?" asks the husky one.

"Nope." I have about forty bucks on me. It's all I have.

I keep giving them the cold shoulder. I hope they're not armed. I continue to walk. I'm about a hundred feet from the train now. In my mind I keep telling myself not to let them know I'm scared. Then I'd really be in trouble. They'd demand my cash. Be cool. Keep them guessing.

"Man, fuck this guy!" I hear over my shoulder.

This is dumb. It's all a dumb game. We were all babies once. Why do we play these stupid games? These kids want to embrace the negative stereotype of the bad black dudes. I check my blind spot. They're young, angry, and likely riding on another stereotype: that all white people are rich, weak, and racist.

I'm almost below the stairs to the train platform.

At this point I have left them no choice. I've refused to play the game. I have called their bluff. There is nothing left for them to do. As I walk looking straight ahead a shape swings into my peripheral. A flash of light goes off in my skull. Just like the bike accident a light bursts out of the darkness.

The skinny one has sucker-punched me. Right in the same damned eye. The cursed eye where I just had stitches. As he connects another right hook he yells, "Bam!" A word-bubble like in a nineteen seventies Batman episode explodes in my head: BAM. I fall to the pavement.

When I bounce up I turn around. "Alright you fucks!" I'm going to lose but maybe I can make it cost them. But I'm dizzy. The yellow lights swirl. I hear footsteps and laughing.

Then a voice, "Hey you ok?"

When I gain focus I see the would-be muggers running north. The husky one turns and flips me off. I turn around and see a small crowd has stopped under the El watching the scene. A middle-aged dude in a white t-shirt extends his hand and helps me out of the street and back on the curb. It's the loose squares man who's always hustling by the train.

He asks again, "You ok?"

"Yeah man. I'll be alright."

He picks up my hat and hands it to me.

"Thanks."

The crowd goes about their business. I feel for my wallet. It's still there. As I walk across Lake Avenue I dust myself off and climb the stairs into the station. I'm just glad I didn't have any instruments with me today.

On the train I'm staring out the window. Between the lights flashing by I see my reflection in the window. My eye is swelling up again. My jaw hurts. There's a fresh gash on top of the scars from the bike accident.

At Ashland Avenue I transfer to the Pink Line. I'm going to Pilsen the closest neighborhood I know well. My adrenaline is pumping. I have that sick pulsing feeling under my skin that I always get when I'm angry. I'm turning red. I'm shaking. There are some all night Mexican diners where I can get something to eat and cool off.

All my faith in good karma is boiling away. I really thought if I am nice to people they'll be nice to me. I really thought gangsters only bothered rival gangs. I really thought it would be common sense that I wouldn't be worth trying to mug just by looking at me. What a fool I am. If I were dressed like a businessman sporting a Rolex down Pulaski I would say I was asking for it. But my shirt is full of grease from work. My cuffs are burnt from the pizza oven. The helms of my slacks are torn.

People have warned me about living in the hood. Most of the time I felt like they were exaggerating just to show how street smart they were. At best there is a strange note of pride as people tell streetwise stories like: look at what I've seen, Chicago is tough, and I'm tough too. Great. At worst people raise their eyebrows and say something like "I'm not racist but..." and then they say something racist out the side of their mouth like, "It's not safe there. You can tell by looking around... It's pretty shady around there... don't you think?"

My head hurts. I'm rubbing my temples. I don't want to become one of those snotty yuppies judging whole blocks at a time. I'm not going to let this one experience change me. If I want people to judge me as an individual, on a case-by-case basis, I will have to do the same. Most of the people in Garfield Park I've met were nice. Those guys chose to be bad. No one is born bad.

Taking a deep breath I start thinking about when I was their age. Growing up in Wisconsin my friends and I wore our hair long, dressed in black, at the most we'd carry a knife but never use it. We were pretty scary if it was still the nineteen fifties. In parts of Wisconsin it still seems like it is. We'd sell pot. We'd get drunk, go for joy rides, and smash mailboxes with baseball bats. We'd fight each other but always fair fights. No one actually got hurt. We destroyed some material possessions sure, but we never really hurt anyone... maybe just ourselves. Still we were easy targets for the local cops who were bored of writing speeding tickets.

Before my headache has even gone away I begin to realize that if the circumstances were a little different I could have easily been just like the kids who slugged me. If I grew up on the West Side and the only job available was selling smack on the corner for the older guys I'd probably take the gig. It's not much of a leap from selling bags of grass in high school to selling bags of powder. I'd probably resent white people too when they own everything and hold most of the power downtown. Back home me and my guys resented the preppy kids. They had more money. It seemed like they never got molested or thrown in jail. They were more white bread than we were. Of course the difference is that at any time I could easily look preppy if I wanted to. At any time I could cut my hair and try to be what society wanted me to be. I chose to be the way I was. Just like those kids who made the choice to attack me. I asked them why? For fun... That's why. Not because of who I am, but what I seem to symbolize.

In the grand scheme of things they still have fewer choices than I do. They just wanted to prove that they were men. The bar of what it takes to be man might be more extreme on the West Side than where I'm from. They just wanted to know what it felt like to use what little power they have. When I was eighteen I was the same in many ways. I wanted to show I was a man. Of course that was before I learned that a real man doesn't flex his muscle on the street. It takes a lot more strength to love than to hate.

Back in Wisconsin racism seemed like something that happened in a book. It was something that happened far away and long ago. Living in Chicago I know now that is wrong. Racism is alive and well. It's so much easier to judge a whole group of people than take the time to get to know them as individuals one by one. William Blake said, "To generalize is to be an idiot." Even positive generalities are racist. Like all Asians are good at math, or that all black people are good dancers… It's all still stereotypes. Racism isn't something in a sepia photo. As the technological revolution pushes us to move faster and faster no one has time to get to know each other. We should approach each person we meet with an open mind. But this doesn't happen. It's easier just to assume. As I get off the train on 18th Street I tell myself I'm not going to let three assholes turn me into a racist.

After getting some tacos at one of the only places still open on Ashland I find myself in front of my old apartment. The lights are on. Silhouettes are moving behind the shades. My only chance to get out of the elements is to make the attic. I haven't been here in months. Round the block I go, up the back alley, and I squeeze between the buildings. As I reach the side door I can hear my ex talking and laughing with someone with a deep voice. As I tiptoe up the wooden stairwell between apartments a chill goes through me every time there's a pause in the conversation behind the wall. Feeling my way up to the top level in the dark I paw around for the doorknob to the attic. When I clutch the knob and twist it doesn't budge. The door is locked. I pull. The frame shakes. At this point I don't even bother being quiet. Stomping down the stairs I go back outside. The voices hush and shush as I pass my old door.

Police lights strobe across the brick buildings by the gas station on Paulina like some kind of sick nightclub. The flashing blues and reds illuminate and blind in alternating waves. As I pass they seem to x-ray my skull. A young man's body is lying in the road limp and lifeless. The officers unravel yellow crime scene tape as casually as unspooling measuring tape for a new table in a room. It's the third time I've seen a dead body. The first time it's disturbing. The second time concerning. The third time the most disturbing thing is that I'm not disturbed by it anymore. The fact that I'm used to it is the sick thing. I don't want to become numb. I don't want to become hard. I don't want to seem uncaring. The fact is a person can get used to almost anything. As babies we start life crying. Then life wraps our brains in scar tissue. Most leave this world wide-eyed, aware, staring through space, or mercifully, peacefully in sleep. Not the case for this poor soul. He probably never saw it coming. He's young enough to have felt invincible. Young enough to have his life flash before his eyes twice before the light slithered away.

At the corner of Ashland and Roosevelt an old lady sitting on a bench turns to me and asks, "Do you need a woman?" She pushes a swollen tongue out between her gums. The tongue is white and chalky. Her eyes roll back in her head as she chews her tongue at me insinuating something.

Across the street I go inside the Jewel and get a bottle of Canadian Club just as the clerk is about to pull the accordion gate around the liquor aisle. Having paid for my hooch I disappear into the darkness behind the store and into the vacant lots leading up to the rail-yard. Two years ago this area got some press when the City of Chicago first privatized the parking meters. To meet the quota of meters to be man-ufactured for the transition hundreds of these new machines were lined up and down the vacant lots. These streets are pot-holed like the moon. This is no man's land. I sip my whisky as I pass the worthless meters in a place that no one would ever park. It was just another scandal in a town that eats scandals for breakfast.

I first explored this area when I lived in Pilsen. One of my blues history books gave an address to the first house Muddy Waters lived in when he came to Chicago from Mississippi. It was somewhere near 14th and Wood Street. Living nearby and having to take longer and longer walks to avoid fighting with my ex I thought I'd check it out. But the home of the blues legend appeared to have been torn down long ago.

After a good hit from my bottle a clump of trees catches my eye. I need a place to hide. I need a dark place far from cops and crooks alike. Pushing aside a branch I walk into an open space under a small canopy of trees. There are cement steps leading down into an old foundation. A house was once here. The place has been occupied recently. It is a regular hobo jungle. There are rusty cans, broken glass, dirty blankets, and a large metal object in the middle. It looks like a potbelly stove but as my eyes adjust to the darkness I can see more clearly. The object is a sculpture. It's a metal bust of a scarecrow. It has a pointed hat and a pointed nose. It's painted green and the word LEO is inscribed below an insidious grin.

Brushing away some leaves I sit cross-legged and stare point blank at the cosmic fiend. Taking a swig of whisky I fantasize this is Muddy Water's house. Maybe he wrote songs on this very spot.

As I sip the sweet soma the bottle extends like a telescope. Peering down to the bottom I see the moonlight swirl in tiny reflections. I see myself coming back to the spot two years later to verify the existence of the scarecrow, if only to my own mind. He is gone. So are the long cornrows of useless parking meters. The whole area is under a sea of cement. It's now a Costco parking lot sealed away forever. In the meantime I sit, sip, and stare back at the scarecrow. With one eye open I drift in and out of sleep in a sort of delirium.

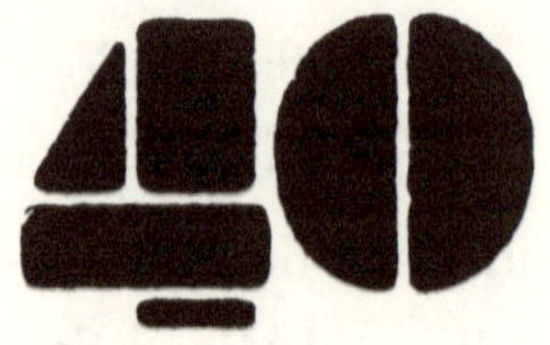

Before I got my busking license on Sundays I would play the Maxwell Street Market. Due to the history of Maxwell Street it is the only place in the city that a musician can play without buying the street performers license. This flea market has been happening for over a hundred years down by Jefferson and Roosevelt. Buskers had been playing the blues at the market before the blues was ever recorded. During what's called the Great Migration black people left the South in droves for the cities in the North. New York, Detroit, Chicago, and all the towns along the Rust Belt promised good jobs working in the factories. It was the promise of a better life.

Since Chicago is a straight shot north of Mississippi it's no wonder the majority of Delta blues musicians who left the farm for the industrialized cities of the North ended up here. Likewise their music became mechanized when the musicians traded their acoustic guitars for electric guitars needed to compete with the ruckus and roar of the city. This is how the electric Chicago blues sound was born. From the train depot downtown people who just arrived from the South wandered into the grid. The first friendly neighborhood where black people were welcomed was affectionately called "Jew Town" in the area around Maxwell Street.

Sometimes you still see ghosts from this era. Once I was

strumming my guitar when a bone thin old woman wearing an ill-fitting sundress danced by on one foot. Her long Einstein like hair was white as snow and she hoisted a massive Bible above her head. Fascinated I watched her dance barefoot in a circle. The Bible seemed impossibly big for her frail arms. Then the crowd panned right and left and swallowed her up in the sea of people.

Always after getting a pastrami on rye from Manny's Deli I would try to shake some scratch at the famous Maxwell Street flea market. There're always carts, booths, tents, and tables filled with tools, toys, fresh produce, art, candles, clothes, soaps, and honestly a lot of junk. Surreal configurations of metal heaped in piles with no obvious purpose lined the displays. As I watched people barter, beg, and buy I'd strum my old guitar wishing I had a louder instrument that could compete with all the bustle and banter.

Presently it's the second week in September. I'm standing in line at the food bank in Evanston with poet Sid Yiddish. Something had caught my eye in the Chicago Reader last week. So I ripped out the page and folded it in my wallet. Standing with Sid I show him the clipping. At the Best Buy off Maxwell Street there is a screening of a new documentary about Chicago blues called *Cheat You Fair*. Bluesman Fernando Jones is going to perform. The filmmakers are going to show clips of the film. Cool. But what really got my attention was that they are raffling off a brand new Fender Delta Blues Resonator.

It's a bright, shiny, perfectly crafted piece of American wood and steel. This is not just a valuable piece of equipment, but the guitar of my dreams. It is the ideal guitar for recording country-blues. It's the perfect axe for busking on loud city streets. The resonator disk provides a natural acoustic amplification mechanism without having to plug into anything. Resonators have that haunting Mississippi blues sound, that chilling clash of brass slide against steel strings that shimmers up the spine and into the imagination. It's a sacred sound to America the way we think the sitar is a sacred sound to India. When that slide twangs across the strings I can hear barbwire through a keyhole peeking at that great rusted sunset beyond the sky.

Taking all the poetic license I please I say as much to Sid at the food bank. He hands me back the clipping. The raffle is next Wednesday.

"Why? Do you think you're really going to win?"

"Actually I think I will." I say this matter-a-factly with no boast or longing. I really feel like I will win this guitar. After all these months hitting streaks of good luck and streaks of bad I feel it in my bones. After predicting all the green lights as I coasted on that bike… after all the corners calling me this way and that seemingly at random… all the streetwise shamanism has come to this crossroads. I tell him I'm due.

"After all that's happened lately the world is about to turn."

"This doesn't sound like you," Sid smirks. "You usually have a skeptical sense of humor like my people. You usually have a more scientific worldview."

"Sometimes clinging to logic is just a defense from going insane. You know what I mean?"

"Sure. People have been calling me a mad poet for years."

"I'm about to cut my damn ear off if something doesn't give."

Wednesday rolls around. I arrive early. I sit in front. They have moved a few shelves and set up a projector and a PA system right in the middle of Best Buy. I look around: gadgets, gizmos, big screen TVs… all the empty promises for happiness that digital culture gives modern man. Is this where the magic will strike? Is this the crossroads? Are souls for sale here? There are big yellow signs: Deal. Sale. Buy Now. Plasma. High speed. Mega-pixel… all buzzwords. There's too many lies here. There's no soul here.

An older black lady sits down next to me. She's early too. The presentation isn't due to begin for another thirty minutes. The woman is dressed in her Sunday best. She's wearing a dark green dress and a church hat with a broad brim. She has strange jade earrings. The design makes them look like Mayan carvings.

Her earrings remind me of traveling to Mexico with my old friend Israel Alpizar. When we were still in school we stayed with his grandparents up in the mountains outside Tula. There we made a short film about shamanism and Mesoamerican culture. While entering a cave in the side of a large mesa called the Cave of Diablo I had found an obsidian arrowhead. Made of black volcanic glass it winked at me in the sun. Locals said the cave was haunted by the devil. In the 1800s bandits used the cave as a hideout. Israel said the part about the outlaws was true, but all the legends about the devil was a rumor spread by the local Catholic church to keep people away from what was really on the mesa: Peyote. Needless to say we did not stay away. We climbed to the top of the mesa. Strange gods formed in the clouds. We tried to film what only our eyes could see and the video camera could never record. As I sit and remember Mexico I smile to myself.

The woman is pleasantly texting on her phone. I lean over and tell her, "I like your earrings."

"Why thank you!"

The lady and I make small talk. We talk about the weather, what kind of food we like, the spike in crime over the summer. Normally I would never do this. Most of the time I feel inhibited. I've been a lone wolf most of my life. I act cool just because I'm introverted. This is one of the reasons why I waste so much of my pocket money on alcohol. Most people drink socially. Sometimes I drink to be social at all. But these last months I have shaken off the last of that country boy shyness by playing guitar on the street, hustling, and chatting people up.

The filmmakers and the musicians arrive.

Fernando Jones comes in wearing a wide brim hat and a loud bluesman suit. He plugs in his guitar and starts tuning up.

"What's all this?" the woman asks me. I tell her about the music, the documentary, and the raffle.

"Oh I was just sitting down to rest my feet."

Fernando Jones starts the show with a high wail. A man sporting a soul patch bobs along on bass. It's great to hear some swampy blues blasting away in the middle of a sterile store like Best Buy. Shoppers stop and rubberneck wondering what all the howling is about.

What amazes me most about Fernando Jones is that he is without ego. He doesn't show off with endless guitar solos. He gets everyone involved. He wants everyone to participate. He knows how to get everyone to sing along. At the expense of the song he'll walk into the audience and ask anyone within reach to strum the guitar for him. As he wanders into the small crowd he tells the bass player to go ahead and take the lead vocals. Mr. Jones understands that the blues isn't about idolizing the performer, like it is in pop music, but getting everyone on the same level. If you break down the line between the stage and the audience you have magic. Otherwise you might as well be at home watching TV.

Next the filmmakers give a little talk and play some clips of the documentary *Cheat You Fair* on the projector. There's all this great footage of the flea market in the sixties and seventies. The director explains the title. "It's an old saying on Maxwell Street. Some of the wares for sale there might be hot. Some of the items might not be worth what they are being sold for. Everyone understands that they are being hustled a bit, but no one really cares because it never gets to the point where anyone is really getting ripped off." After a clip of Robert Nighthawk telling it like it is on his electric guitar I lean over and tell my new friend that I've played music on Maxwell Street myself.

"Oh, good for you," she says.

Finally it's time for the main event: the raffle. Fernando Jones pulls out the Fender Resonator. It's even more beautiful in person. The amber sunburst finish makes it look like it was forged in the sun. The silver disk in the body of the guitar flashes under the corporate track lighting of Best Buy.

The director unravels a spool of red raffle tickets. Everyone gets one free ticket just for being there. Starting with me in the front I tear off my ticket. Next my friend sitting by me tears hers as he continues through the crowd.

"I got number eighty two."

"Mine's eighty three," she says.

"Would you believe I was born in nineteen eighty three?"

"Oh no," she smiles. "You're gonna make me feel old. Let's just say I'm closer to being eighty three years total."

The director gets on the PA and announces, "If anyone would like to purchase a DVD copy of the movie for twenty dollars you'll receive an extra raffle ticket." People line up to get the DVD along with an extra ticket. Some people are buying one, two, three copies along with one, two, three extra tickets.

I think: cheat you fair indeed. More tickets means the odds of winning goes up exponentially. As usual I'm broke. I can't increase my chances for the guitar like everyone else. As this goes on I noticed a sign by the DVDs that states: Purchase of this DVD will NOT increase your chances to win the raffle... So much for that.

I look around. Most of the crowd are dressed like tourists. Some are shoppers with bags of gizmos still in hand. The only people that look like they even play guitar are students from Fernando's class. He explained he teaches a class on the blues at Columbia College. Despite the hand over fist exchange of cash, DVDs, and little red raffle tickets I know nobody wants the guitar more than I do. No one needs it more than I do.

The director opens up a second box filled with DVDs. He's clearing out his inventory. You gotta respect a good hustle but at this moment my confidence about winning the raffle wanes.

"Oh my," the woman next to me says. "How long is this going to take?"

"I don't know."

"Well it's getting too late for me. Here you take my ticket. I don't need no guitar." I thank her up and down. Now at least I have two tickets in the game. It looks like they are finally going to start the drawing. A large fish bowl is passed around. One half of each ticket is torn and placed in the bowl. I rub mine together for luck, tear, and drop. I look over my shoulder for the lady in the jade earrings. I want to tell her they are starting. Are you sure you want to leave? But there's no sign of her. POOF. She's gone.

The big moment is here.

The director asks Fernando Jones if he would do the honors and pull the winning ticket? Mr. Jones shakes his head. "I have my students here. I'll never hear the end of it if one of the kids wins when the others don't."

The director motions to a slender lady in black who has been weaving around the whole event taking pictures with a bulky professional camera. She furrows her brow and reluctantly steps up. Obviously she's working. She just wants to do her job and go home. But for that reason she's probably the only person here without a raffle ticket or part of the show.

"What do I do?" she asks with a distinguished Russian accent.

The director smiles at her. "Just reach in and pick one."

He gives the bowl one final shake. She reaches in and snaps her hand back. Her camera dangles around her neck as she holds the ticket with both hands close to her eyes.

She mumbles, "Eighty three."

There are groans of disappointment. Half the crowd is getting up to leave. But I'm not sure I heard correctly. What happened?

"Eighty three?" I ask. "Did you say eighty three? Oh my God!"

Walking up to them in a daze the director confirms my ticket stub. The winner is the ticket the old woman had so kindly given me: eighty three.

The director looks up from the ticket and smiles, "Bingo."

In a blur the guitar is in my hands. They are nudging me gently to line up with Mr. Jones and the filmmakers for photos. Positioned between them the photographer is back to work bending down on one knee snapping the shutter. The flash strobes away in my face. I smile nervously. I'm not used to being a winner.

The photographer's lens cap snaps on. The crowd drifts away like a riptide. Fernando Jones slaps me on the back and I almost fall over. The director hands me the bulky box the resonator came in. Then he's gone too.

Standing there with my treasure a pimply kid in a blue Best Buy vest starts folding up the chairs. A janitor impatiently sweeps around me.

Now my feet are moving. I gallop away with my magic guitar in its big awkward box. Out in the parking lot I call Sid Yiddish. I want to tell him I told you so. Wait until he hears this, the Doubting Thomas… But when he answers the phone the heart of the matter comes out. I start blubbering. The words turn into sobs.

"Wes is that you? Are you okay? Are you hurt?"

"No, no, no…"

He says, "It's all right. It's all right. Let it out. Take your time."

I manage to spit out: "I… I felt like I was going to win… and then I did…"

Finally I choke out what happened.

"Good for you Wes. No one deserves it more than you. You're gonna make a great record now."

I tell Sid I'm sorry about all the times I was impatient with him. Back when we were in a band I would make little jokes at his expense. I tell I am sorry about all the times I was sarcastic with him. I tell him he really is my good friend. We talk for a while. For once it isn't about the past or the future, or plans, or poems, or songs, or gigs, or no gigs… just the moment… now and forever.

Walking down Roosevelt not knowing where I'm going it's getting dark. I want to go to the practice space as fast as possible and get started.

As I cross the Roosevelt Bridge over the river I rise over the vacant lots and over the smokestacks. I watch the lights of the Loop dance up to the stars. The moon comes out smiling. I'm so happy I punch the air with my fist. My brain is on fire. My feet are floating. The water in the river below shimmers. I feel a million electric beams streaming out my pores. The pavement melts away under my feet.

When I get to the other side of the bridge a new feeling rises in my gut. I feel scared. I have won and lost before. Luck has come and gone before. But I never felt so strongly that something would happen and then it did. It felt like magic. It felt like intention. I've read my share of mysticism, shamanism, and ceremonial magic. I've met psychedelic crusaders who believe consciousness precedes matter. I've repeated what they've said at parties. I've explained this philosophy over cocktails. I've written poems using these elements. But in my core I never believed in all that mind over matter shit… not really. All that New Age philosophy is a beautiful hippie dream, but hard times in Chicago has kicked a lot of that art school pretention out of me.

Stopping on the corner of State and Roosevelt I try to catch my breath. I don't feel so good anymore. What if all that mystic bullshit is true? What if I have been wrong all this time? Then what else am I wrong about? Maybe there is a god? Maybe there is a devil? Perhaps they're both inside of me?

I feel sick. I feel nauseous like I'm going to throw up. I feel paranoid. What if I am more powerful than I know? What if I made all this happen? The guitar… sleeping outdoors… the free bike… the bike accident… even getting beat up… all of it. I wanted to have an adventure and boy I got what I asked for. I wanted this to happen… I wanted this… I wanted to be free. I wanted to do whatever I wanted. Is this what it looks like? Free will functioning in a deterministic framework? All the whispers of fate and faith fill my ears. As I stand motionless holding my new guitar I am gagging on my own cynicism. I don't want to believe in this stuff. That would mean everything is up to me. That means everything is my fault. That means I have to be on my guard all the time. Even the bad stuff I made happen with my will. Was I punishing myself? I might be free, horribly free, but can one ever be free from one's self?

The blues is surrounded with amulets, mojos, daddy-jacks, Santeria, Voodoo. The songs and lives of bluesmen are filled with sexual spells, evil women, selling your soul to the devil for fame, and redemption with god. Push a psychic pin into the ether… you always get what you wanted… though you may have wanted the wrong things… Best Buy indeed.

Still standing on the corner I start talking out loud. I'm that guy on the street talking to himself. I'm talking to the universe. I'm talking to whatever is behind the great vale… I have my magic guitar. What more do I want? What more can I make happen? But be careful. What if it backfires like a monkey's paw? Be careful what you wish for. Don't do anything. Don't move. Stay still. Think before you say anything. Think before you even think!

Is this the fear of being powerful? That the magic actually works? Or maybe it is the fear that I'm not actually charmed, infallible, or fated. Maybe it was just luck. And what's luck? What's fate? What's faith? What's destiny? These are just words defined by more words. We grasp at these inter-dimensional forces with our little words.

I'm inside out. What's worse? Being powerless and thrown about in the cosmic currents chaotically riding on waves of faith and luck? Or having the responsibility of ruling the waves, storms, swells, or calm waters all responding to my inner whims?

Oh god or devil, Earth or universe, love and life thank you. If you just keep helping me I'll be good. I just want to make things. I just want to write songs. I just want to write things that make people laugh, cry, feel good, and think about the world in different ways. I don't want anything more. I don't want the impossible. I don't want to live forever. I don't want immortality. I don't want strange powers. I don't even want to believe in all this stuff. It's all too much. I don't want there to be an afterlife. Really? Live forever? Is a man's work never done?

No, I just want to make things, have a blast and then go to bed with no worries. I just want to find love, have a great life, here on this planet, and then go to sleep forever. The Earth is enough. Beauty is enough. Love is enough. Life is enough. Let whatever I make live on. That's it. Let whatever I leave behind make the biggest wave. Let whatever I make catch fire and have a life of its' own. That's my prayer. I'll be good. I promise. I'll drink less. I'll eat better. I'll really practice guitar day and night. I'll take better care of myself. I'll be nicer to people. Whatever it takes. Great. Fine. Deal? Agreed. But now what?

I feel down into myself. I fear my luck is running out. I feel like my karma is at the end of a cycle. Maybe it's the paranoia, but I want to get my new guitar off the street. I feel like something is watching me. I feel like this sinner is at one end of the pendulum, and it's about to swing back. A good thing happens and then a bad thing comes along. Even-steven forever. Despite the cause or the philosophic reasons this is the way things are despite whether the karma comes from the inside or the outside, from the subconscious or the universe. I had just tempted fate once by walking my plasma-screen monitor through streets of want and need. Maybe those kids who slugged me were a sign? Maybe those would-be muggers were a warning? Or maybe that's all gibberish. Maybe I've been hit on the head one too many times. People always search for philosophy to explain what they are feeling, and right now I feel magical. It's beautiful, but disorientating. Whatever the reason I change my mind about lugging my new treasure to the hood. Suddenly I'm not so bold. Suddenly I have something to lose.

Guitar Mike, my old band mate, lives nearby. I scurry to his building and ring his buzzer. Nothing. I think: what am I doing? I call him on his phone and get his voicemail. I leave him a message howling for joy.

I text Trudy. Nothing.

Finally someone answers the phone. It's Matt Jensen. I tell him what happened.

"Hey buddy can I crash with you tonight? … Yeah? … No I never really worry about myself, but tonight I just wanna get my new guitar off the street… Yeah I'm materialistic now… Yeah being a property owner has made me find religion… Right? I know… Crazy… Say I appreciate it. I'll bring over some food… Great… What you want? Gyros sound good? … Cool." I hit the Red Line.

It's a beautiful Indian summer's eve. I order two gyros plates at the little diner where Clark meets Halsted. As I wait I sit outside at the bus stop in the soft air with my prize. On the end of the bench I spot a bottle. It's a pint of blackberry brandy. I check it. It's unopened. I'm about to pocket it when I think: nice try universe. I said I would be good. I place it back on the bench. The dude in the paper hat slaps the bell. "Order up!" My food is ready. The grease from the fries drips through the bag. This ain't no healthy choice either.

At Matt's we sit cross-legged on the floor and munch our food. I relive the story for him. "You want to celebrate?" he asks.

"Yeah but I told myself I wasn't going to drink so much."

"Ok. That's cool."

"Plus I only have food money until the end of the week anyway."

I'm pacing around. I pick up the guitar. Put it down again. I'm not sure if I can sleep. I'm too excited.

"Tell you what. I've been saving some cigars for a special occasion." Matt starts digging around in his desk. "They're called Bongani's. They're made in Africa."

After our feast we adjourn like gents to the fire escape and light up. Leaning on the railing we puff and tap our ash into the alley below. My mind quiets again. I tap my stogy and a fat cherry descends like a firefly. It lands by some liter size bottles down below. Pointing at the bottles I tell Matt about the black berry brandy I found.

Matt chokes on his smoke laughing. "What the fuck is going on with you? You're like a genie. You gotta go down there and see if you summoned some booze."

Inside I descend the back stairs and push out the rusty door into the alley. Sure enough there's a full bottle of gin and a bottle of vodka peacefully sitting by the recycling bin. Are these temptations? Are these my desires manifesting? Are these tests? Contradictions bounce in my mind. Most likely someone else in the building had the same idea of sobering up a bit and cleaned out their liquor cabinet. Rather than discard good hooch into the dirty bin they left it for the next alley cat to come along. God, devil, Dionysus, or myself… someone is saying have your night. It's time to celebrate.

Back inside Matt can't believe it. He has some lime concentrate and we pour the gin over ice to make Lime Rickeys. Cheers.

"What's going on with you? You're having the luckiest day. Can you manifest a girlfriend for me?"

"I'll try. Right after I find one."

Matt shakes his head. "We've got to test this! Here let's play a game of black jack and see what happens."

"Ok."

He pulls out a pack of Bicycles, shuffles, and deals the cards. I bust over twenty-one three times in a row. Apparently the streak is over. But I don't need luck anymore. Now I create my own luck.

I've decided. There are no coincidences. I've made up my mind. I'm *making* up my mind.

More and more I have become Cousin Bones. I have become the character I created. Now at open mics I sign up as Cousin Bones. At the practice space the recording of my demo is rolling along swiftly under the name Cousin Bones. The songs are sounding good with my magic guitar. Before when my band was called Cousin Bones we'd write songs that told stories, now that I am Cousin Bones the stories are written in the first person. For Halloween I don't even wear a costume. At parties I just wear what is now my normal clothes: my flat cap, my overalls, and my new guitar slung around my waist. No one questions it. No one asks: what are you supposed to be? It's mind over matter.

Out of the blue Trudy asks me out for Halloween night. She just turned twenty-one and wants to see all the bars. Following her and her roommate's text messages like a trail of breadcrumbs from place to place I finally catch up with them at the Flatiron Building in Wicker Park. It's crowded inside. It's hot. It's sweaty. I prefer my old man bars. All her roommates are holding court at a table in the back. I recognize her roommate Chloe. I sit down and look for Trudy. Then I see her standing nearby.

Dressed as a zombie nurse Trudy is making out with some skinny hipster. Her roommates see her too. They see me see this. The roommate dressed in a Wonder Woman costume starts calling her name. "Trudy!

Trudy! Wes is here." But the music is too loud. I get up and leave. She's young. She's still spreading her wings. Let her live her life. My bike messenger friends have told me about a house party on the other side of the park.

Twenty minutes later I'm getting texts from Trudy: I'm so sorry… Come hang out with us… We're going to the Mutiny… Wait, now we're going to a party…

Next she butt dials me in a cab. I can hear the girls yelling over each other giving the cab driver conflicting directions. I'm used to this. My name is at the end of the alphabet. When your name is Wes everyone butt dials you. When this happens sometimes I eavesdrop on the phantom caller. But I don't listen long to Trudy. I hang up. What is she? Another temptation? A siren? Did I manifest her too? Perhaps. Trudy is the polar opposite of my ex-girlfriend in every way. Just like I wanted. Did I conjure her? Linda my ex was always uptight and jealous. She wanted to fight all the time. Trudy is almost too laissez faire. Her attitude is lets just hang out and have fun. You can have me but you can't really have me. This brings its own headaches. I tell myself: I'm a bluesman. I get jealous.

Finding the house party across the park is easy. It's a rager. The crowd is leaping to the Misfits. Kids are dressed in drag and draped in kitsch. The hosts have taken Halloween to its roots. The remains of a pagan feast fume in the kitchen. Two goat carcasses are plucked dry on the table. Goat ribs stick out like beams of a rotted pirate ship. The severed heads of the thorny beasts hang skinned and impaled on poles. Snot and brains ooze out the skulls.

Unable to find Nicolai, Byorn, or the rest of the bike messengers I end up in the backyard where a campfire flickers and the vibe is more chill. That is until two guys dressed as Nazi Officers stroll across the yard. They have all the props: hats with S.S. insignias and armbands with swastikas.

I put down my beer. "Pretty tasteless costumes."

"Oh they're not costumes."

One of the hosts is sitting by the fire. He stands up and says, "Get the fuck out of my party!"

The Nazi punks sneer but comply.

Back inside Metallica is blasting on the stereo. The goat heads have been plucked from the spires and are being paraded around in the mosh-pit. Dead snot oozes down from the goats in ten-inch strands.

Swiping another beer from the fridge I hit the sidewalk. I can hear my phone buzzing in my overalls. Trudy texts me. They're on Damen. They're close by. What the hell? The cab rolls up. It's full. The cabbie pops the trunk and I set my guitar down inside. Then I squeeze into the backseat. Trudy sits on my lap.

The girls are singing and talking and calling and texting. They're having a great night. It's a real Hallows Eve to remember as long as they don't black out. Happy birthday Satan. The ladies take turns speaking in the voice of their costume. Wonder Woman flexes her arms, and the zombie nurse growls. We laugh. I'm in character too. I'm Cousin Bones.

"Are any of your friends single?" I ask Trudy. "I want to find my friend Matt a girlfriend."

"We're all single!" she cries.

After going in circles for twenty minutes Trudy says to the gang, "The bars are about to close anyway. Let's just go back to the apartment."

There's groans and conjecture but we end up telling the cabbie to head to Logan Square. At the curb we exit the cab like a clown car. Everyone falls out the door in a pile. From behind the zombie make-up full of scars and rot Trudy whispers in my ear and leads me upstairs by the hand.

Later as I enter a deep sleep a red-hot alarm goes off in the center of my head. I spring up like a mousetrap. "My guitar!"

Trudy stirs. "What are you talking about?"

"My guitar! I left it in the cab."

"Oh shit," she says rubbing her eyes.

Fishing my phone out of my overalls I ask her, "Do you remember what cab company it was?"

"I don't know." Trudy gets up sleepily, puts on a robe, and crosses the hallway. In the bathroom she starts washing the zombie make-up off her face.

"Was it Yellow? Checker? Flash Cab? What are those maroon ones? Carriage Cab?"

"It was yellow!" she yells from across the hall.

Using Trudy's laptop I go out onto the screen porch and look up every cab company in Chicago. Starting with Yellow Cab I call each one and make lost and found reports. I describe the guitar. I give the pick-up spot and the drop off. I even describe the other passengers. "There was a zombie nurse… a Wonder Woman… I think someone was a cat… I was in overalls…" It all sounds so stupid. How are they going to find my guitar in a city of over three million people and how many cabs? On Halloween? The most chaotic party night of the year…

After all the calls out on the porch I sit in the dark and stew. That guitar was a gift. It felt like the universe gave it to me, and I fucked it up. It's the only nice thing I have. I feel like I was meant to have it. I'm not Cousin Bones. I'm not a bluesman. I'm no genie. No shaman. I am not magical. I'm an idiot. I'm the village idiot. I'm a fucking moron.

As I quietly verbally abuse myself on the porch I see one of Trudy's roommates through the screen window leading back into the kitchen. She stumbles to the fridge in her underwear and opens to the door. As she takes a long pull from a quart of orange juice the light from the fridge pours through the window onto my face. I see it's Wonder

Woman. When she sees me her eyes bulge thinking: who's this dirty old man in my house?

Suddenly my phone lights up.

"Hello?"

"Uh yeah hi there. This is Doug calling from Yellow Cab. Are you the guy who called about the missing guitar?"

"Yeah yeah, that's me!"

"Can you describe it again?"

I do.

"Okay great. The driver found it…"

"Thank you! Thank you!"

"No problem. It was just a matter of getting on the radio and announcing your lost and found report."

"You're the best! Man, you're the best."

"He's on the way to where you were dropped off. You are still there correct?"

"Yeah I'm here."

"Now, it is expected that you pay the fare from where the driver stopped and checked the trunk back to your address. Okay?"

"Good. Great. I'll pay him whatever."

"Great. Happy Halloween."

Trudy is long asleep, but Wonder Woman lends me her keys so I can go outside and meet the cabbie. Outside sitting on the curb I sit picking my head. I wasn't watching the signs. I was ignoring all the signals. I have to be more careful.

I remember what Shanghai Mike said about the Robert Johnson myth. "The devil's bargain is a suckers bet. The deal always backfires. The devil always comes to collect. There are no shortcuts. There are no easy answers."

All this mind over matter shit means nothing if you don't follow through with the actual work. You can dress up in a costume all you want but it means nothing without the music.

I need to practice. I need to record my songs. I need to express all the things Chicago has taught me.

The cab pulls up. The driver is a nice little grey man with round glasses. He pops the trunk and smiles, "I knew it had to be you guys."

"Thank you so much sir." I pay the meter plus a thirty-dollar tip, which is practically everything I have. There will be no beer money for a while. I have to stay focused.

Not sure which cross street this is. The signs have been taken down. Each corner has a new building. I sense they are vacant. The walls of these new skyscrapers are made of mirrors. As I pluck the banjo the notes bounce up to the empty sky. I catch my reflection in one of the monoliths. I'm white as a ghost. My skin looks like dried fruit. I just came from the plasma clinic. It seemed to take longer than usual. During the second cycle when they return my blood to my arm the liquid appeared brown in the tube. It didn't seem alarming because a sense of euphoria followed.

A cop car pulls up to the curb. Tammy is in the backseat. What kind of trumped up charge did they pin on Tammy? But her door opens. She stumbles to her feet, "That's him! He tried to force himself on me!" Waves of fear flood my body.

The officer is out of the squad too. "Alright there buddy," he starts in a thick Chicago accent. "Let me see your street performers license." He resembles the man with the flattop who gave me a polygraph during that job interview months ago, but it's hard to tell. His aviators are mirrored.

"Sure officer." I point to the cup on the sidewalk, but my license isn't there. It should be in its spot clipped to the rim. The cop crosses his arms. "Hold on. I got it." I search my guitar case. I search my pockets.

I can't seem to find it. My hands get stuck in my pants. It's as if my pockets are sewn around my wrists. I struggle in my slacks.

"See," Tammy cries. "He's playing with himself! He's a pervert."

The cop unfolds his arms. He reaches around his belt for his cuffs. "Best you come down to the station. We'll have your license on file downtown."

Fear snaps like a reflex. Now I am running. There is no use thinking about it. I'm not going to lose Shanghai Mike's banjo.

"Stop! You fucking punk! Stop! I'll shoot!"

I pump my limbs. Sweat pours out of my skin. The stench of whisky follows me like a perfume. I look down. The banjo is in one hand. The needle from the plasma clinic is stuck in the other arm. The tube dangles in the air as I run.

As I cut through a vacant lot I sneak a glance behind me. The cop is nowhere to be seen, but a gang of kids is chasing me. "Narc! … Po-po! …5-0!" they yell. The runners pause to pick up rocks and hurl them at me. Stones fall around me. I dart around old tires and a burning mattress. To my right is an entrance to a tunnel under the Metra tracks. The gate is ajar. I slide through the opening finding shelter from the flying stones. Scrambling in the shadows I find some steps.

It's dark down here. Pipes drip overhead. Lights covered in cobwebs flicker from the ceiling. Hot steam press machines fume in the patches of light. There is a steel door in the side of the wall. The handle has a lock with a punch code. I key in numbers but the door won't budge.

I look at the graffiti on the walls. It's as if the tags are codes telling me which way to turn. There's a stencil that says: SOLVE. A piece of graffiti says: COUSIN BONES. Seeing this I lose my footing. I splash into water. Clinging to the banjo like a tiny raft I float in black water. The current pours through brick tunnels. Waves crest reflecting lights ahead. Riding the banjo I come to a subway station. Have the

CTA tunnels flooded? The platform is filled with commuters in rubber Halloween masks. Ghouls, demons, vampires, zombies grin at me as I wash pass.

At the next station I see Brett the owner of the practice space. He's on the platform with all my stuff. All my bags of clothes, books, instruments are stacked in a neat row. "Found all your stuff shithead! It's mine now." I try to yell back at him but the current drags me on.

Approaching another station there are four figures on the platform. As I grow near I see who they are: it's SOLVE, Tommy James, Mr. Fish, and Kenny. I call out to them, but they don't seem to hear me. On the opposite platform a light approaches in the tunnel. They turn to meet their train and disappear in the haze.

The next patch of light is not a station at all. I see my ex-girlfriend Linda in a spotlight. She has cut her wrists again. She holds them out to me. She has an odd smile on her face as if she is flirting with me. Blood drips down her forearms. "Go on. You can lick them." She motions her open wrists to me like some sort of bizarre foreplay. She drips blood on my face. She covers me in the hot liquid. I cry out. My mouth is filled. I am drowning. Infused with the taste of metal I find myself going under.

When I come to the surface I am in a whirlpool. The sewer surges like a dirty galaxy. I am stuck rotating around a black hole in slow motion. Above a shape solidifies out of the darkness. A dark tower made of three tiers comes into focus. Three judges sit stoically on three benches high as the Sears Tower. Their heads hover in space and nod down towards me. As I swirl below I see that the panel of judges consists of Howling Wolf, John Lee Hooker, and Robert Johnson. I wave towards them. I'm met with stiff lips and narrowing eyes. The three bluesmen seem to be in deep thought as they consider this squirming specimen.

To my left I hear a loud speaker. It's the Preacher from State Street. He's in a rowboat. As always he's dressed in his black suit and red bow tie. Two altar boys heave the heavy oars as the Preacher orates from a megaphone. "This boy stands accused of stealing black music from the blues gods. He's been passing himself off as a bluesman." It seems the Preacher is the prosecutor.

I jump when I feel a hand on my shoulder. My neck clicks to my right. I see Ken, my college recruiter, next to me. He floats in the murky water because his body is in the shape of a guitar, but it's him all right. His sandy blonde hair and wispy mustache adorn his head, which bobs in the water at the end of the guitar neck.

"What are you doing here?"

"I'm your public defender." Ken motions to some papers resting on the resonator disk in the belly of the guitar. "Sign here and all the charges will be dropped. Student loans gone, you'll be debt free, and people will like your music."

"What's the catch?"

He smiles like a coiling snake.

"How can I sell my soul when I'm not sure souls exist?"

"Then it's an easy bargain. You won't miss what you don't believe in."

"I want to find my soul, not lose it." I push his papers into the grimy water. They disappear like octopi in spools of bleeding ink. Meanwhile the guitar is filling with water. It goes under along with Ken's urgent eyes. Bubbles bounce from the abyss. Somehow this fuels the whirlpool, which begins to gain momentum.

As the water spins more violently the Preacher demands the altar boys to row harder. Over the megaphone he chants, "Stroke, stroke, stroke… It's getting harder now!"

I peer up at the three bluesmen draped in black robes. Behind the judges' bench is a crucifix. It seems to grow. As it comes into focus I begin to sense this is no artist depiction. The figure is alive. Christ on the cross writhes in pain. My stomach goes cold. Telepathically I feel the words: You write songs about problems? Fathom this. Blood and tears fill the void. I spiral into the black hole in the center of the whirlpool.

A pair of red eyes glows in the darkness. A rat made of tar moves closer in slow motion. His body is long. It extends and contracts as he inches forward. When he grins his teeth glow. It crawls towards me like a sloth as if to hypnotize me. His paws have suction cups on the ends. Like some sort of supernatural salamander a transparent tongue extends and licks his eyelid. The tongue frames the eye and serves as a monocle to get a better look at me. He grins as he reaches towards me tar dripping from his suction cups.

Feeling another rodent run over me I shake out of the nightmare. I sit up. Awake again. The demo is almost done. My magic guitar sounds better than anything I could have imagined. But I can't sleep very well in the practice space. I'm running a space heater now to stay warm. As it gets colder more mice are coming inside. I wake up at night throwing shoes and fighting them off. The carpet smells like rodent feces. I've come to realize I won't be able to make it through the winter here.

In the morning I call Matt. I tell him my latest plans. Kenny at the Gallery has agreed to let me put on a big weekend show. My old friend from school Israel Alpizar has a great new band called Donoma. They're going to come down from Wisconsin after having success playing Summerfest in Milwaukee. Since I'm the acoustic act I'm going to open up the show. Donoma is a big powerful rock band with some psychedelic elements. I told them how The Smashing Pumpkins got their start at the Gallery back in the day. They're excited. Shanghai Mike is going to MC and perform some spoken word pieces. The gig will also serve as the release party for my demo. I ask Matt if he'd be willing to run video projectors during the show.

"I'd love to. Sounds fun."

"Get this. We're calling it Psychedelic Puke Fest."

He laughs, "That's crazy."

"You know what? I think this is going to be the last hurrah for me."

"What do you mean?"

"If I stay here I'm gonna get sick or freeze to death."

"Man that sucks."

"After the fest I'm gonna jump ship."

"What are you going to do?"

"Maybe hop a train to New Orleans."

"That sounds like one of your songs."

"Yeah. More likely take a Greyhound bus ride back to Wisconsin with my tail between my legs."

"Damn. Well, I guess most of our friends from college have left Chicago. Either moved to L.A. or back to their hometowns."

First I have a gig with poets Janet Kuypers and Sid Yiddish on the border of Wisconsin at some roadhouse. To my surprise Trudy asks to go on the trip. Sid, Trudy, and I stuff into Sid's little blue Saturn still on the donut and drive up to the border. She hears me do my songs for the first time. The next day Trudy and I take the Metra back to Chicago whooping it up over a pint of whisky as we watch the world fly by. At Union Station downtown she says, "Let's just do it. Let's be exclusive. You should come live with me."

"What will your roommates think of that?"

"Oh, they love you. Don't worry about it. We'll adopt you."

So I move in. It's warm. It's peaceful. Frost is forming on the windows like elaborate coral and floral, but that's on the other side of the glass.

Still I'm wary that this could end as fast it begins. So I keep paying for the practice space. Trudy's roommates have boyfriends now too. Though Wonder Woman seems to take longer to decide who she's going to hibernate with. All of us go down the block to The Street Side bar. Using her mascara Trudy draws a caricature of me on a cocktail napkin. "Can I use this as the cover art for my demo?" Her roommate Chloe is majoring in photography and takes some promo pics of me in my Cousin Bones gear.

It's December. It's time for Psychedelic Puke Fest at The Gallery Cabaret. I am at my favorite place. I have my magic guitar. I'm dressed in my hat and overalls. I'm selling copies of my solo demo: Blues Bum. I am happy.

Most importantly all my friends are here. Matt is running the projections. Crazed visions crawl across the walls that seem to interpret the music. Trudy is here with all her roommates. Israel Alpizar and his band are playing next. My old band mate Guitar Mike has come to see me. When I play our old songs he sings along from the crowd. Everyone is here: Shanghai Mike, Sid Yiddish, JT, Nathan Xander, Mr. Blue, even Tammy is here. Of course Kenny is here, Zeola, Nicolai, Bjorn, Bandi, Daniel Stine, Janet Kuypers, Mr. Sunshine, Cathleen Schandelmeier, and somehow even Rodrigo my old plasma clinic buddy has heard about it. All the fellow blues jammers and barflies came out: Mr. Fish, Kay G, Garrett, Nate Marsh, Dobro Joe, Michael McDowell, Little Joey, Texas Fred, Izzy the Head, Cowboy Charlie, Art the Grey Ghost, and even David Russell the drummer from the subway. The only person missing is the old bluesman Tommy James if that was even his real name. And maybe the old woman who gave me the raffle ticket that won me my guitar. I imagine my old friend SOLVE is still with us in some way. Suddenly I feel like I was never really alone.

When I play *Village Idiot* everyone laughs and claps along. When I play *At The Plasma Clinic* everyone sings along with the chorus.

It touches my heart. It doesn't get any better. It's like god kissed me on the end of a breeze. After all the hard times simple pleasures magnify. I don't have any more questions. I know where I've been. I know why I'm here. I'm a lucky bum. I am going to be alright. All my friends are going to be alright. Together Chicago is going to make it through another winter.

LOW CARB SPEC
ONLY 7.00 + TA
4 EGGS
HAM
BACON
FRUI
ORAN
Lorraine's Diner
Breakfast
Lunch
Dinner
Lorraine's Diner
WE HAVE BITCHY WAITRESSES AND DIRTY DISHES - BUT DAMN GOOD FOOD!
MLET SPECIAL
ONLY $6.00 + T
ONION
GREEN
OPEN
24
HOURS
ATM
inside
OPEN
24
HOURS
ATM
inside
NO
TURN
ON RED
7AM-7PM
ATM
DOUBLE
DEAL
STEAK &
EGGS
OPEN
ATM
"LORRAINE'S DINER
1959 CHICA
OPEN 24 HRS
HOME OF THE B
STEAK & EGG
BISCUITS & GR

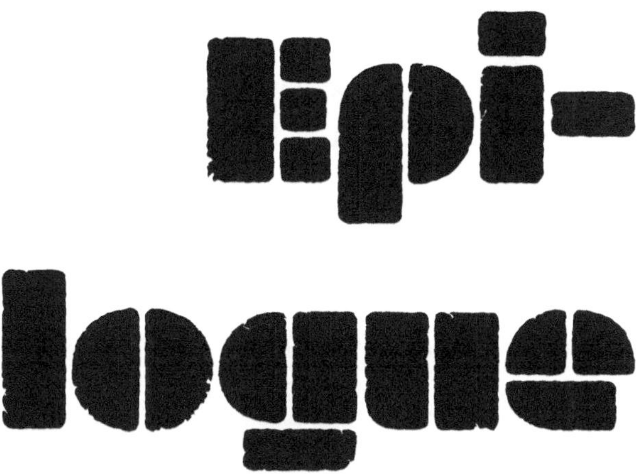

After my set at Psychedelic Puke Fest at the Gallery Cabaret I found myself sitting next to Sid Yiddish at the bar. As he nursed a club soda he asked me, "So you moved in with Trudy eh?"

"Yup."

"Does she have a mother or an aunt? Someone my age?"

"Yeah back east somewhere."

"Is it like the old Chicago joke that young ladies always pick a dude to date during the winter? That way they have a warm body to curl up against only to dump the poor schmo in the spring." I think: Sid you Doubting Thomas.

"Maybe," I say. "Or more likely the other old Chicago joke."

"Which one?"

"What do you call a musician without a girlfriend?"

"What?

"Homeless."

That's the whole season in a nutshell. Fucking punch lines.

After New Year's Eve and 2011 began I used Trudy's laptop to apply for jobs on Craigslist where I landed a full-time job dispatching taxi. As it turned out it was the same cab company where I had drunkenly left my guitar in the trunk of a cab on Halloween. Doug, the dispatcher who found my magic guitar, became my coworker and I would buy him lunch regularly. Once I had a full time job again I was back on my feet. My new college age roommates were pleased. I gave each of the girls fifty bucks a month, which is a lot when you're still in school. We were flush with groceries through the snows of January and February. If it weren't for them I would have skipped town. Busking would have been impossible during the Chicago winter.

Joining the cab company meant quitting Dominick's and saying goodbye to my friends Bandi, Joy, Roxy, Gloria, Charlotte, Mr. Sunshine, Chet, and Moe. Yet on March 30th 2011 when they tore down the last tower of the Cabrini Green Projects I went down to Halsted and Division. Some of my old co-workers were there watching too. Bandi said she was glad they were gone, but as she said this she had tears in her eyes. I asked her why. She said she didn't know. It was hard growing up there, but still the towers had been her home.

It wasn't long after that Dominick's closed all their locations in Chicago. Jewel-Osco bought most of the stores, some of my co-workers were out of a job, but most of my friends like Bandi merely changed uniforms.

It's a funny old feeling getting lost in the modern world. When I first came to Chicago I was chasing some nostalgia in my heart for a Chicago that was gone long before I was even born. Images of nineteen thirties gangster films reeled in my head full of speakeasies, jazz bands, bums, bohemians, and blues singers. That world was long gone and never really existed as it does in the imagination. But in another sense I found exactly what I was looking for.

Now in just a few years the Chicago I knew so intimately is also gone. The housing projects are gone, Dominick's is gone, most of the cheap diners I ate at are closed. The old brick buildings get torn down. New buildings made of stucco, glass, and plastic pop up in their place. Whole neighborhoods are transformed and modernized waiting for their turn to grow old meanwhile appearing how we once imagined the future should look.

The practice space where I squatted is gone too. The last time I went by all the windows were shattered and the steel door was lying on the curb. Inside I could see the trash fires and hear the rumblings of squatters more desperate than I. Last I checked on Google Maps Street-View the building was demolished completely. Now it's a vacant lot. Over a hundred years of activity gone in a puff of cement dust as if it was never there at all. The surrounding area is still one of the largest open drug markets in the country.

The following summer I had the honor of singing at Blues Fest 2011 in Grant Park downtown. I sat in with Fernando Jones and his band. I sang the lead for a bombastic version of *One Bourbon, One Scotch, One Beer*. I was just a bum at Blues Fest in 2010. The next year I was on stage singing in front of a thousand people.

My old songwriting partner Guitar Mike started showing up again fresh from splitting with his lady. We fell back into form. Soon we brought on a new drummer, a bassist, Dobro Joe on pedal steel, and Art the Grey Ghost on harmonica. Over the next few years in various incarnations we played the club circuit again, and toured to New York playing in Brooklyn and Greenwich Village. Cousin Bones was another ragged band rattling around the country like so many birds singing in the trees.

My friend painter Daniel Stine always joked that my Cousin Bones persona was less a band and more like an elaborate art performance piece. If it was some sort of method acting where I lived the way I did just to write songs about it I wasn't exactly conscious of the process. I wasn't in on the joke. It's the chicken and the egg I say. But if it was some kind of survival mechanism it worked. It got me through the recession. Set your troubles to music and all the hard times sound like adventure. That's the blues.

Thing is I don't know if I can sing. I made up for it with a lot of enthusiasm. Even back then when I was putting everything I had into my music I knew in the back of my mind I just wanted to tell stories. I love Delta blues. I love the stories in those songs. Despite all the energy and the unconscious communication in the music much of the poetry in my songs was lost in my growling vocal delivery.

Maybe the band never met the right business people. Maybe there weren't any music business people left. Maybe we never found an audience since we would change styles every other song from blues, to jazz, to heavy metal. Cousin Bones was always too blues for the rock people, and too rock for the blues people. We were always too hardcore for the art people and too arty for the hardcore people. Though the band never found an audience the other musicians around town saw what we were trying to do and liked our sound. Respect from my peers was worth more to me than any popular success.

Whatever the reason once I found myself chasing my own tail creatively I knew it was time to move on. Waiting till three in the morning again to get paid in another dank bar I knew things had run their course. As an artist I didn't want to repeat myself. I wanted to shed my skin and do the next thing. Otherwise I might still be at one of those old man bars living the same night over and over again like a ghost in limbo. In the end I lost my voice howling on stage night after night, but my voice as a writer grew stronger.

Sid Yiddish was right about one thing. Trudy and I would

break-up in the summer of 2011 after huddling together through the cold months. She slept with the leader of the 77 Punk Gang. This is the same group of assholes whose member stabbed my friend SOLVE to death. This is a level of betrayal worthy of a blues song, but honestly I never had the stomach to exploit the antidote for a song.

With a little persistence everything works out in the end. Not long after the guys and I got back from New York I met my future wife at a poetry reading at the punk club Exit. We traveled to Beale Street in Memphis for a dollar on the Megabus. We traveled to the Mississippi Delta and found the real blues at a juke joint by the river. We took a train to New Orleans and listened to the best street musicians in the world playing in the French Quarter. Finally I had met someone who cared about culture, good songs, good writing, and being open and adventurous in this aching world. We went straight to the source.

Music is a spiritual language. This country is ever transforming. America spins like a storm in the center of a great global village. First there were the Indians. Then came the Spanish, French, English, African Slaves, Irish, Italians, and the rest of the world. The melting pot is a violent brew. Every day in Chicago I'd see the friction of cultures that both burns us and warms us. It takes volatile temperatures to make such great alchemy. Music is what brings us together in the end. Even if you can't understand the words, listen to another cultures' music, and you'll begin to understand. Perhaps future generations will look back at this time and be bewildered at how we're so divided. Nowhere has culture clashed and created more diverse types of music than right here where the sounds snaked up the Mississippi from New Orleans, stopped in Memphis to create rock and roll, and burst into the city lights of Chicago to spread around the world. That swampy and primordial music cuts to the back of my spinal column. Voices of all the angels, devils, preachers, criminals, and workers of Chicago echo in a great chorus.

The last of the Delta bluesmen David "Honey-boy" Edwards died in August of 2011. Many of my old musician friends are gone as well. Most will be forgotten. The world I knew is all but gone. But I can still feel the momentum of the music pushing time forward.

Now my busking days are all just a memory, a tunnel of mirrors, smoke from a fire half forgotten, just faces melting in ice at the bottom of a glass. Like any real life story there is no end. The drama never ends no matter how much I might want it to. The only constant is the music, the passion, the drive to go on. The blues pulses on. The music beats under the skin.

After my squatter days everything life has thrown at me since has felt easier to deal with. After inhaling the streets I have more patience, appreciate what I have, and take more pleasure in the simple things. At the time I was only thinking about the next meal, the next bed, the next song. Still every moment is vital. I am present. Those lost days and nights strengthened my faith in the universe and perhaps more importantly strengthened my faith in myself.

Westley Heine is the author of *12 Chicago Cabbies* and *The Trail of Quetzalcoatl*. His poetry and prose have been published in *The Chicago Reader*, *Gravitas*, *Heroin Love Songs*, *Beatdom*, Dumpster Fire Press, *Gasconade*, and *The Wellington Street Review* among others. He's been a taxi dispatcher, a roadie, a deliveryman, a squatter, a street musician, a grocery clerk, a chambermaid, a novelist, a painter, a metal head, a Boy Scout, an insurance investigator, a jailbird, a farmhand, sold tickets to the symphony, sold plasma, been unemployed, and been a filmmaker. Life is always creating new characters inside him, but always a writer. He grew up in Wisconsin, was lost and found in Chicago, married in Texas, and now resides in Los Angeles. Let in the light. Let out the fire. Instagram: @westleyheine

PHOTO BY ALEXIS RHONE FANCHER

"A broke down history of the blues. Ain't no other map of Chicago like this one. A quest for self. Though I walk through the valley of urban apocalyptic death I shall fear no evil. What does it take to live and be your dream? There is no tribal ceremonial ritual way to escape from being forced to live a status quo do what your conditioned and told to do life to living and being your dream. But a few rare individuals, against all odds, choose to be guided by their deep rooted passion and, regardless of the consequences, go their own damn way. Westley Heine throws the system's rule book out the fucking window. Once I entered the story I couldn't put his book down. BUSKING BLUES: Recollections of a Chicago Street Musician & Squatter is a masterpiece." —Ron Whitehead, U.S. National Beat Poet Laureate

∞

"Provocative and visceral, Busking Blues eviscerates the Chicago streets with a rusty knife... hits like a shot of neon blue morphine icing through your veins. This book will make your teeth curl and your hair fall out. To paraphrase Oscar Wilde: We are all in the gutter... but Westley Heine is looking at the curb."—Leon Horton, *International Times*

∞

"Busking Blues is the devil at the crossroads in the Chicago streets. The novel is full of street life: the art, the music, the graffiti, the smells, survival and most of all the people. Some of the characters make it and wish they didn't, and the ones left behind, leave graffiti scars in street-hearts, a city block long.

Written in the same open tune delta blues style, Busking Blues is a juke-joint day-time juke box filled with desperation, sin and sadness with cocky stubbornness and fortitude on the B side tracks.

Heine's debut novel is the real deal. I can still hear the guitar crying hours after I finished reading. This is the underground, indie hit of the summer." —Dan Denton, Author of *$100-A-Week Motel*

"If you ever dreamt about being a street musician or wondered why anyone would dream of being one, this memoir by Westley Heine is for you. In honest and rocking and often intensely poetic language that evokes Kerouac and Bukowski at their best, Heine pulls us into his wild life trying to make a living playing on street corners in Chicago in 2010. I don't know if Heine can sing, but he sure can write. If you love Chicago, you'll love it even more after reading this!" — John Guzlowski, author of *Echoes of Tattered Tongues*, winner of the Eric Hoffer/Montaigne Award for the most thought-provoking book of 2017.

∞

"With the honesty of a stiff bourbon, Heine recounts his time as a busking Chicago blues player. His transiency helps to transcend old wounds and leads us along the existential path of creative meaning and purpose. A true guide for any aspiring artist on the edge." — Mark Blottner co-director/ producer of "Nelson Algren: The End is Nothing, The Road is All"

∞

"From Henry Miller to Charles Bukowski, the desire to create (and the societal forces working against it) lie at the heart of the artistic experience. Along the way, family, friends, relationships, and simple economic existence often hang in the balance. It's a journey reserved for either the truly mad, or the truly brave.

America has never really respected the arts, other than the select few who make it through the meat grinder to become well known, or perhaps even rich and famous. But it's during the times of struggle and desperation that the richest songs, stories, and paintings come to life. 'Busking Blues: Recollections of a Chicago Street Musician & Squatter,' by Westley Heine, is a chronicle of such trying times, and serves as a paean to perseverance, grit, and inspiration. Beyond a memoir of down-and-out poets, musicians, and madmen, in reading 'Busking Blues' you'll come to know Chicago like only denizens of the streets ever could, along with immersions into Delta Blues, Chicago Blues, and the icons who created that uniquely American music form.

Heine's previous book, '12 Chicago Cabbies,' gave readers an insider view of the hardscrabble world of cabbies working the Windy City. This latest work offers an equally compelling window into the hand-to-mouth existence of the college-educated artist in today's crumbling America. Heine offers busker tales that could only have come from real-life—like his plans to compose and sing original Blues songs based on the quickly offered problems of those passing by on the street.

Joni Mitchell once sang of a street clarinetist playing "so sweet and high," but where the bustling city crowds "knew he had never been on their TV, so they passed his music by." Forget Hollywood blockbuster tales of heroes with super powers. The real ones are all around you, out on the streets of America, and playing before your very eyes. So the next time you pass a street musician, and are drawn-in by what they do, stop and truly listen. Then toss them some scratch. They've given you something special, from their heart, and you should return the favor. You might even read about it in a book one day." — Steven Meloan, Author of *The Kind the Pharaohs Try* and *St. James Infirmary*